Tales Between
Their Legs

Tales Between Their Legs
BOULEVARD *editions*
London 2005

BOULEVARD *editions*
is an imprint of
THE *Erotic* Print Society
Email: eros@eroticprints.org
Web: www.eroticprints.org

ISBN: 1-904989-05-5

Printed and bound in Spain by Bookprint S.L., Barcelona

The Erotic Print Society is a publisher of fine art, photography and fiction
books and limited editions. To find out more please visit us on the web at
www.eroticprints.org or call us for a catalogue (UK only) on 0871 7110 134.

LUCY GOLDEN

Tales Between
Their Legs

*E*PS

CONTENTS

Mandy's Tale: The Wedding

I knew Jeremy and his mother were close. When I first moved in with him, she was coming round to visit regularly, at least once a week, and for me that was once a week too much. It was no surprise that Jeremy's sister, Susannah, having gone away to a university at the other end of the country, had stayed there after her course was over and that her visits home were few and far between. I was very fond of Jeremy, but his mother was an absolute cow, and that was being generous. She was mean with her compliments, mean with her money, mean with her affection, mean in everything she did. Then Susannah announced she was getting married (something Jeremy and I had not bothered with) and you would have thought that she had become an angel incarnate.

That didn't last long. As soon as Mrs Collins became involved, she tried to take over. There was a huge row when Susannah said the wedding would be held in Newcastle where all their friends were, not at home in Sussex where Mrs Collins wanted it. Even so, it had soon become quite a grand affair, whatever Susannah and Terry, her fiancé, wanted: 'If a thing's worth doing, it's worth doing properly,' she spouted endlessly. There was certainly no hope of our avoiding it, or avoiding our all travelling up together in one car. I did manage to take over the booking of our hotel on the basis that I could do it more easily via the internet than Mrs Collins could by phone and that at least was a success. I arranged a nice double room for us with a king-size bed and a small single on an upper floor for Mrs Collins. She meanwhile fussed over what she would wear, her hat, Jeremy's suit, his tie.

~

Halfway up the motorway, she started about the rooms. 'Now what have we got? Did you get a family room, like I suggested?'

'No, they didn't have any free,' I lied, not having even bothered asking. 'But you've got a nice single and I asked them to put Jeremy and me as close as they can.' Once you start lying, it gets quite easy.

'What? We can't have that!'

'Have what?'

'We can't have you two sharing a room at the hotel. You are not married.'

'Mrs Collins, we live together at home; we do share a room there.'

'Oh I know that. Don't think I don't know that. But that doesn't mean I approve. Be that as it may, what you get up to at home is nothing to do with this. Many relatives from both families will be here and you need not think I am being shamed by your loose morals in front of them.'

'Jeremy?' I turned to him for help. 'Please back me up on this?'

'Well, I do rather see Mum's point. Some of the family are quite... old fashioned. Uncle Geoffrey is a preacher, you know.'

'So?'

'Well we don't want to upset them.'

'Oh all right!' I bit my tongue. 'Have the bloody double room. I will probably be much happier on my own.'

'Don't be stupid, child. I can hardly share a room with

Jeremy, can I? No. You and I will have to share and Jeremy will be in the single.'

'But Mrs Collins...'

'That's all there is to it. You should have organised the rooms better and either reserved us a family room or three single rooms.'

The rest of the trip was horrible. The hotel, a Victorian monstrosity was horrible. Supper was horrible. Mrs Collins chattered the entire time, sometimes inviting Jeremy to join in but not often and by keeping the subject to people who might be at the wedding, other family events, Jeremy's childhood, she was able to exclude me totally. 'You're very quiet, Mandy,' she offered once. 'Cat got your tongue?' and then returned to Auntie Dorothy's funeral ten years ago where something had happened or hadn't happened but I had long since stopped listening.

After coffee, we sat for a while in the residents' lounge where some people were watching a programme of which Mrs Collins thoroughly disapproved. 'Good heavens what language!' The other people, a couple with two children, said nothing but I had a horrid feeling that they might be from the groom's family, also here for the wedding. 'I really don't understand why it is necessary to be quite so explicit about these things. Cannot young people keep their clothes on for more than ten minutes at a time?' Thankfully they appeared to be more amused than annoyed by Mrs Collins's outbursts.

Eventually when that finished and a snooker programme started, she had seen enough. 'We don't want any of that, thank you,' and since she had decided to go to bed, I was required to go too. 'I can't have you coming up later and waking me.'

Upstairs in our room it was dreadful. 'Turn off the radiator please, Mandy. I really don't know why they insist on putting the heating so high in these places. I cannot stand to be too hot.' 'Are these sheets clean?' 'Are there no towels in this hotel? The back of the door? Well what a stupid place to put them.' 'I will take a bath before I go to bed.' 'You might as well unpack our things.'

It often is easier to go along with her than argue so I unpacked while she sat applying a range of creams to her face.

'That's a lot!' I said in an attempt to make a conversation that was not about somebody else's failings.

'If a thing's worth doing, it's worth doing properly,' she answered and reached for another jar. On the pretext of taking Jeremy a non-existent toothbrush which had got into our case by mistake, I scuttled out to see him before she could stop me. His was a really miserable, poky little room, boiling hot and with all the windows firmly painted shut; it would have been ideal for Mrs Collins. We managed a quick cuddle before the telephone rang. 'I am about to take my bath and will naturally need to lock the bedroom door before doing so. If you do not wish to be locked out all night you had better come back at once.'

I found her scowling in the middle of the room, still fully dressed but with her hair now a mass of curlers. We had to lock the door carefully and re-check the curtains before it would be safe for her to start taking any clothes off. I turned away and while she was in the bathroom, got ready for bed. Of course I had anticipated sharing with Jeremy, and had even bought a new and quite stunning nightdress for the occasion, but it was not a style of which Mrs Collins would have approved, nor one that I wanted her seeing me in even if she had. I slid into bed, hauled myself over to the very edge and pulled the blankets tight round me. At least I had asked for a king size.

Some thirty minutes later, she emerged in a vast pink dressing gown, swept that off to reveal a thick purple nightdress that could have doubled as a marquee and went to throw open some more windows as well as the curtains, immediately bringing the temperature down another ten degrees. Finally, with considerable huffing, she settled into bed and turned out the light.

She sniffed. 'Goodnight,' and then snored all night, occasionally even drowning out the trains.

The wedding was not actually too bad once it got going. I had never met Susannah before but she was the complete opposite of her mother and we got on rather well. I saw Mrs Collins a few times, tucking into the champagne, gossiping with various aunts and cousins and, from what I could overhear, criticising everyone from the groom downwards. I had been right about my fears over the other family: they were from the groom's side, but beyond a smile and nod, we didn't talk.

At about half past nine Mrs Collins decided that was enough and that we should leave. Having had a very disturbed sleep the night before, I was not all that sorry and Jeremy is not a great socialiser so neither of us argued with her.

She was unusually chatty on the way back to the hotel. 'Well not a bad do, I suppose. Susannah did look gorgeous, though, didn't she? I still wish we had been able to hold it at home as we said; we could have done it so much better. Still, at least I put my foot down over that registry office nonsense; that would have been quite inappropriate.'

Upstairs, all went much as last night. Jeremy and I managed a brief kiss before he was sent off to his attic. Once our bedroom door was shut, Mrs Collins dropped down at the dressing table but this time she started talking to me as she applied the buckets of face cream; complaining about the wedding guests mostly and although she was as critical as ever, for once she wasn't criticising me. Twice she even laughed as she recounted some incident or other and laughter did not come easily to her face.

She emerged from the bathroom in the same dazzling array of curlers but several of them were only hanging on by luck and as she carelessly threw off the dressing gown, several of those flew with it.

'Bugger,' she said which was most unlike her. She came over and tottered into the bed without even opening the window. She lay there with the light on, staring at the ceiling before she turned her face to me.

'I know it wasn't real champagne, but that was very pleasant.' Then she started about her wedding. 'Dear Eric, lovely man he was, you know. Of course girls in those days waited until they were married before they let a man into their bed. So I was quite looking forward to it, I can tell you. He was good to me, Eric was. Kind man and somehow he made everything so much easier for everyone around him; so sad, him going so young. It hasn't been easy, you know, raising two children without him. And I know I get short tempered, I can hear myself doing it, but I just can't stop. I'm still so angry about it, you see. Oh well. No use my chattering on. We've got a long drive tomorrow. Better get some sleep. Did I open the window?'

The total absence of train noise answered that but I tried anyway. 'Yes I think so.'

'I don't think I did, you know. Be a dear and open it for me, would you?'

And in all the months I had known her, I think this was the first time she had ever asked me to do anything. Everything else had always been a command and that made it so much harder to refuse, despite my wearing the nightdress that I had intended only for Jeremy.

Of course she commented the moment she saw it when I got out of bed. 'That's a lovely little nightie, dear. Not much of it though, is there?'

And once I had wrestled the ancient windows open ('And the curtains, dear: let the air circulate.') and turned back to the bed, she could see me from the front as well. 'Ooh!' she said. 'Yes, quite saucy that, isn't it?'

I said nothing, smiled as much as seemed necessary and quickly slid back under the covers but she hadn't finished. 'I expect Jeremy likes that, does he?'

'Actually I don't know that he has seen it.'

'Not seen it? Why ever not?'

'It's new, if you must know. It was going to be a surprise for him on this trip.'

'Oh,' and then she must have realised her role in my plan's failure. 'I see,' and she even sounded sorry. 'That's a shame, because you look just the thing in it, don't you?'

'Thank you.'

'I imagine young men expect more these days. In my day I suppose they'd go to a professional woman if they needed.

Now they don't do that. And I suppose young women know more what's what. I really didn't have very much idea what to expect on my wedding night.'

'No I guess things were quite different then. Shall we go to sleep now, Mrs Collins?'

'I suppose it is better nowadays, but take Susannah, now. There she is: this is her wedding day, the biggest day of her life. But now? It comes to the evening, her wedding night, and instead of something new and wonderful and the entry into womanhood, it's just the same as she has every night.' This was not really a picture I wanted conjured up for me and stayed silent. 'Except her husband is probably sloshed.' Another pause. 'Actually Eric was a bit tiddly on our wedding night; I think he was nervous, poor lamb.'

'Yes, I can imagine he might well have been.'

'We nearly had to leave it till the next day, but it was all right in the end. After he'd had a little rest.'

'Mrs Collins, I really would like to get to sleep. I didn't sleep all that well last night.'

'I was nervous too. I'd never seen a man before, you see. Seems funny now. What with it in the films and even on the television. In those days that didn't happen, not where we lived. They said it did in the cities, but not where we lived.'

'No, I suppose not. Well: Goodnight.'

'Of course he knew much more about all that side of things than I did, from being in the army.'

I reached over and turned the light off, although the hotel sign, car-park lights and street lights kept the room almost bright enough to read in. I rolled back right over to my side and tried to sleep, but I could feel that Mrs Collins hadn't moved or settled. She was still lying half propped up, staring up to the ceiling with her hands under her head. Finally she did lie down, the bed heaving up and down with her movements, but she still hadn't finished.

'It really is very short, that nightdress of yours. I can see your bottom.' Then her hand came out and I felt it on my back, gently running up and down my spine. 'Have you had a nice day, dear?'

'Yes thank you, Mrs Collins. Very nice.'

'Susannah is a lovely girl, isn't she?'

'Yes; she's very friendly.' Still the hand was stroking up and down my back, longer sweeps from my shoulders down to my waist.

'And her Terry seems very pleasant. Nice looking boy.'

'Yes.'

'You looked very pretty, too.'

'Thank you,' but I was utterly amazed: that was the first compliment she had ever paid me.

The hand was still stroking me, if anything even fractionally lower than it had been, and it was nice enough although I couldn't really get to sleep while it continued. The mattress bounced as she moved herself nearer to me. For several minutes the slow stroking continued and I was beginning to think that actually I probably could get to sleep while that went on, when she spoke again.

'Mandy? Does Jeremy ever do it up your bottom?'

For a second I thought I must have misheard her, but no: that was what she had said, I was certain. 'I beg your pardon?'

'Does he ever do it up your bottom?'

'I'm not sure that is any of your business, actually.'

'No, but I am his mother dear.'

'I know that, but it is still a private matter between him and me.'

She was silent for a moment; maybe she was thinking, as I was, that I had answered her question: if the answer had been "no", I would simply have said that. 'Eric was always on at me to do that, but I never let him. Girls didn't in those days, and besides I was afraid it would hurt.' Another silence while the stroking continued. 'Now I will never know.'

Several more minutes passed before she rolled even closer and I was sucked down into the hollow her body made in the bed.

'Mandy? Could I look at you?'

'I'm sorry. What?'

'Could I have a look at you? Only I've never seen a woman properly and I always wanted to.'

I didn't move: stayed lying frozen on my side of the bed. 'I don't think I know what you mean, Mrs Collins.'

'Just to see,' she carried on. 'Of course Jeremy sees you all the time, and so I've kind of wondered what he was seeing.' I felt her pulling at the bed clothes. 'What you are like for him.'

I grabbed the top of the blankets. 'I don't think so, Mrs Collins. I really don't think that would be a good idea.'

'It wouldn't hurt,' she said, still pulling at the bedding, but now she turned on the light and propped herself up on one elbow. 'Seeing as we are both women, and you're practically one of the family.'

'Even so, I don't think so.'

'Why not?'

'Well...'

'I've seen pictures of course...'

'Pictures? Of me?'

'Yes dear. Jeremy showed me some he took at your hotel

on holiday last year. You were sitting by the pool with nothing on your top at all. Very pretty, you looked.'

'I see. Well, that was different.'

'Why is that different? You show yourself off to complete strangers, men as well as women, on holiday and yet you won't give me a little look.' By this time she had tugged at the blankets and lifted them up on her side so that I felt the cold air on my back and bottom. I turned over to confront her.

'That was entirely different.'

'I don't see why. I mean, if I had come on that holiday with you like I suggested...'

'Look, Mrs Collins...'

'There now! That's better, isn't it?' Because in the process of turning I had lost my grasp and she had succeeded in working the blankets right down so that I was now, except for my nightdress, uncovered. I quickly fought to pull the blankets back but did not succeed in getting them much higher than my waist.

'Very pretty, isn't it? Why don't you slip this off?' and she tugged at the neck of my nightdress.

'No, Mrs Collins.'

'Don't make a fuss, love. You wouldn't be so shy if I was Jeremy now, would you?'

'No, but...'

'So. What's the difference? I am just his mother.' To me the difference seemed obvious; to her it clearly wasn't. 'It's only what he sees every day anyway. Besides, to be frank, dear, it's not hiding much. I can see you almost as clearly as if you had nothing on anyway.'

'Oh, all right! All right! I will take it off, then can we get some sleep?' I started pulling the thing up while Mrs Collins immediately busied herself with the tie at the neck. Then she pulled it up over my head and, while she dropped the thing down by her side of the bed, I tugged the blankets up to my shoulders. She immediately pushed them down again until my breasts had appeared.

'There's no need to be shy, dear; not with me, is there?' She smiled, and peered down at me. 'You aren't very big, are you dear?'

'Big?'

'I mean your bosoms.' And this time she reached out and touched me, enclosing my nipple in her fingertips to draw me up. 'They are very pretty and everything, just not very big.'

'I can't help that; that is just how I am.'

Still she continued the same slow milking action and I wished she would leave them alone because, although they may not be big, they are sensitive. 'What size are you, dear?'

'34,' I answered and, before she could probe any further, 'B.'

'Really?' but I don't think she believed me.

'They do look smaller when I am lying down.'

'Yes, I suppose so.' She had moved across to the other breast, but still her fingertips lightly ran up and down the nipple and it had now drawn up erect. 'You don't think Jeremy might like it if you had them made bigger.'

'I don't think he would actually; he has always liked me just as I am. In any case, I certainly have no intention of undergoing anything like that, whatever Jeremy or any man wanted.'

'I would pay for it, if you wanted to.'

'No, thank you, Mrs Collins. I don't want to. Do you think you could stop doing that, please?'

'Isn't it nice?'

'Yes, it is very nice. I would just prefer it if you stopped.'

'Just a kiss then,' and before I could stop her she had bobbed down and planted a single, relatively chaste, kiss on each bright nipple.

'Thank you. Could we go to sleep now?' but her hand, which had so innocently rested just below my breasts while she leaned down to kiss me, was now working its way under the blankets and down my stomach.

'Let's see down here, too.'

I snatched hold of her wrist. 'That is not seeing.'

'All right,' she admitted, drawing her hand back. 'Just look. I won't touch you.'

I don't know why I let her. If a line was going to be drawn, I think here would have been the place to draw it, but I let it pass. She seemed lonely; I felt sorry for her; we were a long way from home. There were many reasons, none of them good enough, none of them worth a moment's consideration in the cold light of day, but this wasn't the cold light of day and I simply lifted my hand off the blanket.

'Thank you, Mandy,' and she eased the covers down to my thighs.

Again, she peered at me. 'Is this...?' she asked. 'I mean, have you shaved some of this?'

'Yes.'

'I read about that in a magazine at the hairdressers. It is all the thing in America apparently; all the film stars do it. I never thought you might.' She was peering closer. 'Why do you?'

'I think it looks nicer and,' and this should please her, 'Jeremy likes it.'

'Does he? Why?'

'It's not so scratchy.'

She was silent a moment. 'Do you mean when he is kissing you there?'

'Yes.'

'Eric once wanted to kiss me there. I told him not to be disgusting.' Another silence. 'Is that nice, him doing that?'

'Do you mean to say you've never...?' But one glance at her face gave me the answer.

'There's only ever been Eric.'

'I see. Well, yes, Mrs Collins: it is very nice. Perhaps the nicest thing of all.'

In the silence she blinked a couple of times. 'I've missed a lot I suppose.'

'It's not too late.'

'Ha! I'm fifty-four, Mandy. Who wants to sleep with a woman of fifty-four?'

'A man of fifty-four? They do exist, you know.'

'Maybe,' and she paused again. 'Can I see you properly, Mandy?'

I knew well enough what she meant by 'properly' and so I lifted my knees up and let them fall open as she pushed herself further down the bed. I didn't watch her, beyond a quick glance down the bed to see her face, concentrating, frowning, framed between my legs as she examined me.

'Can I open you, dear? I would like to see inside.'

I didn't agree, but I let my thighs drift even further apart as her fingers came up, slithered down my lips and then, with one hand on each side, she gently peeled me open.

How far inside had she meant? I had assumed she wanted to open my outer lips, that they would be sticking together and she wanted to see my inside ones. But already her fingers were sliding up and down those too, parting them, exposing my clit and one finger was tracing up and down between them.

She smiled up at me. 'It's very pretty, your front bottom,' but when I simply laughed she blushed. 'Isn't that what you call it?' I shook my head. 'What then?'

'My cunt.'

'Mandy! That's very crude!'

'That's what it is, Mrs Collins: a cunt.'

'I suppose so. Well. All right. It's very pretty, your cunt.' She giggled. 'Do you know what, Mandy? I do believe that is the first time I have ever spoken that word!' And she grinned to herself while her finger continued tracing lightly up and down between my lips. I don't know why I let her really, except that I had let her do everything else; she seemed so eager it would have been mean to stop her; I was missing Jeremy; another list of inadequate reasons that persuaded me at the time. Perhaps she wasn't the only one who had been tucking into the wedding wine.

Once her finger dropped lower, down to the delicate place below my cunt and hovered there a moment, running inquisitive little circles and timid little darts up and down.

'So, Mandy? Does Jeremy ever do it up your bottom?'

This time I did answer. 'Sometimes, yes.'

'Doesn't it hurt?'

'Not if you are careful and take your time.' She considered this. 'And use plenty of lubricant,' I added. 'Then it is very nice.'

'I see,' and the finger returned to running up and down my lips, slowly, smoothly and extremely seductively. I felt myself weakening, softening, moistening, opening.

'You said "look",' I reminded her but she gave no response.

'Mrs Collins?' I tried again. 'You said "look".' But still there was no reaction: the finger continued sliding up and down me right from the tip of my clit, along the whole length of my lips and down to the join where, unless she stopped soon, there would be a little drop of juice forming.

Or maybe it had gathered there already, because the finger was definitely running more deeply there, and then without warning, it slid right up inside me. Automatically I squeezed and she grinned at me.

It didn't stay up there long. She returned to the previous movement, the same slow, steady pace, which was nice, although it was never going to be nice enough. For several minutes I let her continue, unable to bring myself to ask for more. Finally the frustration became too much. 'It's nicest just up at the top.'

'Oh. Oh, all right dear,' and she did concentrate a bit more round the top of my cunt, but still too vague, still not enough. I reached down, took hold of her hand and showed her where my clit was and where I needed to be rubbed. After that it was much better.

'If it's all right, dear...'

'It is,' I answered; this really was not the time to listen to more of her thoughts and doubts.

'No, I mean if it's all right with you, I shouldn't like to kiss you down there.'

'That's quite all right, Mrs Collins. What you are doing now is really very nice.'

'That's good, dear, because I would like to make it nice for you, if that's all right.'

And it was very all right; it was really quite wonderful, and I just lay back and let her do it. I couldn't watch her. There was something too bizarre about the sight: this middle-aged woman in a garish balloon nightdress, curlers hanging onto stray bits of her hair, kneeling beside me and staring intently between my legs while she steadily masturbated me. But I didn't have to watch, and what I could feel was glorious: maybe she was making up for lost years; maybe this was her normal determination ("If a thing's worth doing, ..."), but whatever the reason, what she was doing was good. I wanted to try to retain some distance, to keep the image of independence which I had always fought to retain with her, but I could not. I felt my hips rising to meet her, my thighs trembling and opening to give her more and better access to any part of me that she wanted to explore. I could no longer keep still, or silent, and squeezed my own breasts because I love having them stroked at any time and at this time, while she was doing that to my clit and my whole body felt to be on fire, it was the best thing ever of any time in all eternity.

Afterwards, I lay back, getting my breath while she stayed slowly running her fingertips across me and once, only once, bobbing down to kiss me right on the tip of my clit. But I straightened out, brought my legs back down and tried to return to something like the aloofness that I had always tried to maintain with her. She was kneeling there, her face half in shadow, but staring down at the spot between my legs where our whole concentration had just been focussed. And she looked so lost.

I sat up, reached for her shoulders and pushed her down onto the bed, back up onto the pillow. Then I took hold of the hem of that dreadful purple nightdress. 'Right: you now.'

Jeremy and his mother are still close, and she still comes round to visit once a week. Now, more often than not, her visits are on the night of his evening class.

ANGIE'S TALE: HANDY

'**O**kay, but first you have to take your clothes off.'

'What? No way!'

'You made us do it!'

'Yes, but that was ages ago. Besides, that was just a game!' argued Angie.

'So is this,' and Kathy settled down to wait.

'Graham,' Angie turned to me and wailed, 'you aren't going to let them do this to me, are you?'

⁓

Angie and I had managed to get a weekend away for once at a village on the Dorset coast where we have often been before. We always stay in a little Bed & Breakfast which has comfy beds, thick walls (we both work hard and often work late during the week) and does good breakfasts. On the Saturday we planned a pub lunch and a walk. It was a glorious June day: pure blue sky: brilliant sunshine: excellent lunch: lovely pub, and the prospect of a long walk along the headland later. To top it all off, as we sat in the beer garden, rather an attractive woman was peering over in our direction: early twenties, tall, not far off six feet I would guess, with thick blonde hair, a rather fine bosom, and the legs which appeared below her short skirt were long, slender and magnificent. I was not the only man in the pub garden to have noticed her. More than that, it became clear as she threaded through the tables, that she was heading straight for us.

'Angela?'

'Yes.' Both Angie and I turned to look at her, Angie with a frown that suddenly cleared and just as suddenly reappeared, me with the thought that if she was a friend of Angie's, I wish I'd been introduced before.

'Angela! I knew it was you! It's me! Charley!' Angie was still holding the blank look. 'Charlotte Bolton! From St Theresa's?'

'Oh yes.' But there was much less enthusiasm on Angie's side than on Charlotte's. 'Hi.' No, Angie was not pleased at all, and I couldn't work out why. I vaguely remembered talk of this "Charley" but not as someone who had caused any particular problems. 'How are you?'

'Fine. Great! God, what a surprise! How good to see you!'

'What are you, um? What brings you here?'

'I'm staying with Kathy for the weekend; you remember Kathy! Kathy Miller? Anyway, she has bought a cottage just along the cliffs. She is just parking the car. Hey!' and she started waving across the pub garden, attracting the attention of everyone except the petite young woman who had appeared in the far corner and was now examining the blackboard of "Specials!!!". Charlotte headed across the garden still waving.

'Shit!' which was the first time I had heard Angie swear in many months.

'What is the matter? Who is she?'

'We were at sixth form college together. I'm just not all that keen to resurrect all the school days business.'

'Why not? I'd like to meet some of your friends.'

'Yes well I wouldn't. I've put all that behind me now. Can we pretend we are just visiting? Don't tell them we're staying here, eh?'

'Why ever not?'

'Angie!' and the other woman, Kathy presumably, leaned down to plant kisses on both Angie's cheeks. 'This is brilliant because we would have waited ages for a table otherwise. You don't mind if we join you, do you?'

'No, of course not,' and Angie shifted along her bench and further into the corner.

The two women were looking over at me with half smiles. 'And this is...?' asked Charlotte.

'Oh sorry. This is Graham.' The due round of handshakes followed. They settled down at the table and I went off to get some drinks and leave them to reminisce. When I came back, the reminiscences did not seem to be going all that well.

'But Angie, you were a total bitch!'

'I wasn't!'

'You bloody were! The things you used to make us do!'

'Those were the rules of the club. Everybody did it.'

'You didn't!'

'Well they were for when new people joined.'

'Exactly! So everybody except you.'

'Oh, it was only a game! You make it sound dreadful.'

'Some of the stuff was!'

'Yes, you made me walk across the footbridge over the dual carriageway stark naked.'

'There was nobody about! Everyone else was in lectures.'

'Come on! At least a dozen cars drove underneath and they all saw me!' Kathy laughed at the memory, but it was only a half forgiving laugh. 'Besides, then I was late for lectures and got a detention.'

The conversation drifted away to other aspects of college life, although Kathy kept coming back to this "Batman" club.

'Why "Batman"?' I asked.

'She made us all wear these stupid Batman badges. God, we were so proud of ourselves.'

By this time Angie and I had finished our meals, the other two having only just started, and she stood up. 'I'm just going to the loo, Graham, then I think we should be going.'

Kathy dived in. 'I don't think we should allow you go to the loo, should we Charley? You were always stopping us!'

'Rubbish!' but I know Angie well, and again I got the impression she was not as certain as she pretended.

'Oh you did! You had this thing about anyone having a pee. Half the time you made them do it in front of everyone else.'

'You liar! That happened twice.'

'Much more than that. I can think of at least four times when I was there.'

'She's right, Angie.' Now even Charlotte was joining in. 'I spent hours in agony not wanting to admit I needed a pee because I was afraid you would do something weird.'

'That's silly!'

'You made Linda Williamson drink some.'

'I certainly did not!'

'Well she said you did.'

'I did not!' Angie repeated but she was blushing as she hurried off through the tables.

The silence was a little awkward until Charlotte returned to mundane topics. 'So what are you doing this afternoon?'

'Just a walk,' I explained, 'along the shore and up to the headland.' They didn't seem like walking types and I assumed this would put them off but it proved just the opposite when Kathy explained that was where her cottage was. She and Steven – a husband or partner: the relationship was never explained – had just bought one of the old coastguard cottages. Were they pleased with it? Well, it had cost an absolute fortune, specially considering the place is a total dump that needs complete renovation. Still, Steven's friend Gary – or maybe it was Barry – is in the business and he says it will be worth a goldmine in a couple of years. Anyway, we simply must come and see it. In fact, why didn't we all walk up there? They could leave the car here and come down this evening to collect it.

'Well I'm not really sure that...' I started.

'No it would be great! Here,' and Charlotte was already standing up, 'let me get you both a drink while we finish our lunch.' She was off before I could stop her.

When Angie came back, she wasn't pleased; I had been afraid she wouldn't be but short of being flatly rude, there was little we could do to escape. Angie looked quite grim as we sat waiting for them to finish eating and at last set off: me trailing along behind and the three girls up ahead until the path narrowed when Kathy dropped back and joined me.

'So does she bully you too?'

'No!'

'She was an absolute terror to us. I don't know why we went along with it. There was just something about her that made you obey. We all swore we would get revenge one day.'

'Angie doesn't talk about her schools much.' Not much was an exaggeration: she did not talk about them at all, and not at all with such determination that I had always been intrigued and quietly suspicious.

The coastguard cottages formed a neat row of six, deliberately sited to give the occupiers the best possible lookout across the bay, and it was on the grass directly in front of them that Angie and I would normally take a breather after the hard climb up from the shore before dropping down into the next bay and beginning the long wind across country back to the village and home. Kathy's cottage turned out to be the end one and it certainly was in awful condition. It needed complete rewiring, replumbing and redecorating, there was not even hot water since the water heater had apparently been condemned. On this visit, almost their first since buying the place, they were still effectively camping and so far had done little to make the place more comfortable beyond scattering it with the weekend newspapers.

Kathy started to organise tea for everyone, except that they had forgotten to buy any water and nobody fancied the rusty brown sludge that was trickling out of the kitchen tap.

'Okay. Who's for some white wine?' and the cork was out almost before we had time to answer.

I took my glass outside to have a cigarette in the long narrow garden but the kitchen window was open and I could hear the raised voices.

'No, Angie. You will have to wait. You made us wait: now you'll have to do the same. Half an hour, I think.'

'This is silly!'

And some thirty minutes later, they still did not want to let Angie off. 'Come on, the time must be up by now!'

'Oh, I don't know. What do you think, Graham?'

I knew what I thought: I wanted to see where this game was heading. Disloyal? Perhaps, but I could step in at any time if it started going too far, and in the meantime, it was just a game, wasn't it? 'Oh, I don't know. Maybe just a little longer.'

'Graham! You bastard!' but actually there was more sparkle than anger in Angie's protest and she quickly turned back to address Kathy again. 'What happens when the time is up?'

'We'll have to see, won't we?' Kathy stared round, wide-eyed. 'In the club you were either sent somewhere public to do it, like in the middle of the courtyard, or else you had to do it with everyone else watching you.'

'Unless you were Linda Williamson,' added Charlotte, 'in which case you were made to drink it.'

'It wasn't like that!' protested Angie.

'Aha! So you don't deny it happened then.'

'I didn't make her drink it.'

'That's what you say!'

'Look, she had gone in the bowl as normal but there were only the two of us there and she said "I wonder what it tastes like" and so I just said she should try it.'

'And did she?'

'Yes.'

'Yuck!'

'She only dipped the tip of her finger in and licked it.'

'Even so...'

'Yes well, all right but look I really need to go to the loo.' And I think she did; Angie had put down her glass, empty of course, and was squirming.

'Well now. Let me see. Charley, come with me a moment, and we will decide.'

Kathy led Charlotte out, clutching her hand in a way that looked almost possessive. 'Just a mo!' they chirped as they closed the kitchen door behind them.

'Angie? What is all this about?'

She blushed. 'They are just being silly. I mean this was all years ago. And it's not true. Most of it...'

'Do you want to leave?'

'I don't know that we can, can we? I mean they've invited us here.'

'We could, Angie. They can't stop us.'

She paused at this, glanced at the closed kitchen door and would not look at me. 'Do you want to?'

But before I could reply, the girls had returned. 'Right,' said Kathy, 'we have decided that you can go to the loo in a minute. First you have to take your clothes off.'

'What? No way!'

'You made us do it!'

'Yes, but that was ages ago. Besides, that was just a game!' argued Angie.

'So is this,' and Kathy settled down to wait.

'Graham,' Angie turned to me and wailed, 'you aren't going to let them do this to me, are you?'

Charlotte jumped in before I could answer. 'Those are the rules, Angie. If you want to go to the loo, you have to take your clothes off.'

'Well I won't!'

'Then you can't go to the loo.'

'But please...'

Kathy did not stir. 'Those are the rules.'

'All right! All right!' Angie conceded eventually. 'I'll take my clothes off, but that is as fas as I am going.'

She pulled off her socks and trainers and stood up to peel off her tee-shirt; the jeans came next and then she reached round to unhook her bra. I have seen Angie undress many times during the eighteen months we have been together, but it has never been like this. I have never felt such an unbeatable surge, bred from the knowledge that something was starting to happen, and I had no real idea what that something might be. She dropped the bra and turned round to face us. Her long brown hair, tawny, not mousey I kept telling her, framed her little face and her breasts still bore a trace of the tan from last summer – she had not been shy in Tenerife – but the paleness of her body was emphasised by the little black lacy thong which snaked round her waist and down between her thighs. Her nipples were fiercely erect. 'Okay now?'

'No. Certainly not. Take your knickers off.'

'Oh come on, Kathy! That's just silly.'

But Kathy said nothing, just picked up the colour magazine and started thumbing through.

'Charley?' Angie turned to try a different appeal, but Charley just shrugged and poured herself another glass of wine.

'Oh all right then,' and Angie hooked her thumbs into the waistband of her knickers and pulled them down, tossed them over onto the pile and stood with one hip thrust out. 'There you are. Everything. Now are you happy?' She looks wonderful naked, and although she trims her pubic hair, she does not go in for shaving it into unnatural stripes so there is always a sweet but respectable little, fluffy bush to play with.

Kathy looked up, considered her slowly and then turned back to her magazine. 'Good. Now you can go and fetch the glass bowl from the kitchen; put it down here in front of me, and wee into that. It's in the cupboard over the sink.'

Angie looked to be about to refuse but could see it would do her no good and just went out to the kitchen. I did wonder what she would do; beyond the kitchen was the little bathroom;

shabby certainly, but it did at least have a toilet and there was no actual barrier to her going in there. Instead, I heard the cupboard doors opening and shutting and then she was back with the bowl; she set it down and squatted over it. Kathy put down her magazine and Charlotte sat up.

'Okay?' asked Angie.

'Fine,' said Kathy, and almost immediately there was the first golden swirl spinning round the side of the bowl, and we watched it filling up as the stream splashed on down, a stream which went on and on. Finally Angie was done and stood up, feet either side of the bowl and her glorious long legs twisting as she peered round the room.

'Can I have a tissue? If that's not too much trouble.'

Kathy slid out of her chair down onto the floor and crawled across to Angie's clothes where she picked her knickers from off the top of the pile and held them out. 'You can use these. You won't be wearing them for the rest of the day.'

There wasn't much of them; we were on holiday and these lacy little things were designed for show, not function, but Angie took them, bundled them up and wiped herself. Then she carefully picked up the bowl, clutching it against her stomach.

'Can I empty this now?'

'Yes. I don't want it.'

'Hold on,' jumped in Charlotte, suddenly taking much more interest. 'What about Linda Williamson?'

'What about her?'

'Put your fingers in it, Angie.'

'Oh please? That was her idea!'

'That's not what she says. So go on: put your fingers in and lick them.'

'You're sick,' but she manoeuvred the bowl into one hand and tentatively dipped the tips of her fingers into the golden pee. 'It's hot!'

'Now lick them,' and in fact she didn't take any further persuading. She lifted her hand up, put out her tongue and licked off the drips.

'Satisfied? Can I empty it now?'

'Yes,' said Kathy, 'but I want it tipped onto the compost heap at the end of the garden. Take it out there.'

Angie turned and stared out of the window at the long straight garden, little more than wild scrub with random rectangles of even less flat ground marking where beds had once been dug. There were no trees, no shrubs, nothing to obscure the Coastguard's outlook across the bay, and only a three foot high wire mesh fence separating this garden from the next. Without a word, Angie turned and walked out of the front door and began the slow journey down to the end of the garden, completely exposed to all the other cottages, visible to anybody out walking, to anyone on the beach or in a boat, but best of all, completely visible to all of us as she made her careful way down the broken concrete path, the bowl clutched in front of her.

She looked gorgeous, her slender legs and smooth round bottom brilliant in the sunshine, her hair catching the breeze and blowing out towards the sea but her whole body completely uncovered as she made her way down.

She was halfway there when a figure appeared on the clifftop footpath beyond her. Just for a second she faltered when a second figure came into view, and this one stopped. She was a scant ten yards from them and continued, getting closer and closer to where they stood on the path that skirted the bottom fence. She appeared not to be watching them as she finally reached the end of the garden where she stopped, almost within arm's reach, tipped her bowl onto the meagre pile of brown grass cuttings and discarded flowers and then turned to begin the walk back up to the house. Now her small red nipples and the neat triangle of her bush were being displayed to us as she returned, walking at a pace little faster than when she had been trying not to slop the bowl on the way down. Now the wind blew her hair away from her face, showing the bright glow of her cheeks and, when she finally reached the door, the sparkle in her eyes.

'Happy now?' she asked.

'Good,' said Kathy, settling back into her chair. 'Now wash the bowl. Thoroughly.'

'And bring another bottle of wine,' called Charlotte sprawled on the sofa. 'There's a case under the stairs.'

When Angie returned, the bowl washed, the bottle opened, the glasses all refilled, I was starting to get used to her moving naked about the cottage as she attended to the two girls' instructions. Even so, it was not a sight that left me completely unmoved so, since there were no empty seats, I drew her over to sit on my lap where I could kiss her, not too deeply because the girls were both watching us, but she seemed as eager as me.

Kathy yawned, rubbed her hands across the back of her neck and stretched out her hands. 'I want a handy.'

Charlotte glanced up. 'Nobody's stopping you.'

'From Angie,' Kathy added and I had a sudden flash what a "handy" must mean, or at least I thought I did.

'No!' protested Angie. Evidently I was right.

Kathy stood up and took hold of Angie's wrist. 'Come on. Upstairs.'

'No,' repeated Angie but she had already allowed herself to be drawn off my lap as Kathy started leading her up the narrow stairs.

Charlotte and I could hear the boards creaking as the two of them moved about the room above our heads, sometimes a low laugh but then it all settled down and the sequence of sounds was too low for me to interpret. Charlotte was watching me.

'Is a "handy" what I think it is?' I asked.

She nodded. 'I expect so.' She curled her long legs up under her, a manoeuvre which only exposed an even greater expanse of her thigh, and took another drink of wine as she brushed down the short denim skirt. 'I don't know who first brought the term up; it had been somebody's school slang I suppose and it got adopted in the college. Mostly we were doing them for ourselves, but some of the girls did them for each other.'

More creaks and groans of ancient furniture came from above, a few laughs and conversation too low to make out.

Then Angie's voice, louder: 'No! You said a handy!' I could not make out Kathy's reply but Angie sounded determined. 'I don't care. I'm not doing that.' Another mumble and what sounded strangely like a slap.

'But Kathy...' Angie's tone was wheedling now, as she struggled to defend her line and eventually. 'Just this once. But don't tell Charley, promise?'

Charlotte grinned as the sounds died away to quiet, beyond an unmistakable rhythmic creaking and then a sigh followed by a louder groan, unmistakable in its cause.

As these moans continued, increasing in both frequency and volume, Charlotte grinned at me. 'Here we go again. Kathy always was a screamer.'

And all I could picture was Angie, up there naked, and Kathy, presumably naked too, and the "handy" with which they had started had no longer been enough so the picture was clear: the classic position of two lovers, except that now one of them was my lover, and the other was the rather skinny little woman with straggly auburn hair in whose house we were all sitting. Had Angie ever done this with a woman before? She had always slightly dodged that question, always implying not, but never actually saying it, but the earlier conversation and Charlotte's remarks suggested it had not been unusual at this college of theirs. Furthermore, the sounds from upstairs gave no indication of a tentative exploration. Whatever experience Angie had seemed to be quite satisfying to Kathy. I sat there trying to take it all in, wondering about Angie, about her history and most all just picturing what was happening up there. How was it arranged? Was Angie kneeling or was she lying down? What was Kathy like? Bushy or shaved? Neat, compact and closed up or with generous, exposed lips? And Angie? What did she look like with her head between Kathy's thighs and her tongue lapping at Kathy's clitoris?

The sounds grew more unrestrained and unmistakable and although Charlotte was slumped half asleep in her chair, she stirred and smiled at the occasional, exceptional squeals and once or twice I caught her eye and we grinned across the room to each other. 'Is there anyone in the next door cottage?' I asked.

'Oh yes!' she said. 'But they will be getting used to it.'

'But I thought you only arrived yesterday.'

'Yes,' and she blushed to the very roots of her hair. 'I meant they would have to start getting used to it.'

'I see.' I said. Soon after that Kathy audibly reached the

climax she had been struggling for and the room went silent. I wondered whether we would hear the favour being returned. If we did, then come what may, I was going to creep up the stairs and peer in. I was disappointed when, a few minutes later, footsteps sounded above our heads, down the stairs and Kathy came in, tying a white towelling dressing gown round her waist and followed by Angie, still quite naked.

'Good handy?' asked Charlotte without stirring: eyes shut but a slight smile twitching at her face.

'Very nice,' answered Kathy.

'Yes, sounded good.'

Kathy grinned. 'Piss off. Have one yourself.'

Charlotte opened an eye and fixed on Angie. 'Maybe later. I'm too comfy here.'

'Have it here, then,' persisted Kathy.

'Huh! I'm not doing it with you watching.'

'Why ever not? You watched me!'

'I didn't.'

'You did.'

'When?'

'Last Christmas. With Ben.'

'Oh well. That was different. With Ben.' And she settled back to her half-sleep but a few seconds later stirred again. 'When are the boys due?'

'They said round about three, depending on whether it goes into extra time.'

'The boys?' asked Angie. 'What boys?'

'Didn't we say?' asked Kathy, with an innocence I couldn't believe. 'Ben, that's Charley's partner...'

'No, he's not,' Charlotte butted in.

'All right: Charley's friend, okay?' but Charlotte just

sniffed. 'Anyway he and Steven are coming down later.'

'I see,' and Angie paused. 'Well I'll tell you this: I am getting dressed again before they arrive.'

'Perhaps,' said Kathy, topping up all the wine glasses.

'No,' said Angie. 'I am.'

'Perhaps,' mumbled Charlotte half asleep.

<hr/>

But Angie didn't, couldn't. She had been sent out to the kitchen to fetch yet another bottle of wine when the front door was pushed open and two men, presumably "the boys", appeared in the doorway.

'Twenty-six to fourteen and I need a fuck!' one of them shouted and then stopped dead when he saw me. 'Oh! Hello.'

'Steven!' and Kathy almost jumped into his arms, kissing him with totally uninhibited enthusiasm, her hand running blatantly down the front of his jeans to squeeze him, staying there while she kissed him again. 'I've missed you!'

The other man glanced at me, a touch of suspicion on his face and stepped forward to make his own claim. 'Hello Charley,' and he leaned down to kiss her, one hand cradling her breast as he did it.

'I'm pissed,' she mumbled as she turned her face up to receive and return the kiss but otherwise scarcely moved.

The man looked up and held out a hand to me. 'Hi! I'm Ben.'

So I introduced myself, little helped by Charlotte's explanation. 'He's with Angie.'

'Angie?'

'She's in the kitchen,' and then Kathy was calling for Angie to come and meet the boys.

Kathy waited.

Charlotte giggled.

I held my breath, wondering whether she would.

She did. Completely naked, she pulled open the door and walked out. 'Hello.' The girls both giggled again and for a moment neither of the boys said a thing.

'Hello Angie!' said Ben finally, not bothering to hide his appreciation.

'Hello,' said Steven, going up to shake hands. 'Pretty dress! It suits you.'

'I was just getting some more wine.' Angie held up the bottle, but that seemed to provide all the explanation that her nakedness required.

'Good,' said Steven, sitting himself down and hauling Kathy onto his lap where she promptly dragged his hand inside her dressing gown. 'So what have you lot been up to while you have been waiting for us?'

'Getting pissed,' mumbled Charlotte, 'and Kathy made Angie give her a handy.'

Kathy tried to look sheepish with little success but Steven simply laughed. 'Can you not manage to keep your knickers on for a single day?'

'You weren't here!' she complained, which was no answer at all.

Ben was more interested; he settled down on the arm of the sofa next to Charlotte and began nuzzling up to her: 'And did you have one too?'

'No!'

'Why not?'

'I was waiting for you,' and she began returning his kisses, whispering in his ear and giggling at whatever he was suggesting. I tried not to stare but the other side of the room was little better: Kathy had given up trying to keep her dressing gown tied up so that the thing was soon in danger of falling off completely as Steven's hand roamed freely inside it.

Angie brought glasses for the boys, but when Steven struggled up to take his, Kathy's dressing gown fell open, exposing her small breasts entirely and she made no attempt to cover them up.

The other two were still whispering, or at least, Ben was whispering. Charlotte, on her fifth glass of wine, had abandoned discretion. 'Get off! I'm sleeping,' and she pushed him away, although without too much determination. 'Can't you wait? Get Angie to do it then!' she said and then 'Of course she will: she has to. Those are the rules, aren't they, Angie?'

Nobody had stated what they were talking about, but everyone knew. Kathy twisted round on Steven's lap, an excited grin lighting up her face and her dressing gown little better than gathered round her waist.

'Yes. The rules are that Angie has to do whatever she is told, aren't they, Angie?' Kathy didn't even wait for a response, bubbling on with almost childish excitement. 'And if Steven wants one afterwards, you'll do that too, won't you?'

We all looked at Angie and she kept her head down, staring at the floor. 'Yes,' she finally whispered.

If Steven was surprised, he gave no indication that he would refuse the offer. Ben, however, was already on his feet. 'Come on then, Angie. Let's go upstairs.'

'Oh no,' interrupted Charlotte, stirring lazily and crossing her legs. 'You have to stay here. I don't trust you upstairs. You'd be fucking her the second you got out of sight.'

'I wouldn't!'

'Yes you would! You fucked Kathy the first chance you got. I don't trust you.'

'That was your idea! Please, Charley? I don't want to do it with all you lot here.'

'Nope!' and she patted the sofa next to her. 'Here where I can keep an eye on you or not at all.'

'Oh bloody hell!' and he sat down where she had directed, parted his knees and waited.

Angie had stopped. Standing naked in the middle of the room, a wine bottle clutched against her chest like a charm she hoped would save her, I was almost moved to intervene and take her home, except that two things stopped me. First, nobody had actually forced her to this; she had taken off her clothes of her own free will, and at the very beginning she had seemed as reluctant to leave as I was. Second, for all her hesitation, Angie's nipples were as hard and excited as I have ever seen them.

While she stood there, everyone else settled down to watch. Kathy, leaning back into Steven's shoulder, had pulled her dressing gown back up onto her shoulders; she turned and smiled at him: a quick kiss in anticipation. Charlotte was still keeping a wary eye on Ben. And me? I was now as caught up as anyone; I had missed seeing Angie with Kathy; I did not want to miss seeing what she did to Ben. I leaned forward, partly to see better, mostly to hide from Angie the erection that had followed this latest instruction to her.

'Get on with it, Angie!' said Charlotte. 'Don't keep the poor man waiting!'

This time she did glance at me before she took the last few steps forward, knelt down between his thighs and then, after a breath, reached up to his belt.

She has done this for me often enough, although I would hesitate to be quite so imperiously uncooperative, but I have never seen her do it to anyone else. I have never seen anyone do it to someone else before, and yet here she was: my Angie, kneeling naked at the man's feet and unzipping his fly. He had the decency to lift his hips to allow her to pull his jeans down to his ankles, and again for his underpants, but otherwise he sat back, entirely relaxed, a small contented smile on his face and watched her.

She pushed the shirt up his stomach and there was his penis, curled up on a nest of black wiry hair, waiting for her. Delicately she picked it up, the whole thing fitted into her hand and she gently eased back his foreskin. By the time she had rolled it up and back two or three times more, the change was unmistakable: it no longer fitted into her hand. The head was pushing hopefully out of the top of her fist, her fingers which had been cosily wrapped round it could now barely meet. Ben sighed, carelessly draped an arm round Charlotte's shoulders and prepared to enjoy himself. For a moment I felt a sudden jealously and turned away.

That was little help. The scene was reflected back to me in the reaction on both the other faces: Steven's hand slowly creeping round to open up Kathy's dressing gown again: to cradle a single small breast in his palm, knowing I could see every single movement he made as his thump flicked her nipple back up to erect, and when that was not enough he casually, oh so very casually, slid the rest of the dressing gown down off her shoulders to expose her breasts entirely. And I know that Steven knew I was watching.

I heard another sigh from Ben, satisfied, but he was evidently an optimist. 'I think I'm a bit too dry,' he complained.

'Ben!' Charlotte's sharp retort had a tone of tolerating the misdeeds of a naughty puppy, and maybe Angie knew it was not too serious. She leaned forward and, just for a second, wrapped her mouth round the head, letting it reappear wet and shining before she resumed the gentle stroking with her hands, but they grinned together at having outmanoeuvred Charlotte and I turned away again.

Steven whispered into Kathy's ear: something: nothing. I could not make out what he said and he knew that, but she smiled, giggled, glancing briefly at me as she squirmed her legs together at whatever promise he had made, and when his hand slid down the next time, leaving her breasts uncovered but heading down between her thighs, she did not stop him. He tugged lightly at the dressing gown belt but it was caught under her bottom and so she pulled it out, letting him pull it free; the side flopped away to reveal the rest of her and now I had the answer to one of the questions I had been wondering about earlier: not shaved, but very neatly trimmed. Just for a second she could not keep from glancing over to me. Was she aware how much of her I was now seeing? Not just seeing, but openly watching? Maybe, but I don't believe she cared as much as I did.

And beside me, flickering in the corner of my eye, it was all still going on: Angie kneeling there, bent over, her bottom pushed out, her hands wrapped round this other man's erection and working it with as smooth and irresistible a motion as she ever applies to me. I kept watching: to see exactly what she was doing and how; trying not to make comparisons of size, or of her reaction, whether she was enjoying the contact as much as she would do if it were me. And when I turned away, there were Steven and Angie, she still on his lap but her thighs now spread either side of his, completely opening herself so that his hand could roam freely between her legs, his fingers openly digging down between her lips, masturbating her without the slightest qualms. And they had as few inhibitions over watching Angie and Ben as they did over allowing all of us to watch them. Only Charlotte, for all her display of possessive jealously earlier, seemed unconcerned, even uninterested. She was sitting right next to Ben on the sofa, their legs touching, but she was carelessly slouching down, her legs stretched out in front of her, and much of the time with her eyes half shut as if she found herself in front of a rather dull televison programme that she had seen before but had not the energy to switch off. Her whole body was jiggled by Ben's increasingly urgent movements, but beyond an occasional deep sigh, she showed not the slightest concern over what was going on.

Steven now had both arms encircling Kathy's waist, his hands burrowed deep between her legs, his fingers working steadily and evidently effectively: her face was twisting, her hands gripping his thighs as she pressed herself harder down against him. Next to me, Ben's breath had been getting increasingly short and suddenly he groaned out a quiet 'Oh fuck!' and when I looked round he was ejaculating; long streams flying up onto his stomach as Angie's fists continued their frantic pace.

When it stopped, Ben lay back staring at the ceiling. 'Fuck!'

'Here!' called Kathy, and tossed a cloth over to Angie. 'Clean him up.' Only it wasn't a cloth: it was her knickers again, left on the floor from when she had wiped herself with them earlier. Even so, Angie did as she was told: carefully and gently wiping round Ben's softening erection, his stomach, and, when that was done, pulling up his pants and trousers. Finally dressed, he sat up as Angie climbed back to her feet.

'Charley next!' Ben announced.

'Yes!' cheered Kathy. 'Come on, Charley. Your turn!'

'No, I don't want one,' she replied, settling back into her half-doze. 'I'm going to sleep, and I will probably take Ben upstairs later.'

'Too late! Your turn now!' insisted Kathy, hopping off Steven's lap and, with her dressing gown flowing round her like wings, scooting across to Charlotte on the sofa.

'Come on, Charley,' said Ben. 'You know you want to!' but he had already started grabbing for the zip on the side of her skirt.

'No!' protested Charlotte and now she did sit up, batting his hands away. 'Oh come on! I'm not in the mood. I'm going to sleep.' She twisted over to keep the zip safely out of reach underneath her, but now Kathy was joining in too and her hands went straight up Charlotte's skirt and reappeared tugging a pair of flimsy pink knickers down her legs. When Charlotte tried to grab at those, Ben was back tugging at the skirt.

And all this while Angie was standing naked in the middle of the living room staring, her knickers clutched in one hand; I was watching, appalled, horrified and shamefully excited at the prospect of what seemed, with increasing certainty, to be Angie's next task.

Charley was still fighting Ben off but by this stage he had the zip of her skirt half undone and was tugging at the waistband to pull it down over her hips. This alone aroused her determination: 'Careful! You'll tear it!' And she reached down herself to finish unzipping it. 'Okay,' she said as Ben slid the small skirt down and off, 'but I'm not taking my top off!'

Ben and Kathy had already won their battle and had just about stopped but this burst of defiance reinspired them. One glance was exchanged and they were both at Charlotte's sweat shirt pulling this up, one restraining her hands while the other tugged at the sleeves, and since they showed less concern over damage to her clothes than she did, they soon had the top off. By this point she barely even resisted the attack on her bra, allowing herself to be pulled forward so that Ben could reach round and, after an age of fumbling, Kathy in despair could finally come and unhook it. They hauled it away, waving it as a trophy and left her there, quite naked, while she continued low, indistinct and entirely unconvincing protests. These would have been more credible if she had not promptly lain back in the sofa, her arms spread wide, her legs apart and her body freely displayed to the whole room.

I have always been proud of Angie: she is very attractive: Charlotte was simply stunning. Her breasts were much bigger than I had realized, but so wonderfully smooth and even, now gently resting on a narrow chest that seemed barely strong enough to support them. The nipples, softly and warmly pink, had perked up a little but modestly, ready if called upon but not overly assertive. Her stomach lay smooth and silky and she was completely shaved, with the tips of a pair of pink lips peering out towards us. You could understand why she had no misgivings about being seen naked; she could stand comparison with anybody.

And when I glanced round at Angie, still standing, still waiting, still naked in the middle of the room, she too was staring down at the person who she had now been told to caress, and she stared with a surprised longing that had wiped all other considerations from her face. Nobody else spoke, but Charlotte was looking up at her, swaying her knees wider and closer, wider and closer, as the two of them prepared for what they had been told they must do. And it ended with Charlotte swaying her legs wider, and staying there; finally she opened wide her eyes.

'Well get on with it, Angie, if that is what those perverts want.'

The room went completely quiet and then Angie stepped forward, knelt back down again, reached out once to run her fingertips over the lips on offer and then, without being asked for anything further, she leaned down to bury her face in Charlotte's pussy.

It was almost more than I could stand to watch. It would be a very dull man who had not at some time imagined seeing his lover in the arms of another woman, let alone one as beautiful as this. Ben was still sitting there while the scene was played out beside him and he would occasionally reach over to stroke Charlotte's breasts, or to lift up Angie's hair so that he could see better what her lips and tongue were doing. On the other side, Kathy had stayed perched on the sofa arm, her dressing gown first hanging entirely loose but soon shrugged off entirely, while she also casually stroked Charlotte with one hand, and as casually caressed herself with the other. Between them sprawled Charlotte, a serene smile on her face, her arms and legs flung wide while she received the attentions of these three people as if she was accustomed to this, expected it and deserved it.

I was already aroused, I admit that; the whole situation as it had gradually grown: the implications of the various relationships among the four people in the cottage: the easy way all that had come to light. The implication too that my own Angie, someone whom I thought I knew well, had so involved and sensuous a past, a past to which she had never admitted. Now, lying with her head buried between Charlotte's thighs she was a different person.

Charlotte was clearly enjoying everything that Angie was doing. Her thighs were quivering, her chest heaving and her nipples had puckered up to tight little scarlet berries.

Without opening her eyes and by only the slightest movement of her neck, Charlotte tilted up her chin. 'Kiss me,' she said to nobody in particular and although they both moved, Ben was too slow. Kathy had already dropped down beside her and her mouth was clamped to her friend's. The contrasts between the two of them could hardly have been greater: their heights, their colouring, their builds, yet they seemed to fit together perfectly. From where I was sitting, I could see their lips moving, and their tongues as they kissed. More than that, Kathy's hands were playing with her breasts, rolling, pinching and squeezing them, and reaching down also to dig her hands into Angie's hair. I suddenly looked round and realized that the three men, Steven, Ben and I, were all completely left out while the three girls were completely engrossed in each other. We were all fully clothed; the three girls were naked. I grinned round at the realization, although whether they knew what I meant I have no idea. From what had been said, this kind of event was not at all unusual in their lives.

Charlotte was moaning softly, a steady purring like a contented cat as she slowly lifted her hips better against Angie's tongue. The purrs grew shorter and faster, finally joining into an almost continuous rumble until she grabbed

Ben's arm on one side, Kathy's shoulder on the other, digging her fingers into their skin, finally going quite rigid and letting out one long gentle wail.

She lay back, pulled her hands back and lay back in exactly the same position she had been in ten minutes before. 'Hmm! That was nice!'

Kathy bent down to pick up her dressing gown, although she didn't bother to put it on as she sauntered back to Steven's lap.

Angie sat back on her heels, her hands resting on Charlotte's knees, her face wet and shining but a look of real pride in her eyes. I reached for her, pulled her up onto my lap and kissed her, a glorious deep warm kiss in which I tasted Charlotte on her lips, and felt her excitement in the way she squirmed her bottom down into my lap; she could have been in no doubt as to how I was feeling and even reached down to make sure. She giggled, and kissed me some more.

'Now what?' asked Ben.

'More wine,' murmured Charlotte, 'and I need a pee.'

Steven and Kathy pulled apart, Kathy resting her head on his shoulder and leaving him to speak. 'Apparently Angie caused Kathy to get a detention.'

'More wine,' repeated Charlotte, this time just twisting her legs over.

'So?' asked Ben.

'So we think Angie should be paid back.'

'The slipper?' asked Ben.

'The slipper!' said Steven.

I felt Angie shudder on my lap, but when she turned back round to me there was no real fear in her eyes. And when she leaned down to kiss me again, there was more desire than anything else.

'Good idea!' Kathy was certainly enthusiastic. 'Angie, go up to my room and get my bedroom slippers. Well, we will only need one of them actually.'

'And bring more wine,' added Charlotte, still lying spread out, completely naked, completely unconcerned. 'And a potty.'

Angie climbed off my lap and set off upstairs. I heard her moving about in the room above us for some while, before she called down, 'I can't find them.'

'Oh bloody hell!' said Kathy and stalked off up. A few seconds later there were some muffled voices, then Angie: 'Well I didn't look there!' a loud slap, a squeal and Kathy came back down looking very pleased with herself as she returned to her perch on Steven's lap. A short while later Angie appeared, clutching one slipper and still rubbing her bottom.

'Me first!' claimed Kathy. 'How many of us are there? Five? That means... Bugger! Only three each! Well come here for your three, Angie.'

She obviously knew the routine: from what they had all been saying, it seemed likely that she had devised it. Angie walked over and presented Kathy with the slipper; then she turned her back and bent over, staring across at me as she waited to receive the strokes.

Kathy was not easy on her. The three fell in quick succession with a retort like gunfire each time. Angie winced at every one, her knees giving way as she struggled to absorb it and then she straightened up again, ready to take the next. Even so, her eyes were shining when she stood up after the third to take the slipper back.

'You next, Steven?' and when he sat up to get ready, Angie

meekly passed the slipper across. I do think Steven was a little gentler, but Angie was still blinking back tears by the time those three had been delivered. I wasn't the only one to notice.

'Wimp!' said Kathy, 'Now Charley.'

'I'm asleep.'

'Then wake up. This is fun.'

And Charlotte did wake up. When Angie carried the slipper across to her, she arranged her at the best angle and then Charlotte slammed the slipper down as hard as she could so that Angie squealed after each one, her eyes red and filling with tears.

Ben was no more sympathetic. He took the slipper – part of the ritual seemed to be that the victim had to take it from each person and pass it on to the next – bent her down almost across his lap and whipped the slipper down, all three strokes carefully and deliberately on the same cheek, in the same place, with the same stinging slap.

'And now Graham,' said Kathy.

'Me?' I really had not thought that I would be expected to take part; I had been little more than a spectator to any of this, but Angie already had the slipper and was holding it out to me. 'I'm not sure that I should...' I started but Angie wouldn't move and she merely offered the slipper a little more firmly towards me. So I took it.

She turned and bent over in front of me, presenting her bottom and for the first time I was able to see properly what it now looked like. It was red: very red absolutely all over although there was one patch, right in the middle of her left cheek, that was even more inflamed than the rest.

She was bent over, and I could reach her, but it would

be awkward. And she had... Well she hadn't lied to me, but then she hadn't told me the truth either: about St Theresa's College; about her friends there; about her experience before we had met; particularly her experience with other girls. More than that, this afternoon had revealed a side to her, a range of fantasies that I had not known about at all, and she had not been honest with me about them. And I had never spanked her, not even the lightest slap in play, although there had been many times when I had found her face down on the bed and thought that if I didn't know better, I would believe she was offering herself up for a spanking. I had resisted the urge then, fighting it down for lack of any sign from her that it would not have been abhorrent. So many nights wasted; so much time to make up.

'Not like that,' I said. 'I have waited a long time for this and I am going to do it properly. I want you flat across my lap and you are not getting three: you will receive twelve.'

'Yes, Graham,' she whispered and lowered herself down, stretching herself out ready to receive them. 'Please, not too hard.'

'They will be as hard as I determine.'

'Yes, Graham.'

The other two girls, still naked, gathered round to watch; Kathy squatting down within arm's reach so as not to miss anything. Ben and Steven stayed in their seats but they sat forward to see better as I began to lay them on.

'Count them out,' I said and brought the first one down. It made a wonderful deep slap and her whole bottom quivered but she gasped out one, and two and three and on. Every stroke was made to count and every stroke she did count even though by five she was counting through tears. She almost lost control completely by nine but I did not let up and the sight of our small audience, watching silent and enraptured, spurred me on; Kathy of course already had her hand back between her legs, shamelessly masturbating as she crouched in front of us, although it was not until nearly the end that I realized her other hand was stroking Angie's breasts at the same time.

Angie kept her count all the way to twelve: even the one for luck which I added afterwards and when that was done she lay with her bottom upturned to us, a picture of perfect glowing beauty. Her eyes, when I dragged her up onto my lap a minute or two later, sparkled, a picture of perfect gleaming exhilaration. I sat her with my back to me, her legs hooked outside mine so that I could swing my legs apart and open hers to all of them. Kathy, still squatting directly in front of us, immediately took the invitation, slid her hand all the way up Angie's thigh and a single finger pushed straight into her. Angie gasped and clutched my hand.

'Steven,' wheedled Kathy, scampering back to Steven, snuggling up to him, rubbing her little breasts against his chest and pushing that same glistening hand down the front of his trousers, 'why don't we take Angie upstairs?'

But this time I did step in. 'No. I am going to take Angie home,' and I felt Angie's hand squeeze a fraction tighter. 'We have some unfinished business.' She turned, grinning at me, hugged me close and kissed me. 'Although I could bring her back tomorrow, if you like.' The hug tightened so I could hardly breathe.

LOUISE'S FIRST TALE: LOVE CHAMPIONS

Neil and I had been planning this Round-the-World trip for ages, but inevitably, once we were actually on the road, we found more places we wanted to see and more countries we wanted to visit. The cost soon left our budget behind, galloped away out of our control and by half-way round we were having to work whenever, wherever at whatever we could to keep going. In Japan, which was horrifically expensive, the money ran out altogether. Still, there are other ways to make money and the most accessible in Japan was the range of bizarre television contests which give out massive prizes for very little work. This had the advantage of being legal – you don't need a work permit to enter a competition, nor to win a prize – and I thought that our 'foreignness' would give us an added interest which would help us to be accepted.

The thing you notice immediately in Japan (in fact all across the Far East) is that everyone has black hair. The girls also tend to have fairly small busts.

The thing you notice immediately about me is that I'm the opposite. I have blonde hair and rather a lot of it, and a good size (and good shaped) bust: 36D to be precise, and it would be silly to deny that on several occasions during our trip we had been successful in getting lifts, meals and hospitality (as well as jobs) purely because of those assets. Now maybe I should be more feminist and militant about this, but it would have been utterly naive to think that my degree in business studies coupled with work experience at the Water Company

Call Centre and six weeks at the Miner's Arms in Leeds was going to carry much weight 12,000 miles away in a foreign country surrounded by people whose language made as much sense to me as mine did to them: none at all.

What did make sense to them, what was intelligible in any language, was my blonde hair and ample bustline.

We tried for various quiz shows, including one that was similar to the European *Big Brother* where I thought we might stand a chance, but the language problem prevented it. I'm sure we could have sailed through any of the silly quizzes if only we had understood a single word of what was getting everyone else so excited.

But at the open audition for one of these, when we had again, most apologetically, been rejected, the producer called us aside and whispered that he might be able to offer us a place on another show he produced if we were interested. He invited us to wait in his office and promised to tell us all about it as soon as he had finished dealing with this quiz.

We were conducted through a tangle of corridors and waited in his office while the sounds of hope and despair rang round the rest of the studio building. Although the office was not big (nowhere in Japan is space wasted), this was more than an office: you could have lived there. It had a desk and all the usual office furniture but also, in a small alcove off the office, a bed and tiny bathroom with a shower, a basin and toilet. It seemed to epitomise the efficiency of the Japanese way of life and their devotion to their employers which would lead them to sleep at the office if that was necessary to get the job done.

We waited there, with tempered optimism in view of the many disappointments previously, for over half an hour before the man came bustling in, introduced himself as Mr

Kan, shook my hand, scrutinised my chest and finally sat down behind his desk.

'No, this show not for you. So sorry. But I do many shows and maybe I have one better. It is called *Love Champions*.'

We had never heard of it, but that didn't matter; we were too short of time to be choosey.

'You never see this show?'

'No, we don't watch much television.'

'Ah! Very popular on adult cable. Many people like it very much.'

'Adult channel?'

'Yes.'

'I see. So what does it involve?'

'It is contest with two couples, see which is sexiest on television.' He grinned broadly.

'How is that judged?' I was getting a little bit suspicious but also intrigued at this revelation of an unexpected side to the culture in what is – in so many respects – a very strait-laced society.

'They just do love and judges say which is better.'

'Do love?'

'Yes. That's all.'

'You mean make love? Have sex? On television?'

'Yes, and couple who judges think is best one, they win much prize.'

I didn't even need to consult Neil. 'I see. Well thanks for the offer but I don't think we'll do that.'

We stood up to leave but Mr Kan had not finished. 'For you, western couple is only once before on show. They win prize, so maybe you win too. Very much prize.'

'How much?'

He hedged about and finally, after some negotiation,

quoted an amount that was not far short of fifteen hundred pounds, but with a guaranteed sum of just under a thousand pounds even if we didn't win. This was beginning to get tempting: after all, there was nobody who knew us in the whole of Japan, and on a small late night adult channel: the possibility of being recognised was almost nil.

'And what exactly happens?' Neil's curiosity was aroused now.

'What I say. You just do sex.'

'That's all?'

'Yes, and we make film to show televison.'

'So we just do whatever we like? I mean you aren't suddenly going to want us to do something weird?'

'No, very normal. In Japan, people do not like strange things. Japanese are very honourable people. Very ancient traditions of honour.'

'Yes,' Neil mused, 'except for a penchant for watching other people screwing.'

'Anyway,' I pushed on, wanting a good deal more reassurance if I was even going to consider this suggestion. 'It is just the two of us doing it? We don't find that a couple of your friends have been invited to join in?'

'Or their dogs?' added Neil.

'Oh no,' he assured us earnestly, 'no dogs. Just you two.'

'Nobody else touches us at all?' I was determined to get this straight.

'No! I tell you! No! Just normal.'

'Normal,' I repeated, realising that this crazy idea was actually beginning to sound rather appealing and so trying to assure myself that it really was "normal".

'Yes!' he said again, 'but if you want to win...'

'Aha! I thought there'd be something more. If we want to win, what?'

'It must be good. Interesting to see for the judges.'

I glossed over that. 'How long do we have to perform for?'

'Show last one hour. We start with little interview, who you names, how are you old, this things, all that maybe five minutes. So maybe fifteen minutes or twenty minutes you do sex. Other couple the same. Then judges say who won.'

I glanced across to Neil and that was all it took; Mr Kan could see we were wavering. 'Okay? Show goes on Friday. We film Thursday, you come here at five o'clock. Yes? You like?' He was so eager.

Neil and I exchanged a glance again and for an inexplicable reason, yes we did like. So we agreed. We signed the contract then and there, to include first the release which they needed and second to specify the prize money he had agreed and ensure that we got paid to take part. I didn't want any arguments afterwards. As we were leaving, Mr Kan clutched my hand between his hot clammy palms and explained how pleased he was that such a beautiful girl was to be on his show. He even hinted, hints which I chose to misunderstand, that there were other ways of ensuring we won the big prize, even that we could go on to take part in the finals of a big international competition which he was – he claimed – even now planning. I thanked him, said I would certainly consider it and retrieved my hand.

As we walked out into the blazing sun, I could not suppress a surge of confidence: as he had admitted, western couples were rare so we would be starting with a huge advantage. Neil and I left the televison studios and headed down for the nearest bar, laughing loudly enough, but I'm sure that inside he was just as anxious as I was about what we'd let ourselves in for.

~

We arrived at the studio on the Thursday and met the show's two presenters, a couple who were not a great deal older than us, yet seemed much like the presenters of any populist TV show in any country. They handed us over to a very young assistant, a sweet innocent little girl who was to act as our interpreter and guide. She said her name was Kiki and, dressed in a short straight skirt, white blouse and jacket, a combination that looked horribly like my old school uniform, I was beginning to wonder why she wasn't in school herself, and certainly why she was able to work on a show like this. Then she spoke of having been to university in Seattle, and of a husband who was still there studying for an MA, and it was a shock to realise that she must have been at least twenty-two: she was actually older than either Neil or me.

She took us down to the dressing room which we were to share with the couple who would be our competitors. They were Japanese, young, and again I had to remind myself they must be older than they looked, but there was no possibility of any conversation. They spoke virtually no English at all beyond greetings and slang picked up from films and records, but I don't think there would have been much we could say. Neither of them looked happy, and the girl in particular clutched continuously at her boyfriend's hand, staring at Kiki and us through wide eyes and clamped lips. We were introduced to the three judges: there were two men and one woman, but they seemed a quite ridiculously staid trio; one of the men didn't even bother to get off his mobile phone to greet us and the other two both looked utterly bored by the whole business. On balance, if those were to be the people who would assess my competence as a lover, I was not worried. Halfway through this, Mr Kan reappeared in his tailored suit and fresh-laundered shirt, grinning the same implacable grin, and there was no question but that his interest was a good deal less academic. He smiled broadly, rows of expensive gleaming teeth, and again grasped my hand between his to recite how much he was looking forward to the evening and to our performance. He repeated his offer to include us in other shows, and without rejecting his kindness, I said we would have to see how we got on in this one first.

After these strained introductions, Kiki took all four of us, the competitors, up to show us round the studio. That was the first real shock.

It was huge, a full-size studio, but completely dominated by a canopied bed so over-elaborate that I couldn't decide whether I was more amused or terrified. It was at least king-size and low to the floor, but it was a mass of pink bows and hearts, strewn with piles of lacy pink pillows with a lacy pink canopy over the top equally decorated with bows and hearts and little pairs of bells. The whole ensemble made up the worst imaginable cross between Saint Valentine's Day kitsch and cheap wedding stationery that it would be possible to imagine. So much effort and work had obviously been put into preparing the thing, and the effect was appalling. But next to that, only ten or twelve feet away from the side of the bed, was the neat semi-circular desk at which the judges would sit to gauge our competence. It might as easily have been used to adjudicate on an ice-skating championship or to accommodate a panel game but with its simple functional austerity, the exact opposite to the bed, it looked ridiculous. To add to the banality, three chairs were lined up behind it and a row of three neat writing pads lay waiting for the judges to make whatever notes they felt to be necessary on particular aspects of our performance. The other couple clutched each other and whispered.

But there was worse.

There were the cameras. One was mounted on a swivel on the head of the bed, another similarly on the foot, one suspended inside the canopy directly overhead and two on low tripods, angled up from the corners. And there were two others, standard trolley-mounted things such as I had often seen in television studios, which would presumably be brought round to home in on whichever area they thought was most deserving. In all I counted seven cameras that could be aimed at us from one angle or another. Nothing we did would be allowed to pass unseen.

And still there was worse.

Beyond the bed was the auditorium, gaping like an empty mouth, whose rows of empty seats waited for a live audience. I looked at Neil and his face showed the same shock I was feeling. He turned to Kiki.

'Is there an audience here during the filming?'

'Oh yes!'

'Shit!' I suppose I should have expected it, the producer had said something about it being filmed live, but I hadn't really taken in the full implications of his words at the time.

Neil put his arm round my shoulders. 'Don't worry. They're a long way off.'

'Oh yes!' Kiki announced proudly, 'and we have big screens!'

Following her gaze upwards we saw them: huge white rectangles as if for a rock concert were suspended above the stage, and I counted seven of them. Seven screens presumably meant one for every camera, that whatever we did, it would be visible to at least one camera position and would then be relayed onto these giant squares for the entertainment of the live and television audiences. I felt sick.

Other than that, and another cluster of four seats on the opposite side, the stage was quite bare. There was to be nothing to distract the audience, the viewers or the judges from the action on the dreadful bed.

Neil and I made our way back to the dressing room in silence, where we sat, both lost in our own thoughts, and waited. The other couple exchanged occasional comments that we did not understand but they never let go of each others' hands and looked more miserable than ever. We tried making conversation, but a succession of nods and forced smiles quickly showed that this would get nowhere and we lapsed back into silence. For half an hour we all listened to the last of the setting up being completed: shouts and calls as the equipment and music was tested and then stopped before suddenly it started up again with renewed determination, only to be drowned under a stampede of rushing feet. I pictured the excited gathering dashing for the best seats above us and began to understand the feelings of a condemned man hearing the sound of his scaffold being erected. A few minutes later our sweet little assistant returned. 'The audience is just going in, okay?' and something, presumably the same, in Japanese.

The Japanese couple clutched each other even tighter: they were to go on first and evidently liked that prospect no better than I would have done, so when a few minutes later

Kiki was back yet again to deliver a quick smile to us and a few words to the other couple, she led them away, although not before they had both taken off their shoes and socks. I didn't realise that the custom for Japanese houses applied here too.

We heard voices, announcements, cheers, silence, applause, more cheers, more silence and the routine went on and on until eventually, after about ten minutes, a different music started, something which you might, if you had liked the idea of a pink candy floss bed, you might have thought was appropriate music to watch a terrified young couple making love by. I reached for Neil's hand and tried to picture what might be happening up there as the music welled and faded and while the audience alternately cheered and fell silent. Finally, as the music finished, drowned in loud roars of applause, Kiki appeared in the doorway, bright, professional and untroubled.

'Ready now, okay? Advertisements last five minutes and we go up. It is best you take off shoes and socks here.'

'Yes, of course. I'm sorry.' This was certainly no time to show our coarseness by upsetting local sensibilities, but she just frowned.

'It looks very clumsy to do that later when you start. When you go upstairs,' she continued as Neil and I started unlacing our trainers, 'first you go on stage and the judges make a few questions, then...' she shrugged. 'As you like.' And smiled. 'Have fun.'

'Yes, but do people just, you know,' I started, but I couldn't really think what it was I was trying to ask, 'do it? You know, like for real? Or do they aim for more of a display? More like a show?'

She shrugged; the question didn't interest her. 'Some one

way. Some another.' Then she glanced round. 'I think they like to think it is real, you know?'

'Right,' I nodded. 'Thank you,' and trailed behind her towards the stairs, the click of her smart shoes contrasting with the silence of our bare feet. 'What's the audience like?' I just wanted to keep some sort of conversation going.

'Okay.' She turned and wrinkled her nose. 'Maybe not so happy. First ones,' and she nodded her head up the stairs ahead of us, 'first ones stayed in for the ending. Audience don't like that; they want to see.'

'What? See what?' I was lost.

She turned without a shred of embarrassment. 'You call it "The Money Shot" I think? They like to see the man come, see him do it outside, spill his sperm on you. Not do it inside woman's pussy where they don't see anything.' Her degree had obviously included precise English terminology for a specific range of parts of the body.

'Ah!' I said, not at all pleased that I now understood. 'I see.'

'Yes,' she continued. 'If you do outside, I think you win.'

'Thanks,' I said. 'If we do, we'll buy you dinner.'

She giggled. 'No, I mean it!' I stressed. 'If we win, it will be because of your help, so you definitely deserve a thank you. I'll come and find you.' I don't know quite what was driving me. It wasn't just generosity, perhaps curiosity at this strange and rather sweet looking girl who seemed so young and yet was so much more worldly wise than us in this.

'Oh no! No!' She was genuinely upset at the prospect. 'So sorry, but I have duties afterwards.' She was adamant but I would have pressed on except that we had reached the side of the stage.

It was still the interval. All the lights were up, brighter out there than where we huddled in the protection of the wings, so that the auditorium was now illuminated and we could see the crowd milling about eating ice-cream and drinking fluorescent pink slush from huge paper cups, and it was a real mix of people. Perhaps there were not quite as many women as men, but almost, and there were as many young people as old. The two presenters were also having a break, being fussed round by make-up girls and hair-stylists. Two other girls, thankfully, were changing the bed linen, and although the new set was no more tasteful than the last, at least it would be clean. The panel of judges had gone into a huddle round their note pads; two were middle-aged men but the third, the woman, was noticeably younger, barely thirty, and she peered across at me with a look that seemed horribly like hunger. I quickly turned away.

Kiki stood behind us. 'I tell you when it is time to go. You cross over and sit on those chairs,' she indicated the empty seats on the far side of the stage, a little cluster of four like any chat show set, 'and the presenters will make the introductions. This all speaking in English, we dub Japanese before broadcast tomorrow.'

We digested this but she was going on. 'I will stay here and show you the time with these cards, see?' She held up four big cards saying "15", "10", "5" and "3". 'This will show you how much time is left. Okay?'

Butterflies were working overtime in my stomach. My heart was pounding, my hands felt clammy and as I reached for Neil, his palm was no better. I had often dreamed of being on television; I had never dreamed it would be for an occasion such as this. A floor manager appeared with a clipboard and called something over. Kiki answered him, presumably confirming we were ready and then the man called for silence, the two presenters picked up their clipboards, put on their smiles and the theme music started again. Some more words, more applause, more big smiles and they turned to grin welcomes at us.

'Go!'

I simply couldn't move. Kiki pushed me in the back and I stayed still but she shoved harder, so hard that I could only keep from falling on my face by taking a step forward. And then another.

On stage the world was lost in the glare of the stage lights, the roar of applause from a sea of invisible faces (choreographed, I noticed, by other uniformed girls on each side of the auditorium) and then at last we had made it. We were safely across the stage and being ushered into the seats by the presenters, Neil and I in the middle with the man next to him and the woman next to me.

The interviews started off as banal as at any quiz show on any channel I had ever seen. We agreed that those were our names, told them our ages, a bit about our home towns and what we would do if we won the first prize. I did not say that we only wanted to earn enough for the flights home, and instead I explained that we wanted to stay longer in Japan, to see more of the beautiful countryside, explore its rich culture and meet its warm and wonderful people. They nodded understandingly at that.

If all these questions were trite, they were at least innocent. But then both our interviewers paused a moment, the man leaned forward and, with a deep earnestness on his face, addressed himself to Neil alone. The questions had turned more personal. How many girls had he slept with before me? What had appealed to him about me? How long had it been after we had met that we first had sex? How often did we have sex now? How did I compare with his previous partners? They were growing increasingly intrusive but were all asked with such solemn seriousness, as if this were part of a scientific study, and without a hint of prurience so that the answers came easily enough.

Then he paused, he was done, and like the figures on a weather house, as he leaned back in his seat, the woman leaned forward, swivelling round to face me. It was my turn.

'Now Louise, we don't have many western girls on this show, so it is particularly valuable to have you here this evening and to be able to get answers to some of the questions which many of our audience will be asking themselves. I hope you will be able to help us.' She smiled. I smiled and said I hoped so too, but on the intrusiveness scale, she started where he had stopped.

She began with physical things; the size of my breasts, whether my hair was really blonde and whether my body hair was also blonde. Then it moved on. What did I like best sexually? How many men I had slept with? Which was my favourite position? It was known that western girls were very liberal and had dozens of partners, possibly three or four at one time, how many had I had? Whether I liked having sex with girls, the answer to which was probed for some while since this was something which Japanese people would never do. Next we moved on to how much I masturbated, whether I liked a big vibrator or a small one, and so on. I felt myself viewing all this as if from a distance and realised that I should not be surprised that their questions were so personal, nor that hers were so much more personal than Neil's had been; after all the whole show was about stripping away our privacy and making us display to the whole world the most intimate of actions. Somehow I got through, and answered them all in some way or another, not always truthfully, but I have to keep some privacy.

Then she sat back and thanked me before the two of them, in over-rehearsed harmony, stood up to take each of us by the arm and lead us across towards the waiting bed. Then they released us, stepped away, and left us there. It was time.

I don't know whether Neil had considered what we were supposed to do next but I certainly had not. Were we both just supposed to strip off? Were we meant to start kissing and undress slowly? If we weren't careful we could easily be still waiting there when Kiki was standing on the side wildly flapping her "three minutes" card. Neil would happily spend the whole hour indulging his breast fixation and I wouldn't mind much: I like having them stroked, but we had to remember that we only had a few minutes to win the prize, and Neil was just standing there, peering vaguely about him.

So I put my arms round him and snogged him. He accepted that happily enough – well who wouldn't? – but he didn't make any further move, seemed totally unconcerned that time was slipping by, and that we had a huge audience and a panel of three judges to keep happy.

So I sat down on the side of the bed, pulled Neil down beside me and we started kissing again, but this time I pushed away the sounds and the bright lights, the audience and cameras, and just carried on as if nobody else was there. I brought his hands up to my breasts and he started stroking me straightaway and then sliding down to slip his hands under my top. But reaching my breasts would not impress any of our watchers, so I pulled my top up myself, right up and over my head, tossed it away, and sat there in a black bra that was probably big enough on its own to hold the breasts of all the other women there: the compere, the assistant and the interpreter, all in one. The audience was quiet now. They may not have understood much of the interview, but there was no translation problem in what was happening now as Neil massaged across my breasts.

'Undo it,' I whispered and at last he did, freeing the constraining straps to let my breasts out to face the audience and I heard the intake of breath at the way they stayed, pointing straight out at them all, the nipples huge as plums and erect, the aureolas dark and smooth and prominent. How could anybody feel anything but pride in that situation? The combined awe of two or three hundred people as they were presented with my breasts and I still had more to show them. We were still kissing as I unbuttoned Neil's shirt and pulled that off and then I pulled away and lay out flat on the bed. Above us a good expanse of the screens was visible and I realised just how exposed we were to the eyes of the cameras and the eyes of the audience. It was intoxicating but Neil had leant down to suckle my breasts, and with all those eyes on me, waiting for me, I wanted to be completely naked, to let them see everything.

So I stayed lying there and reached down myself to loose the popper of my Levis, unzip the fly and push them slowly down my legs. Very slowly, I edged the denim lower and lower while everyone waited for the top of my knickers to appear. Perhaps they expected they would match the bra and were watching for the first hint of black lace; instead, the first thing they saw – relayed onto a massive screen above my head - was the top of a bar of warm golden fur. I don't wear knickers,

I haven't worn them for years.

The gasp, and cheer, came all across the auditorium and I half turned towards the line of judges to let them see too as I shoved the jeans down the rest of the way and pulled them right off. Kiki had been right about shoes.

For a moment I lay there and let everyone see the golden triangle. I don't shave or trim it as so many girls do these days, but then it is naturally thin and very curly so you can see enough of my lips to be tempting without the whole lot being offered right away. Underneath it is short and still hides little, so I leave that too, and Neil likes it that way. He says it smells of me.

So now I was naked, and the trolley cameras had come rolling up closer, one at my side and one down at the end of the bed, and for that one I drew my legs up and then slowly opened them as wide as I could while the camera moved in ever closer. I reached down to stroke myself, rubbing along the lips and up round my clit before I curled a finger down and pushed it up into the warm wetness inside. Out again to show the audience, my knuckles glistening in the bright lights while the cameras zoomed up so close they were almost touching me, before I dipped it back in, wet it again, and rubbed it across my clit.

But from the corner of my eye I saw Kiki setting up the "15" board.

I pushed Neil off my breasts and sat up so that I could now reach down to unfasten his jeans and pull them off, and as Neil now agrees with me about underwear, his cock immediately appeared, bobbing in the air, pink and glorious but only half-erect. As he settled down on his back, I caught it in my fist and knelt down to take it in my mouth seeing the trolley cameras closing in on us from both sides. One was right in front of me, so I made a big display for that, taking as much as I could into my mouth and then licking the whole length of his erection, right to the tip and then back down to his balls. But the other camera had moved round behind me, and although I could no longer see the screens, I could picture well enough what they would be showing with me kneeling there, my bottom stuck out and my legs partly separated. I reached my free hand down to go on playing with myself, and at the same time opened my legs wider. The camera moved in a little closer.

Neil's cock was growing steadily in my mouth, thickening and lengthening and it was getting more and more difficult to keep much of it controlled, so I released it and I knew that would impress them too, because when, as now, it is fully erect, Neil has a magnificent cock, not only solid and thick but as long as any I have ever known. But I was now kneeling across the bed, and when I glanced up, I found the line of judges directly in front of me, all craning hungrily forward across their little desk, their gazes fixed intently on my hands wrapped round the erection and – when my tongue slipped out to lap at the smooth head – two of them subconsciously copied the motion. For a few minutes I stayed there, watching them watching me, as I licked and slipped the head back into my mouth while my hands worked slow strokes up and down the shaft.

I was getting eager for something too and so I turned round above him to take up the classic "69" position which would let the judges still see clearly, and would also let one camera continue to film me licking his cock and give the other one an even better view between my open legs as Neil started to lick me, chewing on my lips and sucking at my clit, nipping at the hood and pulling at it. His fingers meanwhile were flapping at my lips and then pushing up inside me to work round in growing circles that opened me up inside in a way that began those glorious low tremors and which would soon have the juice visibly dribbling out of me. I do get very wet.

I suppose I should have stopped him and done something to play more to the crowd, but it felt too good, and besides, they were getting a good enough look at my bottom.

So instead I continued playing to the judges and to the camera in front of me, taking as much of Neil's cock into my mouth at one time as I could and alternating this with making long sweeps with the flat of my tongue right up its whole length while the big wet shining head bobbed about against my mouth and cheeks and the whole thing got bigger and harder and I knew he was going to reach a stage where he could not hold off.

I moved down to nibble his balls, taking each in turn right into my mouth and rolling round its sack with my tongue before popping it back out again and moving on to the other one. Then lower still, running round the little star of his anus, and just as that was nicely wet, feeling him do the same thing to me and the tip of his finger, wet with my juice, press through into my bottom.

But there was a swirl of movement at the side of the stage and Kiki held up the "10" board.

I began to panic; it had seemed like seconds had passed and we still had much to do. I lifted away, swivelled round and rolled over onto my back next to Neil, opening my legs to him in an invitation as ancient as mankind, but it was an invitation that the cameras picked up first, closing in again to examine the wet lips and open warmth, the whole thing repeated above my head on one of the screens, surrounded by other views of us, of the two of us moving naked across the bed, of Neil's cock, and of my breasts, close-ups of my breasts, of the erect nipples and smooth round sides where they dipped to either side of my chest and lay waiting.

'Come on,' I whispered, but saw the image above my head where a lip-reader could have understood, 'fuck me.'

Now Neil was there, positioning himself between my legs, his cock bobbing wildly, wet at the head with my spit and perhaps his own anticipation, tapping up my thigh to where my open pussy waited, glistening and shining in the clear light. And then it was there, up on the screen in front of me, an incredible sight which I had never seen before. His cock came knocking up my thigh, nudging against my lips and at last pushing in, filling me gloriously and rubbing me all along the places I most wanted to be rubbed. And his balls were slapping below that, every push in jarring me, and he was propped up on his arms but had twisted down to take my nipple in his mouth and that left room so I could slide my own hand down and feel my own clit there, wet and greedy for attention, and I could roll that between my fingertips.

But I was still enthralled by the view straight in front of me, spread across acres of brilliant screen, where the whole scene was repeated: one breast rocking with every jolt from Neil's hips; the other breast quivering but held at the nipple by Neil's teeth; and then my legs spread wide and welcoming and my lips stretched apart by Neil's glorious cock, clinging to him as he emerged slowly and shining from so deep inside me until only the tip was still inside. Then pushing back, enfolding the lips into me, as the whole length pushed in and disappeared deep, deep within. Out again. And back, slow wonderful strokes that Neil can keep on for hours and which bring me to the quivering edge of insanity.

I wanted to stay there too, but we had an audience to entertain, and I was now as much a part of the audience as anyone. I pushed him off me and over onto his back, turned round and stood up over him. For a few seconds, I just stood there in the full glare of the lights, my skin wet and shining with sweat, with Neil's spit and, starting to trickle down my thigh, my own excitement. I reached down and pulled my lips open, waited while the trolley camera charged in to capture this and strummed across the head of my clit as the huge glass eyes of the camera devoured my display.

Then I squatted down over him, my legs wide apart to keep open the judges' view, letting them go on seeing everything, down over his hips and then caught his eager erection in my fist and lowered myself the rest of the way, stuffing it into me.

I realized that the audience were totally quiet now, but still the cameras circled round, stalking, hunting for the best shots, probing for the glimpses of openness and action, hoping for something extra, perhaps something that even we had not intended. But I love this position, when I can be in control and yet he can reach up to hold my breasts, squeezing at the nipples and trying to get me to finish him. But I can also get easy access to my clit, to stroke myself as gently or as hard as I like, or to my own bottom so that I can caress that, and when I feel in the mood, push a finger in there as well.

And yet here it was better than all that, because I could look up and also see it all: see perfect pictures of his cock sliding in and out of me, of the tight stretch of skin round my anus, and of my fingers twiddling round my clit as the juice leaked out with every forward thrust.

And the line of judges was there. The one woman with her

eyes narrowed as she enviously followed the steady driving of his huge erection in and out of me. And the three men, seeing Neil's hands on my round breasts, squeezing me and pulling at the nipples, so much bigger than the breasts of any local girls.

And on the side, Kiki was watching too, looking shocked as I squatted there so gloriously naked, masturbating while the cameras circled round, watching and recording, and while the audience sat in rapt silence, missing nothing of the scene that was shown on the stage in front of them and on the seven huge screens above our heads. But while I watched her watching me, Kiki changed the board again. I don't know when she had put up the "5" but now I saw her drop that down and the "3" appeared. We were running out of time.

I wanted so much to let that continue and for a few moments I increased the tempo to bring Neil up to almost the point he could not resist but then slowly, ever so slowly, I straightened my legs so that most of Neil's length was visible, still squeezing my muscles round the head for a minute and then I stood right up and he slipped free, his erection taut and bursting, waving blindly in the air as if seeking a home. I spun round and took him back into my mouth, finding that glorious taste that is mostly me, but also the little announcement that he is nearly there. For a few moments I let him get used to that new position, let the cameras arrange themselves for the best angles and then, with only a few squeezes of my hands, my tongue lapping round the ridge, my lips running smoothly across the head he grunted and his body went rigid. As I felt the first spurt moving up his cock I pulled back and shut my eyes, vaguely aware of the gasp from out beyond the lights as I let the first jets shoot up over my breasts, gloriously sticky as I smeared it into my skin, and then squirmed down to catch the rest on my face, across my cheeks, my eyes, my nose and my mouth, jet after jet covering me until there was no more and his erection was beginning to soften in my hand.

And at last I released him, lay back and concentrated on myself. It took only a few moments, watching myself on the great screen above me, seeing Neil lying beside me, the judges peering down, the cameras pushing in close, my face and hair covered with Neil's spunk and me lying in the middle of it all, my legs spread wide, my hands between my thighs, my clit erect and hyper sensitive and I just wanted it all to go on for ever, although it never could as the rapture of the climax engulfed me, and I heard myself screeching out at the crowds and the lenses and the humiliation of so blatant and glorious an exhibition.

The next sound was huge applause, and peering down I could see the little uniformed stage managers stirring up the audience, although I do not believe they were needed, and as the presenter stepped forward to speak to the hundreds in the audience and the millions beyond the cameras, Kiki appeared with a silk dressing gown for each of us – and some tissues for me to wipe my face – and led us over to the chairs where we had previously been interviewed and where we were soon joined by the Japanese couple, in similar dressing gowns. We exchanged nervous smiles and nods but there was little we could say so we sat in a neat row, sipping tea while the last section of advertisements were run and the judges huddled together to prepare their verdict.

The comperes' make-up was redone, the judges returned to their desk, the bed was tidied, the trolley cameras took up station at the front of the stage and then the final segment started. This was again all in Japanese so I have no idea what they were saying but the subject of their discussions was perfectly clear because it came up on the screens above us.

First they considered the Japanese couple, opening with a shot of the two of them kneeling nervously on the bed as they began their show. Then it speeded it through and stopped again where they started to undress: the shot showed the girl with her hand down inside the boy's waistband and although I could not understand the comment, it was apparently unfavourable. The poor girl was sitting beside me and she gasped and buried her face in her hands and her body shook while her partner (husband, I think, for I now saw she was wearing a ring) stared impassively at the screen. This moved on: through her being undressed, and it whisked past with only a very brief pause to consider her breasts when they first appeared and on to when her neat white knickers were pulled down and her thick black triangle of pubic hair appeared, completely hiding her pussy. Then the boy, his first nakedness with a very small cock barely showing through his own thick bush of hair. But then she had taken it in her hand, and in her mouth and soon worked it to a much more impressive erection, but as soon as she had done so, he turned her round, bent her forward and pushed his cock into her and that was the last we saw of it. They went through a very imaginative range of positions, with her kneeling, standing, bending, sitting; with him on top, her on top, side by side; even one where she lay curled right up on her shoulders with her legs bent down by her ears and him spinning round on top of her. It was impressive, athletic and imaginative, but it wasn't erotic and I could sense the disappointment when he reached a very obvious climax lying on his back with her sitting astride him. Even when she quickly lifted off, letting his cock slip out of her to be followed by a trickle of semen, the lack of enthusiasm from the audience showed they felt they had been cheated.

The film came to an end, the audience was stirred into giving a big round of applause and the judges moved on to our performance. I could hardly bring myself to watch.

They were so serious, the three of them, so intense as they sat and discussed whether they thought we were any good at making love together, as if we were new to it, as if we hadn't done it hundreds of times before. But this was the first time under these conditions, in the certain knowledge of other people being assembled for the sole purpose of watching us, and with a view to making a critical analysis of our abilities, our enthusiasm, our competence and our potential. This must be the most humiliating judgement ever imposed on another person. Supposing their conclusion was that we were no good? Would we be forbidden from ever doing this again?

But in front of us and on the screens above our heads, the assessment had started and they were slowly working through our performance. They reached the moment when my breasts came free, and for several seconds, a shot of my breasts filled the whole of all seven screens while a succession of commentaries from each of the judges entertained the audience and conveyed nothing to us. For one brief moment, the screens flashed back to the Japanese girl's breasts and when, on a comment from one of the judges, the whole audience burst into laughter, the poor girl hid her face again. Then it was back to us again, me naked and long loving shots of my pubic hair, from the front, from the top, from underneath. When the woman judge gave her commentary, she even walked across to where we were sitting, reached out a hand to help me to my feet and asked me to take off the dressing gown again.

How could I decline, offered another chance to show myself to so many people? I dropped it on my chair, feeling my nipples erect as I turned to show them everything, and feeling my pussy moisten again when the woman reached down to run her fingers through my bush and tease at the hairs, pulling them out straight. I could not tell what point she was making, but then she made the Japanese girl stand up too, and remove her dressing gown, so we both stood there, side by side and quite naked, while the woman toyed with my hair and then the other girl's and then mine again. I could see now that hers was quite straight, and it seemed to be much less springy, softer and more like head hair, so that I was rather intrigued and wished I could have felt her hair myself.

When she was done, we were not allowed to sit down again because now the other two judges both wanted to come out and make the same comparison. One of them made much of the differences in our breasts, weighing mine in his hand and then running a fingertip beneath the little swelling that was all the other girl had. He tweaked at my nipple, pulling it out and stroking it, and doing the same to her tiny buds. Then they moved on to our pubic hair: feeling at mine, feeling at hers; teasing the tight curls on my stomach and twirling the long strands on her, but when one of them wanted to examine more closely the curls on our lips, we were made to return to the garish pink bed, walking naked across the wide stage, and lie down side by side with our legs wide apart while they pulled at the hairs and in the process probed at the lips themselves, peeling them open and pulling back at the hood over my clit. All this again relayed onto the screens above us so I could watch every detail of them playing with the other girl's pussy, of her tiny clit that barely showed, just as she could watch them playing with mine as it gleamed in the full glare of the light.

Finally released, we were allowed to return to our seats and retrieve our dressing gowns while the analysis of our lovemaking continued. The next point of particular interest was when I took Neil in my mouth and there were several minutes of that, shot from the front to show my lips wrapped round his cock, and from the back to show my own open cheeks, the swollen lips of my pussy and even the wrinkled opening of my anus. From this it moved on to when we had both been going down on each other, when his mouth had been nipping at me, pulling at the skin, but it was only now that I could see the consequence. His lips had been pulling at the hood itself, peeling it away, so that the pink tip of my actual clit was exposed to the camera's lens, and now, enlarged to monstrous proportions, was shown in slow motion as it glistened across the massive screens above us and then his finger had dipped deep into me and then probed towards, round and finally into the brown star of my bottom.

They cut between scenes of the different positions we had used: him on top, me on top, and there were long slow motion replays of my squatting over him before the finale, the part which they focussed on most, when Neil's erection slipped out of my pussy and I took it back into my mouth, brought him, on steadily higher and higher until he finally climaxed all over me, squirting his semen up over my breasts and then all across my face. That was the picture which was left on the giant screens as their analysis of our abilities came to an end: a close up of my face, rapturously happy, with Neil's sperm spattered across my cheeks and mouth and running down to where I was trying to catch it on my tongue.

There was a pause after this, the judges went into a huddle, conferred seriously and earnestly, glancing across at both us and the other couple, but finally they handed an envelope to the woman presenter who brought us all out to centre stage to read it. We had won.

Immediately Kiki appeared from the side with sashes and Neil and I had to take off our dressing gowns again while the sashes were dropped over our heads. *Love Champions* in pink letters flowed between the dotted hearts as the sashes were carefully arranged across our bodies, draped neatly between (not across) my breasts and lined up on our hips to ensure that they did not cover any part that the audience might still want to see. We were led forward to take a bow, while the audience clapped and cheered and whistled. One of the trolley cameras had been lurking at the back, but I saw it come forward to film our bow from behind, and get one last glimpse between my legs before we were led off. From the side, we watched as the other couple then took their bow, and although there was to be no sash for them, they were still relieved of their dressing gowns and led forward quite naked to receive a very respectable applause from the audience before the four of us were finally free and could hurry back down to the safety of our dressing room. Quickly we dressed, no words exchanged although the silence was broken by occasional sniffles from the other girl and they quickly hurried out with barely a glance back. I didn't know what their arrangements had been and whether they had negotiated any payment if they did not win. Quite possibly they had not, so they had only humiliated themselves in front of a huge audience for nothing, while their family and friends, work colleagues and neighbours were much more likely to hear about the event, perhaps had even been told in advance and were either in the studio audience or sitting mesmerised in front of their television at home. Their distress was hardly surprising, but there was nothing we could do. We silently finished dressing, gathered up our things and set off to collect our prize.

But the studio was already completely dark and both Kiki and Mr Kan had disappeared.

Louise's Second Tale: Love Rats

I suppose we should have expected this, but we had to be quick. It was getting late and already the building was emptying steadily. Of course, nobody we met spoke English and to find our way to Mr Kan's office we had to rely on directions from a range of people, several of whom had either no idea what we wanted or no intention of helping us, but after several wrong turnings we eventually found our way back through the maze to his office. The immediate response to my knock, shouted out in Japanese, I took as a signal to enter and opened the door.

Perhaps I should not have done so. Perhaps the response called out from beyond the partition had been to tell us to go away, but I didn't think so then and anyway it was now too late. I pushed open the door and walked in with Neil right behind me. And we stopped. Stopped dead like bad actors in some pantomime show.

There was Mr Kan, the producer, standing proudly in the centre of the room, leaning back as he perched on the edge of the desk, his legs splayed wide and victorious. But his cock was sticking straight out of the front of his trousers and there, kneeling on the floor in front of him, was the girl who had just lost the contest, entirely naked. Her head had turned towards us at the sound of the door opening, and her wide eyes stared. She gasped – we heard that – and froze with her tiny fists wrapped round the short fat erection pushing out from the front of Mr Kan's pants. Her husband was sitting hunched on the sofa just behind her, and he too had turned to stare as we came in, and next to him sat Kiki.

At first nobody moved. In my determination not to be cheated, I had shoved open the door and barged straight in with Neil immediately following. So now we also stood there, as shocked at what we had found as the four people in the room were at our interruption.

The first to react was the girl kneeling naked on the floor. With a jolt, she was startled back into life, perhaps my expression alerted her to the picture she presented to us, for she snatched her hands away as if scalded, and tried ineffectively to cover her nakedness. The close grip of her hands, the wet shining head on the end of a proud erection, all of it told too clear a story of the events that had been unfolding during the minutes since the two of them had left us in the dressing room.

But if she was mortified, Mr Kan was entirely unabashed. 'Ah!' he said. 'Miss Louise!' and then after only a moment's pause, turned to mutter something to the girl in Japanese. She, with an apologetic, or possibly humiliated, glance towards us – first Neil and then more specifically and entreatingly me – reached out for the glistening erection which was waving in front of her face and took it back into her grasp and began to ease her hands up and down its length. Following a second command barked at her by Mr Kan, and with a second glance across to us, she brought it back to her mouth. For a second a little pink tongue emerged and the tip of the tongue lapped delicately at the tip of the erection before she shut her eyes and enclosed the smooth head in her lips.

Mr Kan studied the action for a moment and then turned back to us. 'You have come for your prize, yes?'

'Er, yes,' I answered, adding 'if this isn't an inconvenient moment.'

'Ah no.' He still had not grasped irony. 'You wait one moment. Please! Please sit!' And he pointed at the low sagging sofa, presently littered with discarded clothing. 'I get prize in, Oh!' he had to pause for a moment, but with the crisis controlled, he continued, 'in one minute. You sit down.' He stared down at the bobbing head for a few more seconds, then looked up at us again and grinned. 'I will be finished very soon. She is very good!' and then he turned to direct his grin at the girl's husband, and when there was no response, added a Japanese commentary which made the poor man look even worse.

I suppose we should have left them there: waited outside, for the girl's sake if nothing else, but finding this scene only added to my distrust of Mr Kan. The boy and Kiki moved up to give Neil and me room to perch on the sofa, where I tried to block out the symphony of noises continuing just a few feet in front of me by carefully gathering up the girl's clothes and – to distract myself – folding them in a pile. A little skirt; the blouse; some tights bundled up with a pair of knickers; and, tipped forlornly onto the floor, a bra that could have been made for a Barbie doll.

When that was done, all folded as neatly as I could make them, I glanced up but the scene was still going on. Neil had no qualms about openly watching them, and I had little choice. So close I could almost have touched them, and hypnotised by the sickening arrogance of the man as he took his pleasure in the girl's mouth while we sat there, I was simultaneously repelled and hooked: disgusted but could not look away. Perhaps my standards had been changed by the last hour, by the fact that we had ourselves just been watched making love, watched by who knows how many hundreds of people live and with any number of millions seeing us later on television. Recording us, I suddenly thought; and playing back our love-making in slow motion, and freeze-frame to get the most they could out of every humiliating little second. How long would it be before selections were being emailed across the country, even across the world, perhaps to turn up in some dreadful compilation on cable television in Britain?

But it was clear now that the girl kneeling naked on the floor in front of us was not like that. She was not trying for a prize, and her embarrassed and apologetic glance round towards us as we settled down to wait, her shamed refusal to glance towards her husband, all of this confirmed my first impression of the arrangements. For us, being western had ensured payment. For them, there was an extra sacrifice.

So she knelt at his feet, her hands wrapped round his erection, her eyes twisted shut as she moved her lips up and down its long length. Mr Kan twined his hands in her thick hair, holding and directing her and yet could not resist looking across to us from time to time, the smile for all of us and mostly for the husband as he gloried in this exhibition of his power. How the boy was managing I could not imagine, but I returned Mr Kan's stares to deny him any gloating at my expense. Besides Neil and I came fresh from an exhibition of our own, so we could scarcely claim either innocence or outrage. I had been doing this act on Neil less than half an hour ago, and from the expression on Mr Kan's face, perhaps more competently than this girl in front of us.

Suddenly he pushed her away and enfolded his cock in his own fist as she first stared up in dismay into his face, but then bit her lip and her focus moved down to the quivering head right in front of her as she settled back to wait the outcome of a process which was evidently familiar to them both. His hand tipped under her chin to tilt up her head, a single word was grunted and she opened wide her eyes, opened wide her mouth, pushed out her tongue and waited. The man was now pounding at his fat shining erection with fierce determination, the growls rising up from his throat until suddenly he stopped that too and lay the tip of his cock on her tongue while it twitched twice and delicately lay two, three, four, five streams of sperm in a neat pool. For a second he stirred round the inside of her mouth with his cock as the last dribbles seeped out until, still holding her under the chin, he pulled back a moment to allow her to close her mouth and swallow, before she obediently opened her mouth again, showed the sperm all gone and obediently licked clean the shining pink round head that was proffered back to her.

Eventually he was satisfied and with a firm pat on the side of her face he moved away. 'Okay,' he muttered and she scrabbled to her feet, reaching for her clothes. Standing on one leg as she tried to get her knickers back on, Mr Kan watched casually then stopped her. He turned to Neil.

'You would like?' A vague sweep of the hand embraced the girl, Neil's crotch and the space on the floor in front of him where the girl would have to kneel. For a couple of seconds the whole room stopped in silence; I think it took that long for Neil to realize what he was being offered. In the meantime, Mr Kan waited as patiently as a generous host would, Kiki did not look up, and the young couple were frozen in miserable dread.

'No!' Neil finally understood. 'I mean no thank you...' He tried to smile at the girl, to reject Mr Kan and not her, but I don't think she cared so long as she was not required to stay there a moment longer.

Mr Kan appeared disappointed at Neil's refusal; disappointed and also surprised. 'No? Perhaps you like to see them doing fucking? Private? Here, for us?'

'No,' repeated Neil. 'No thank you.'

The young couple were staring, evidently unsure what was being discussed and glancing to Kiki for a translation, knowing only that something was being offered to these two foreigners and whatever it was, was unlikely to be anything pleasant for either of them. Mr Kan's next offer needed no translation. He snatched the knickers out of the girl's hands and tossed them to the floor before taking hold of her shoulder to turn her round and bend her flat over the desk beside him. His hands on her bottom dragged the pinched little cheeks apart.

'Here?' he offered Neil. 'Very good! Very tight!'

'No!' repeated Neil and this time the sharpness finally penetrated Mr Kan's determination. With a reluctant sigh, he allowed the girl to stand up, but even so, she was no sooner scrabbling for her knickers and trying to climb into them again than he growled something else which caused her to stop immediately, snatch the rest of her clothes from my hands and, clutching the bundle to her skinny little chest, she scampered out of the door. With one disgusted glance round at the rest of us, all complicit by our presence in her humiliation, the young man scurried after her.

Mr Kan watched them go in silence, still leaning back against his desk, still with his flies undone and his wilting cock hanging out for us all to behold. However immediately the door had closed, he grumbled to Kiki who got to her feet, sidled out to the little bathroom and returned a few minutes later with a bowl and some neat cloths. In turn, she knelt at his feet, gingerly took his cock in one hand and carefully began washing it. Again, he muttered a couple of words to her and she carefully put down the bowl and cloth and headed back to the bathroom, head down, unable to look at us. This time she returned with a small china urn and having knelt back down, she held it up, again took his cock cautiously between finger and thumb to guide the head into the urn and a couple of seconds later we heard his piss flowing loudly. When he was finished, still without a word, she carefully carried the thing back out to the bathroom, came back to her place and resumed washing his cock, wiping it all over, patting it dry with a second cloth – during which I got the impression it was beginning to stiffen once more – and then she quickly tucked it back into his pants and zipped up his fly.

During the whole process, Mr Kan stared gloomily down at her but did not offer a single word of thanks. While she was taking out the bowl and cloths, he turned his bristling smile towards us, a patronising nod to me and a man-to-man leer towards Neil. 'Now, you want to take your prize.'

I despised his eagerness to draw us into his callousness, and despised too my inability to demonstrate his failure. Watching Kiki in the little corner bathroom, remembering the pale little figure that he had just sent naked out into the corridors, I wanted to hug them, to show them we were not all so repulsive, to apologise that Neil had I had been the ones pre-selected to win which had meant – inevitably – that they were pre-selected to lose, whatever they did. I very nearly followed them: only my distrust and determination not to let Mr Kan out of my sight kept me there. 'Here,' I shoved our copy of the contract into Neil's hand knowing that my growing anger would fail us where Neil's calmness would succeed. 'You'd better deal with this, but don't let the bastard get away with anything.' I went to help Kiki, despite her protestations that it was unnecessary, rinsing the bowl and the flannels while she scrubbed her hands.

Mr Kan paid up, surprisingly, and without the slightest quibble but perhaps he just wanted to show us that he was above concerning himself with financial considerations. Even so, he would not let us go immediately.

'You like to do again? Maybe more special?'

'More special?'

'Yes. Not public this time. Private audience. More private. More... special.'

'No, thank you.'

'Very big prize this time.'

'I don't think so, thank you.' I could understand what "special" might mean. Neil is much more literal.

'What kind of "special"?'

'Ah!' Mr Kan charged the opening in our front. 'You would like? Very, very big prize.'

'I imagine,' I explained for Neil's benefit but also to show Mr Kan that I at least understood, 'that "very, very big prize" means very very private and very, very special show. No, thank you.'

'Very enjoyable for young couple.'

'No, thank you.'

'Important people there seeing.'

'No, thank you.'

'You think. Maybe change your mind. Here is my card.' He solemnly presented this to us and we took it with sufficient interest and sufficient appearance of considering his offer that he finally let us go. I stuffed the card into my jeans, put the money more carefully into an inside pocket and Kiki showed us out of the building.

We emerged into a neon-lit clamour of shoppers, tourists, workers and traffic, a turbulence into which Kiki could disappear in minutes. She started awkwardly to say a quick good-bye, and although Neil was content enough, my guilt and self loathing were still so strong that I could not let her go without making some attempt to make amends.

'May we buy you a drink?'

She smiled so very politely. 'No thank you very kindly, but I must go home. My mother will be waiting for my supper.'

'Then have supper with us.' Neil was standing placidly listening but this would not affect him.

'No, sorry, but my mother is waiting.'

'Tomorrow then? Lunchtime?'

'Tomorrow is my day off. Sorry.' The polite smile did not waver so I came straight to the point.

'The other couple? The ones who lost? Do you know how I can contact them?'

'Why?'

'I want to give them half the money.'

'Why?'

'Because they deserve it.'

'No. You won. They lost.'

'I want to give them half anyway.'

The smile began to soften into something almost genuine. 'They would not accept that. They would be ashamed.'

'But I am ashamed.'

'You? Why?'

'Because ... Because it was not fair. The contest was not fair. What Mr Kan made her do afterwards was not fair.' She shrugged, the smile still showing on her mouth as she watched me struggle. 'I feel very bad.'

'There is no need. It happens.'

'It should not.' But she simply shrugged: maybe it should, maybe it shouldn't but life is never fair. Only a fool thinks it might be and only the rich have the luxury of attempting to make it so. Her calm acceptance made me angry: confident of that acquiescence, Mr Kan had exploited it. Worse, he had made me exploit it too and that made me angrier still so that I could feel tears beginning to prick at my eyes. I was so impotent. 'There must be something.' And then the tears began to fall and such a public display of emotion clearly startled, even alarmed, Kiki. Maybe she just did not want to be seen standing in the street with such an ill-mannered westerner.

'Perhaps we have a quick supper.' She grabbed my arm and led me across the street. Neil, entirely ignored, tagging along behind us.

⁓

In a tiny plastic noodle restaurant we perched on little plastic stools, eating with plastic chopsticks from little plastic plates. The food, however, was anything but plastic. Two cooks, supported by two assistants, were working at steaming pots immediately behind the counter and serving straight from the pan onto the plates. We made polite conversation over a couple of plates but Kiki was steering clear of anything difficult and frequently glanced past me at Neil.

'Neil, go and look in the shop windows.'

'Why?'

'There are loads of electrical shops along this street and you know you wanted to get a camcorder while we were here. Go and look at them.'

'Don't we want to look at those together?'

'No,' and I stared straight at him and eventually it sank in.

'Ah! Right. I won't be long,' he called cheerily.

'Be at least half an hour,' I called back and saw, the moment he was gone, Kiki visibly relax. At first I couldn't think where to start so began with the easy bit. 'I am sorry we came in.'

She did her little shrug again. 'You did not know.'

'Even so. I am sorry.' She said nothing. 'Does he always do that?'

'No, not always.' Her chest rose and fell in one deep breath. 'But sometimes.' She glanced across, her eyes glistening, her chin quivering and quickly turned away, clutching the edge of the table. I said nothing and waited. 'It depends. He does not always come to watch when we are filming the programme, but if he comes and if he is excited then maybe he wants something for himself afterwards. Because you were there, western people with yellow hair, that makes him excited. He always wants to have a western girl but never have.' She paused again before finding the strength to continue. 'But sometimes he asks the winning couple to come to his room. Sometimes other one.' She glanced round. 'Sometimes both.'

'And sometimes you?' There was no point in beating about the bush.

'Yes.' She murmured and stared down at the floor.

'And he makes you hold that thing while he pisses?'

'Sometimes,' but this was barely more than a whisper. 'Sometimes worse.'

'Worse?'

'He likes to play games with the girls.'

'What do you mean, "games"?'

'Sometimes he...' for a minute she could not speak at all but then she sat up, faced straight in front of her and spoke out clearly and flatly to take all emotion out of the words and the memories. 'Sometimes he likes to play games like that. He makes them sit in the shower in his office and then he... he goes all over them.'

'Has he done that to you?'

'No. Not yet. But he will.'

'But why don't you refuse?'

The little shrug again, then, 'I cannot refuse. Besides, it is not often me, because I am alone.'

'What do you mean?'

'He likes someone to see. Like today: while the girl does that, her husband must stay and see. He likes that. So I am not interesting, not yet.'

'Why "not yet"?'

'Next month my husband will come home. Then Mr Kan will send for me. Send for both of us.'

So the whole story came out: how she had only been given the job because her father was related to Mr Kan's wife, how he enjoyed his power at the television studio and a film production company he ran, how he would sack her if she did not do as he required and that she could not risk that until her husband came home and got himself a good steady job. Until then, she was trapped. Strangely, she did not regard it as unreasonable that Mr Kan abused his power; that seemed to be an accepted perk of the job.

I tried to apologise repeatedly but, against her insistence that I had nothing to apologise for, my words had no effect. All the same, by the time Neil had returned and she left to make her way home (after proudly presenting her business card, of course), I did feel that I had done as much as I would ever be allowed to do.

We certainly enjoyed the prize money. A big chunk of it went on airline tickets for our return home, but we even put that back a week because now that we had money, we could do so much more than had been possible when we had been broke. We could now spend all we had left of our own money so we bought a DVD player and a camcorder and also travelled around for two days, tried the bullet train, and saw some of the strange Japanese theatre. By the time we returned to Tokyo, we had spent almost all we had won, but we at least had something to show, and we had kept enough to spend our last few nights in Japan in a proper hotel, with a real bathroom: an actual bath and western style loo. Real luxuries after making do for so long with a dribble shower and a squat toilet. Once we had checked in – and christened the bed, and played with the new camcorder, filming each other naked – I dug out Mr Kan's business card, rang the number and arranged that I would go to see him: alone.

When we settled in his nasty little office, his warm handshake was clammy as ever. 'How nice, Louise, how nice. Now: you would like to do this show?'

'Well, we have been thinking about it. What do we have to do exactly?'

'It is more private.'

'Yes, so you said.'

'I have some friends to a quiet restaurant, have a nice dinner and after we finish, then you fucking.'

'I see. That is all, is it? And how much is the "very, very big prize" which you mentioned?'

'Ah, well. That depends what you are doing.'

'I see.'

'Yes. Some things big prize. Some things very big prize!'

'Ah! So nothing, I notice, with a "very, very big prize". And what makes the difference between the two.'

'Well. That depends. First, I have to see if you are suitable.'

'Suitable,' I repeated. This conversation seemed to be heading all one way.

'Yes. You see...'

'But Mr Kan! You have seen.' He shrugged, a cruder version of Kiki's elegant little expression but perhaps the pedigree was revealed. 'Just last week, you, in fact not just you but most of the population of the northern hemisphere, saw me and Neil giving it maximum.'

He smiled in that way which shows he did not understand any part of what I had said but believed a joke might well have been made. 'I have seen that together you and Mr Neil are good. Very good. And I am happy that Mr Neil can manage anything: what man cannot?' He grinned all his teeth at me.

'But you, I am not so sure.' His mouth tried to look doubtful but his eyes could only manage hopeful.

'Why not?'

'Sometimes it is more difficult for a lady to adapt for these things.'

'I see.'

'I need to check.'

'Yes. I see.'

'Everything.'

'Ah.'

He sat there, peering over a cluttered desk and grinning right across his shining face. 'You understand?'

Oh yes; I understood that all right. 'And afterwards?'

'Afterwards?'

'After I let you check.' He looked expectant. 'Check everything.' Expectancy turned to glee. 'Then what?'

'Ah well, then you do show and win big prize.' I noticed that the prize had already shrunk from "very, very big" to "big" and I could see it shrinking further but I needed to keep things sailing smoothly.

'Okay,' I said, albeit with some misgivings in my voice. 'But I don't want these checks being done here.'

He shrugged again. 'It's private.'

'Even so, we'll do it at my hotel.' He looked dubious so I hurried on. 'It is more comfortable and even more private.' He was still unconvinced. 'No-one will come in.' That was something even he could understand.

'Mr Neil?'

'He would understand.'

'When we do this?'

'Well, we leave quite soon...'

'So, do it now?'

I swallowed. 'Okay. You come to my hotel after lunch. Say two o'clock.'

He glanced at his watch, calculating and then nodded. 'Okay. Only until then, no toilet.'

'What?'

'You don't go toilet. When I come, then you can go toilet.' He was still beaming as I closed the door.

~

Unsurprisingly, he was very prompt. Our room was small, well we hadn't won all that much on his damn show and all Tokyo hotels are expensive, but at least it was better than the hostel we had been straying in. He dropped his neat briefcase by the door and peered suspiciously round. 'Mr Neil?'

'He is out. He will be back in half an hour.'

'Half an hour?'

'Yes. You said you needed to check me first. We have half an hour and then he will come to learn about this show you want.'

'Okay.' Perhaps this was better than he had hoped for: he beamed his wide smile again. 'So, first, you undress, yes?'

He had already seen me naked, watching me having sex both in reality and blown up on massive screens so there was no real cause for embarrassment. On the other hand, nobody can be completely unmoved to be asked to undress in front of a man, and although I fully expected his "check" to become tactile as well as visual, I did not know exactly where it was all going to lead. And viewed in a certain way, if you were in a certain mood, there was something quite appealingly masculine in his arrogant, dominating bullying. He took off his jacket, draped it over the back of the only chair, and settled down to watch.

I took my clothes off slowly, carefully folding each one and laying it down neatly, feeling his eyes taking in every new little piece of me that the process revealed. As the pile of clothes grew higher and the amount of visible skin increased, he became steadily quieter, more still and more attentive. Finally, keeping my back to him, I slipped off my knickers, dropped them on top of the rest and turned to face him. He beamed some more.

First he wanted me to sit on the bed while he played with my breasts. I know they are impressive anyway and in this city, were quite extraordinary. Perhaps this had been the main appeal, but he spent several minutes running his hand across them, squeezing the main part of the breast, pinching my nipples and finally, as he leaned closer and closer and clearly could not resist, I pulled his head down to squeeze it between them for a second and then directed him across so he could suckle at one nipple.

Eventually he tired of that, or maybe he worried too much about passing time, but he pulled away and while he sat grinning at me, his hand reached out and took mine, hauled over and pushed it into his own lap.

'I like you!' and although I quickly pulled away, I had not been quick enough to avoid feeling his erection, not all that big, but certainly hard. Even so, he did not persist when I made clear my hands were going nowhere near there.

Next he had me lie down and open my thighs so that he could "check" between my legs. My lips fascinated him and he pulled at them, feeling them growing slippery as his fingers roamed across them, up and down my crease and stopped to play with my clit, pushing the hood back as far as he could until I could feel his cold breath. He glanced up once or twice, perhaps unsure where I would draw the line, and finding no signal, took the next chance. The fingers of one hand spread open my lips so that one finger of the other could be pushed up inside me. Soon a second finger followed while his other hand moved back to my clit, touching, stroking and brushing across that with an exquisite delicacy.

I was unsure quite what he wanted to achieve. If things continued as they were, one hand masturbating me, the other probing slowly, gently, up and down inside, it would not take me too long to come. I could feel I was already wetter and with no conscious move on my part, my hips were starting to lift to meet his strokes. He smiled at this, smiled at me, smiled with smug satisfaction at what he had achieved and continued: circling: pushing: pulling back: stroking. I was looking down the length of my body as he worked me like a robot, my chest was rising and falling with each deep breath and more than once the breath was accompanied by a little moan that I had not intended. At each one, he smiled a little more. And then stopped, and took his hands away.

Now he wanted me turned over, and since there was little doubt what he was going to do, it would have been silly to be difficult. I turned onto my stomach, on my knees and elbows, my knees wide, my bottom lifted, my cheeks open and immediately his fingers homed in on my anus, touched it tentatively, circled it, smaller circles that ended right in the centre where they hesitated before pushing through the tight ring and inside.

'You like that?'

'Sometimes.' Yes, actually, I do, and so did Neil; there is an incredible intimacy and intensity to it but that did not mean I would allow him everything. His fingers probed further.

'Very tight.'

'Yes,' but I wished he would go back to my clit, and when I felt the fingers pulling back out, I thought he might. I was not to be so lucky.

'Toilet now?'

Even Mr Kan was taken aback by our bathroom, but it did not distract him for long. I was sitting astride the loo when he stopped me.

'In the bath,' and he positioned me perched against the wall on one side of the bath with my feet on the side nearer him. He squatted right down in front of me and pushed my knees even wider apart. 'Okay.'

Neil has never shown any interest in my peeing, although I have had lovers before who occasionally liked to watch me. None of them displayed the degree of rapt attention that Mr Kan showed as he stared expectantly. He had to stare for some time, because although I was keen to go, it is much harder when you are twisted awkwardly while someone waits hopefully for you to perform. This time, he was eventually rewarded, but as soon as the first trickle appeared, he immediately put his hand into the stream and held it there until I was finished when he used his fingers to wipe away the last drops.

'Now here?' and he reached through underneath me and tapped on my bottom. That was something I could not do, had never been asked for and certainly was not prepared to offer Mr Kan now.

'No. Sorry.' And I scrambled back out of the bath before this all got too difficult. His eagerness and disappointment raised another possibility though. 'Maybe later,' and he had to settle for that.

I was still rinsing the bath out, Mr Kan taking advantage of my being bent over it to stand behind me and run his hands down my back and over my bottom while I did so, when I heard the bedroom door opening and Neil appeared. Mr Kan was clearly disappointed, but if he had hoped to take things a little further while he had me on my own, I was all the more glad to see Neil arrive.

Neil glanced across from me to Mr Kan and back again, taking in my nakedness, my washing the bath and I could see him failing to make any sensible connection. 'You okay, Lou?'

I do love him when he worries about me. 'Yes. Fine.' And to put his mind at rest: 'I was just having a pee.' Still he seemed unable to fit the pieces together, even with Mr Kan nodding and grinning like a demented puppet.

We reassembled in the bedroom, Neil and me sitting apprehensively on the bed, and Mr Kan took the only chair. I was now as comfortable being naked in front of Mr Kan as I was in front of Neil.

'So,' I started. 'Tell us about this show.'

'Well,' he began, 'it's private...'

His polite detour could take ages before we reached the essentials. 'Yes you explained it was private and very special and also,' it would do no harm to remind him, 'that we would win a "very very big prize".' He looked a little flustered at the recollection but I continued. 'What I want to know is what happens; what we have to do?'

'Like I say. Private dinner for a few gentlemen friends, perhaps some ladies, perhaps not, and after, you fucking. They watch you, but watching closer. Maybe join.'

'Aha!' This sounded more like what I had been expecting.

'Oh no! Not they fucking with you. They just watching, maybe touching.'

'How close are they watching?'

'Like this,' and he waved his hand across the short distance, a scant arm's length, between us.

'And touching? Touching like you were doing just now?'

'Yes!' his beaming grin flooded back. 'Just like!' His fingers even flexed at the memory as he tried to keep from reaching out to touch me again. 'You try? Try now?'

We had expected this, had assumed it would come when Neil and I had discussed and planned how the day might go, so there was no point in making any protest. Besides, after what we had done before, it should not be too difficult.

Neil pulled his sweat shirt over his head, unlaced his trainers, pulled off his socks and then his jeans, all of it tossed over onto the floor, and finally he stood up and pushed off his pants to stand as naked as I was. Already he looked to me to be partially erect.

'Ah!' Mr Kan leaned in closer towards Neil, grinning some more. 'Very good!'

In fact, it was more difficult than I had expected doing it now with an audience of just one; harder than it had been with an audience of, possibly, thousands. He sat so much closer to us that we could never for a moment ignore his presence. We lay down on the bed, Neil lying over me so we could kiss and he could stroke my breasts, and of course Mr Kan reached out to stroke my breast too. Then his hand slid down my body, ruffled briefly through my pubic hair, and then it moved across and the fingers casually enfolded Neil's cock. I had been watching this happening and immediately stopped dead but it took Neil a few seconds to realise that the hand fondling him was not mine. He too stopped, froze and stared down.

Mr Kan still grinned but it seemed just too glassy. 'Japanese people don't do this,' he said, his fingers still encircling Neil's cock which reacted with the usual indiscriminate enthusiasm of any cock. When neither of us reacted to the statement, he explained more. 'One man with another man: never do this.' He shook his head. 'Never.' Well that was a fine thing for him to say but it clearly was not true: he was sitting there, hunched forward in his chair reaching out to Neil, and he patently was "doing this". After a few seconds silence from all three of us, he nodded down towards Neil's groin, grinning again. 'Very big. Very strong.' He looked round to us for confirmation or at least agreement, and continued with a leer to me 'Very nice for ladies!'

And in fact Neil's cock was visibly more erect than when Mr Kan had started; when it comes down to it, a hand is a hand and perhaps Mr Kan had more experience of masturbating a cock, either his own or someone else's than I had. Certainly he gazed with rapture as Neil continued to swell and lengthen to a very satisfying full erection. I wondered whether I should quietly go and leave them to it, but maybe that would make it too overtly a homosexual experience. With me there, it was just a free-ranging threesome. And perhaps Neil had the same thought because he suddenly turned his attention back to me with renewed intensity and started kissing me, deep loving kisses that squashed my breath as he also stroked my breasts, twisted down to suckle them and reached down to caress my clit. For a second I forgot where I was and, automatically reaching down to fondle him too, was momentarily surprised to find Mr Kan's hand there, still steadily working up and down

Neil's cock which was, by now, firmly and fully erect.

'You fuck now.'

I obediently shuffled down flatter onto the bed, Mr Kan pulling my legs wide but he would not leave us to get on with what he had asked. For some time, while he kept one hand firmly gripped round Neil's cock, he also fingered me, peeling open my lips to push his fingers inside me but mostly strumming at my clit, so that before long I no longer cared that this wasn't Neil's hand as I felt myself lifting my hips to offer myself more completely. Even so, it was not enough.

'Fuck me, Neil. Please fuck me.'

'Ah!' Mr Kan was pleased with himself, and maybe he was entitled to be, but he pressed me even flatter, his fingers burrowed about opening me up and then, still holding Neil's cock in his fist, began stuffing it into me.

It's so glorious, that feeling as his erection pushes further and further inside me, opening me up, possessing and controlling me. We had been together for long enough to know each other's rhythms, and to fall into that easy familiarity and intimacy which meant this was going to be good. Even Mr Kan, frantically bobbing about next to us trying to make sure that he did not miss anything, even he could not put me off. However, he clearly was not happy with what he was seeing: his hand slithered in between us to feel my breasts and slid down to stroke my clit again, but there was little room for it and he started grumbling at his inability to see everything he wanted to. Finally he interrupted.

'Maybe better if lady is on top.'

So we rearranged ourselves as he had requested, Neil lying across the bed and me kneeling astride him, facing Mr Kan and Neil's feet and leaning forward on my hands. It is a position that we both like, which lets me see his cock entering me, lets me stroke my clit if I want to, and if Neil, as he sometimes does, takes the opportunity to slide a finger up my bottom, I don't mind at all.

This seemed better to Mr Kan as well and he squatted down, his hands resting on Neil's legs, so that he could peer in and see every stroke we made and every detail. He could not, inevitably, keep his hands to himself and soon he was again stroking my breasts. After a few minutes of this, he moved on down to my clit which, because of the way my legs were spread right across Neil's hips, was on full display. Yet even this did not entertain him for long, and soon his fingers dropped down further to cradle Neil's balls as they rolled in his sack and, when I lifted myself up, his fingers even encircled the base of his cock.

His grinning face turned up to me again. 'Very nice! Very beautiful' and then, what I had expected from the beginning, his hands moved back to his own lap, began fumbling there, unzipped himself and brought out his own cock, fully erect and reasonably thick, but almost pathetically weedy if compared with Neil. Perhaps this was a comparison that he did not make, or maybe one that he enjoyed, but from then, one of Mr Kan's hands stayed steadily masturbating himself while the other roamed across me, either my breasts or between my legs, or just as frequently, over Neil.

I raised myself up until only the very tip of Neil's cock was still inside me and let Mr Kan see almost the whole glistening length and even gave him one more treat than that: I leaned forward, brushed his hand aside, and took hold of his own stubby cock and stroked it myself for a few moments, while Mr Kan's eyes darted from the long rigid erection just pushing into me to the sight of his own cock being pumped by this glorious foreigner's hand. My mouth was close to him and his eyes blinked at the proximity as I whispered in his ear.

'Would you like to see Neil come?' I smiled and squeezed him a little tighter as I continued the slow movements up and down him. 'See his spunk squirting out?' I don't know how much of that last bit Mr Kan understood but he nodded, for once not even grinning.

I lifted right off Neil and sat down beside him, took his long cock in my hands, and after suckling the tip for a few seconds, began a slow steady rhythm, a combination of lips, tongue and hands that would soon have him squirming, and soon after that would be more than he could resist.

Once the squirming stage was reached, I stopped for a second and picked up our new camcorder. 'I'm going to film him!' I whispered to Mr Kan, and this time I was the one grinning. 'Perhaps you would like to have a copy afterwards?'

Again Mr Kan nodded, staring intently as I juggled the camcorder in one hand but continued the caress with the other. It was not at all easy, and after the difficulties had become evident more than once, I released Neil and concentrated on the camera. 'Here,' and I nodded down towards Neil's weaving cock, 'you do that bit.' I zoomed back and filmed as it happened.

Mr Kan was delighted. He immediately released his own stubby penis and grasped Neil's erection with both hands, sliding up and down with a firm relentless enthusiasm that used my wetness for lubrication but his own desires for motivation. I pulled back the zoom enough to show his concentration, the eager expectation on his grinning face and his own pale cock bobbing abandoned in the background.

Neil had shut his eyes, maybe he was trying not to remember who was doing this to him – or maybe he did not care and was enjoying it just as much as if it had been me – but Mr Kan knew exactly what was going on. His hands were working together, an unchanging steady pace which already had Neil panting, groaning, his fists gripping the bedclothes as he clenched his teeth. Mr Kan grinned contentedly at the effect he had achieved and his head dropped lower; for one second his tongue pushed out and touched the very tip of Neil's cock and that was it. Maybe that touch was the last straw, maybe Neil was not even aware what had been done, but instantly the first stream shot from his prick, arched through the air to land on his stomach and was immediately followed by a second and then a further succession until they had formed a small pool. When there was no more to come, the hands finally stilled, but Mr Kan did not relinquish his hold. He simply sat back, smugly satisfied as he cradled Neil's subsiding erection in his two hands. He's odd, Neil: he comes up and goes down quicker than any man I have ever known. I turned off the video. He sat up and looked round, sheepish and embarrassed.

'Okay?' he asked me.

'Fine.'

'Very good!' added Mr Kan. 'Plenty... Plenty!' and for a second he trailed his fingers through the pool that was shimmering in and around Neil's tummy button. Then he sat back to show his own cock defiantly pushing out of the front of his trousers. He grinned again, taking in both me and Neil. 'You would like?' and he took the thing in his fist, offering it up ambiguously to either of us. Neil's response was immediate and definite.

'No, thank you.'

And I actually felt sorry for him despite everything he had done on this and previous days. I sat down in front of him, took his cock in my hand and with a fairly brisk efficiency started to masturbate him. Neil was not pleased, and he quickly got up off the bed, gathered up his clothes and withdrew to the bathroom to dress. Maybe I was wrong to do it, and at least when Mr Kan leaned forward, beaming his arrogant grin and tapped me on the side of the mouth, 'Here?', I refused. It didn't take long, and when I realized he was on the point of coming, I merely moved back out of the way and made no attempt to prevent his spurts dropping onto his suit trousers; let him explain that however he liked. As soon as he was done, his confidence seemed to deflate like a philanderer caught in the wrong bed. Within two minutes, he had stuffed his cock back into his trousers, zipped himself up, grabbed his jacket and gone.

I tapped on the bathroom door. 'Neil? You okay?'

He emerged looking sheepish and thoroughly uncomfortable. 'Thank goodness that's over. I hope you still think it was worth it.'

'Of course!' and the more I thought about it, the more convinced I became. 'Yes, definitely it was worth it.'

And it was, even though the next morning, when I met Kiki back at the same noodle shop, handed her the tape, and explained what it showed, she did not understand at first why I had asked to meet her or why I was now giving it to her.

'It's for you,' I explained. 'Now, when your husband comes

back, if Mr Kan asks you to go to his office in the evening, with that tape you have the power to say no.'

And gradually she understood, clutched the tape to her chest and finally began to smile. Her face cleared, brightened and her eyes glowed with such a gorgeous radiance that when she said, 'Thank you. How can I ever thank you?' I thought it was lucky we were leaving the following day. She did look ever so sweet.

ABBIE'S TALE: THE SELECTORS

'Fuck it, fuck it, fuck it, fuck it. Fuck the fucking lot of them!' and David hurled his cricket bag the length of the hall until it crashed into the kitchen door frame.

I must have looked like some Barbie-doll wife from a television advertisement, standing with our supper in my hands, a welcoming smile draining away from my face. David yanked open the fridge. 'Is there any beer?'

'There's a full box in the garage.' I quickly put down the casserole. 'I'll get some.'

'Is it cold?'

'Well, not... , I mean it always stays fairly cold in the gara...'

'I'm going to the pub.' And the front door slammed behind him with the same ferocity as the cricket bag had hit the doorway at the other end of the hall.

I knew only too well what the problem was: he hadn't been picked for the team again. It did seem so unfair. At his last club he had often opened the batting or, if not, had certainly been in the first three or four. Here he didn't even get on the team when the one thing it needed was a few decent batsmen. That was what let them down in match after match, yet for some reason they always picked people like Gary Sanderston or Mike Harmer: neither of them was as good as David and anyone could see that. I know we hadn't lived in the village long, less than a year, but you would have thought he would have been welcomed as the answer to their prayers, not shunned as a pariah. I was sure it was simply a matter of time and after they had got used to us, he would be playing every week, but David was more suspicious, believing there was some more sinister process at work: a prejudice against him, some secret society or Freemason's Lodge in control, but it just made no sense.

And I couldn't handle David's disappointment week after week so, although I didn't know Gill Harmer well, I had to consult somebody, and I knew her better than any of the rest. As we stood in her little kitchen that Friday morning, clutching mugs of coffee and surrounded by toys, bikes, dogs and laundry, her blunt explanation shook me, almost as much as her cheery acceptance of it as part of village life. Even so, at least I finally knew how the system worked and what needed to be done.

I sat with David while he seethed through the match on Saturday, watching us lose by six wickets: Gary Sanderston scoring sixteen; Mike Harmer clean bowled for three.

'For God's sake! I don't know why I bother with this pissy little club,' and when he stormed off to the clubhouse, I pleaded a headache and left the other wives to deal with the teas and crept home.

The selection committee met in the clubhouse every Tuesday at 7.30 and the team list would be posted on the club noticeboard on the following evening, but that Tuesday I skipped my Pilates and drove out to the cricket club instead.

Once I had turned down the little lane and passed through the belt of trees that surrounded the cricket ground, there was almost no trace of the rest of the world. A couple of aeroplane tracks carved across the pure blue of the huge July sky and families of swifts swept past high above me, but it was so quiet that it was difficult to remember I was barely twenty miles from the centre of London. Half a dozen cars were lined along the top of the car park where there was a band of shade beneath the trees, and over on the far side of the field I could see four or five of the younger members in the nets. The click of the ball reached across to me, with laughter and occasional shouts: a cliche of village life, but exactly what we had moved out of the city to find.

The clubhouse itself was still in full sun and looked at first to be deserted; the bar was closed and all the downstairs rooms empty, but I could hear voices. As I passed the stairs, a sudden burst of laughter tumbled down from the committee room above: it seemed that the selectors' meeting had already begun.

The stairs were guarded by a broad red circle fixed prominently to the wall at the foot: "No Entry. Club Officers Only". I ignored it, crept up and there they all were: Jack Cattermole, Roy Midgley and Derek Hunt.

'That was good,' one of them was saying but their laughter fizzled out as I pushed open the door, and they turned like guilty schoolboys.

'Can we help you?' Jack, the club chairman, took an intercepting step towards me while the other two hastily turned away, fumbling with some envelopes. Jack had two common nicknames: Jack Sprat because of his size, or the Red Sprat because of his colouring, but he had no sense of humour and none of the members ever dared use either to his face.

'I'm Abbie Cornwell, David's wife.'

'Oh yes, Abbie. Yes, of course. David's not here, if you were looking for him.'

'I know he isn't. I wanted to talk to you.'

'Me?' Now Jack looked even more guilty. His suit jacket was dangling over the back of one of the chairs but he pulled at his cuffs and his tie as he regarded me.

'All of you.'

'Okay,' but he sounded wary. 'What about?'

'That rather depends.'

'I see.' A very silly response since he clearly didn't – and couldn't – "see".

'If I am honest and frank with you, will you be honest and frank with me?'

'Well, of course!' That was his solicitor's smile: I recognised it.

'Not just "Of course". I mean really. No games. No bullshit.'

His eyebrows shot up at my choice of words but I needed to meet them on their own terms. 'All right. Yes.'

'And can we keep this entirely confidential? David doesn't know I've come here. I don't want him to know.'

Roy Midgley pulled out a chair and sat down at the long polished table. 'Now here's a turn up!'

'Shut up, Roy!' Jack Cattermole snapped at him. For a minute they stared at each other like stags locking horns: Roy the Fireman, a bare thirty, fit and muscular, sleek and groomed, with supreme self confidence versus Jack Cattermole, around fifty, short, over-weight and with spiky ginger hair yet the established chairman of the club with a following and respect throughout the village. After half a minute or so, Roy sniffed and stepped away; perhaps he felt his point was made, but Jack's eyes followed him coldly until he was satisfied the challenge was over, when he could safely turn his attention back to me and continue.

'Of course, Abbie. Naturally the deliberations of this Selection Committee are always entirely secret. As you can imagine, there is a great deal of competition to get onto the team and we have a hard task making the right decisions: we have to keep all our discussions confidential, it's the only way a club like this can operate. So, please! Come in! Sit down,' and he swept up the team lists from the table. The three of them lined up down their side of the committee table, Jack in the middle, Roy on his right and Derek on his left. I pulled out a chair and sat opposite them, arranging my bag neatly at my feet as if I were attending an interview.

They were all drinking beer straight from the cans but I declined that invitation, even when a glass was added to the offer.

'So?' Jack brought us back to the subject. 'What can we do for you?'

'Why is David never selected?'

'Well, ...' he shuffled a minute.

'He is a better batsman than most of your openers. On two of the three occasions this season when he has been allowed to play, he has pretty well saved the match for you. Why won't you pick him?'

There was a long pause before Derek Hunt finally broke in, 'Well, Abbie,' he passed his open palm across the flat table top, 'we have many good players in the club but of course we can only have eleven men in the team. The opposition would object if we had more!' When I didn't even pretend to laugh, he carried on. 'There are bound to be disappointments.'

'Bullshit.' They all looked up at that. 'You aren't at school now, Derek.' I was becoming braver as I watched their embarrassment chipping away at their certainty. Yes, I could handle them. 'I don't need an Assembly Time lecture.'

He had the grace to acknowledge the touch and smirked. 'It's still true though.'

'You said you'd be frank.'

'Well, I am trying to be. The point is, ...'

Jack came back to rescue him. 'This is more than a cricket team, Abbie. It's a club. It involves everybody doing their bit.'

'David does that. He plays his part in looking after the club house and the grounds.'

'And the wives as well,' added Roy, staring at me.

'I do my share of the teas.'

'We need more than teas,' he said, and the room was suddenly very quiet.

'Who's "we"?' I asked

'Us. The Selection Committee.'

'And what do you need?' There was a pause; I think nobody wanted to be the one to call the hand.

'Entertainment...' and Roy let that hang in the air.

'Entertainment?' I repeated just as a sudden burst of distant laughter from the boys out in the nets drifted in and emphasised the silence in the room. All down one long side of the room a line of windows, open at the top, looked out across the square and over to the nets on the far side.

'Yes.' Roy Midgley had not turned to look but ran his hand back over his neatly cropped hair. He was the youngest of the three, and was still the Club Social Secretary although there were rumours that he had been asked to stand down as Chairman after a scandal five or six years ago which everyone in the village claimed to know all about but nobody could quite define. I didn't entirely trust him. 'You see, Abbie, if you...'

'The deliberations of the Selection Committee,' Jack

Cattermole broke in deliberately, and I suddenly realised he didn't trust Roy Midgley either. 'The deliberations of the Selection Committee are kept quite secret. What occurs within this room is never revealed. Ever.'

'I see.'

'But we take a personal interest in all our players. And expect them – and their families – to take a personal interest in us.'

This time it was a bumble bee banging against the glass that underlined the expectation. It seemed right to wait for it to find its way out before I continued. 'What do you want me to do?' And Roy Midgley sighed, unable to keep the smirk off his face.

'We aren't difficult to please.'

'What do you want me to do?'

'And as I said, what happens in this room stays in this room.' Derek's eyes flicked over to the locked cupboard round which they had been clustered when I came in. No, I was by no means the first to be here; nor had Gill Harmer been.

'What do you want me to do?' I repeated and again the stillness smothered us.

'We'd like you to take your clothes off.' Jack's calm voice finally saying out loud what I had known was going to be said at some point was still a shock: the simplicity, unambiguity of his words cutting through any social niceties. "Load of perverts", Gill Harmer had called them, "but they're harmless enough, and if it keeps the old man happy, well..." She had shrugged. "No worse than any fella when he comes sniffing round and won't take no for an answer, eh, love?" I had been surprised, no embarrassed, at her honesty, but could she be speaking from experience? "Of course I am, love. That's how any of them gets on the team. To start with, anyway." I had just stared at her until she laughed. "Gawd, look at you! Don't be so prim! And that Roy Midgley is quite a lad, for all he's a bastard." She had not been any more precise, but perhaps that was more from my reluctance to ask than hers to answer. My imagination had filled in the gaps.

'Take my clothes off.' I repeated it as much for my benefit as theirs.

'That's right,' said Jack. 'Take your clothes off. What do you say to that?'

'I don't know.' And I didn't. I had come there knowing there was a price to pay and they were being very nice about it. 'I don't know if David would want me to do that.'

'That's the point, you see? He wouldn't know. The deliberations of the Selection Committee are totally secret.' Jack repeated the mantra as if it would gain power in the telling: in a strange way, it did.

'I don't know if I want to.'

'Why not?' asked Roy. 'You are a very attractive woman, in "your prime" as they might say. You have nothing to be ashamed of.' And he was right: I am not ashamed. I know that I do have a good figure, which is not to boast, because it is nothing for which I can claim credit: I am just lucky in that respect. 'Besides,' he went on, 'I don't think you have dropped in here out of the blue, have you? You came with your eyes open. I would guess,' he fetched himself another can of beer and casually tore off the ring pull, 'that you have spoken to one of the other wives, haven't you? Who was it? Debbie McGrath?'

'Gill Harmer.'

'Ah!' he said. 'Gill!' but I could only think of Debbie

McGrath: so demure and perfect that I could hardly imagine she might have... But Roy was still talking. 'And you can't pretend that your pulse isn't beating a little faster at the prospect.' He was right in that too, of course he was. 'Even from here, Abbie, even from here I can see that your nipples are now erect.'

'Roy! That's enough!' Jack snapped at him, but too late.

I blushed and quickly crossed my arms over my chest, covering myself, but Roy just laughed. 'Which they weren't before.'

I felt so stupid sitting there like a shocked virgin, and anyway a shocked virgin should have turned and left by now. I hadn't. I was still there, and that was enough for Roy to continue.

'I wouldn't be surprised if you weren't getting just a little bit wet as well,' and he raised his eyebrows as I blushed again, and I knew and he knew that I could not deny that either.

'If I do that, if I take my clothes off, are you going to...?' but I couldn't find the appropriate words and stopped. To what? "Make love" certainly wasn't right, but I couldn't bring myself to use any blunter euphemism.

'Let's just start there and see how we go, shall we?' Jack Cattermole reasserted his authority. 'Roy, would you mind?' he nodded in my direction and Roy quickly stood up and came round to close the door behind me. Then he turned the key. He smiled at me as he walked back to his seat.

I considered it a little longer, then kicked off my shoes and started to unbutton my shirt.

'Er... Standing up please, Abbie.' Jack smiled apologetically when I frowned. 'We like to see.'

So I stood up and undressed. Their eyes never wavered, and in the quiet of that empty room, I could feel their gaze pawing at me. I had never in my life undressed under such conditions: three men sitting watching me, so large and austere a room with no ambitions to prettiness or femininity. A faint smell of stale beer, of male bodies and sweat which seemed almost to be part of the design, and – so close by, yet completely ignorant of what was happening here – the youth team practising their cricket, their voices and laughter periodically breaking in on our silence.

I pulled back my chair and lay my clothes carefully on its seat: a shirt and then my tee shirt; my tapered black trousers, which I always worry are too tight but David says he likes, each folded carefully and piled neatly; next my bra and finally, in the complete stillness of their staring eyes, my knickers. Now completely naked, I stood and faced them. For some time they didn't say anything, just sat there considering me. I do think they were appreciating what they saw, and nobody can dislike being admired, but they made no effort to make my situation any easier. Eventually Roy asked me to turn round, so I turned and found the view of the cricket pitch spread out before me, while the three men behind me inspected my bottom amid a continual low whispering which managed, as I suppose it was meant to do, to unsettle me.

'Very nice,' Jack finally spoke to me. 'Very nice indeed. You can turn back again now. Now come round here and hop up on the table.'

'Why?'

'We want to have a look at you.'

'But you have looked at me.'

'We want a closer look.' He offered another of his apologetic half smiles. 'Don't be afraid. We won't hurt you.'

I realized the shouts from outside had stopped and suddenly

there came a buzz of voices and a clattering and opening and closing of doors from the changing rooms beneath us. For a few moments we all froze, but the sounds gradually stopped and there had been no footsteps on the stairs.

'Come along, Abbie,' Jack repeated.

'Why on the table?'

'So we can see you better. Come along,' and Roy pushed back his chair and patted the table between him and Jack Cattermole. When I didn't move he patted again, curling up his face into what was meant to look like a playful grin. 'Come on!'

I walked round to stand between the two men. 'How do you want...?'

'Just sit on the edge and swing your legs up. That's the way.' I gasped at the first contact with the smooth varnished surface: despite the evening sunshine, it still sucked the heat out of my skin. My feet didn't reach the floor and that just made me feel weaker, even more in their power.

'Settle back and there we are! Now then, Abbie. Shall we have your legs apart?'

'What for?'

'Well we want to have a look at you, don't we? You are a very attractive girl, and we want to see all of you.'

They stood round waiting, eyes staring, watching me, focussed only on me as I uncrossed my ankles and edged my feet apart.

'A bit more than that!' It seemed quite wide enough to me, and anyway I could feel myself getting wet and knew that would be visible to them if I went any further. And also see my inside lips, which I am not ashamed of, because I have always been told that I have a very pretty pussy, but apparently my inside lips are much more prominent and bigger than most girls' and that has been commented on too. So I sat there, frozen. 'Please?'

I still didn't move, but then I didn't resist either when hands reached out to my thighs, pulling them open, sliding my legs across the polished table. And of course then they saw.

'Oh, now this is nice! This is really nice! What gorgeous lips!' Roy beamed at me and his fingers went down to touch me, playing with me, pinching my lips together and then peeling them open; spreading them back, and then stopping and chuckling. 'You see? I was right about you being wet, wasn't I?' Someone, it could have been Jack, pulled my thighs even further apart, but then he stopped.

'Now, Abbie, who would you like to have first?'

'First?'

'Yes: First.' I said nothing until he carried on. 'Unless you want us all at once, but I would have thought that...'

'No, not all at once.'

'Okay, so who first?'

I looked at the three of them gathered round and knew that I could never answer, because seeing them all waiting, and feeling my response proved one thing clearly: I may have come here for David: I was staying for me.

'I don't know.'

All the while hands were passing up and down my whole body, running easily across my breasts and my stomach and ruffling though my pubic hair. I don't know whose hands were going where and it didn't seem to matter: my whole body was available to them and this was an opportunity which they would not waste. Jack was the worst: his hands had been running up and back along my thigh, the fingertips running closer into my pussy than they should have. Little eyes peered out of his florid face, entirely ringed by an even-coloured ginger fringe where his close-cropped hair led into a beard that ran down round his chin and up to join the other side of the crop.

'I don't know,' I repeated.

There was a moment's silence and then 'Me', said Derek, and he stepped forward while the other two, in perfect unison, took an equal step back, their hands drawing away and relinquishing their contact, although they both stayed where they could watch.

Derek reached for my breasts, stroking them, kneading me, tweaking and pulling at my nipples and then his beery breath came down near my ear.

'Very nice titties, Abbie,' Derek whispered in my ear. 'I do like a good pair of titties. Nice and responsive, with good strong nipples like these.' The head moved away down my body and then my nipples were being drawn into his mouth, a tongue lapping round and tiny nips of his teeth. When I peered down, his hair was thinning at the top and he wasn't unattractive, just a great deal older than anyone I had ever had any kind of sexual relationship with before. He reminded me of the personnel director at work: medium height, medium build, medium everything.

But he was certainly good at what he was doing, and I simply shut my eyes and drifted. He regularly switched across, first stroking one breast while suckling the other and then changing sides. Each time he swapped, one nipple would be left standing up cold from his saliva until his circling fingertips had dried it. Derek was obviously as keen on my breasts as David is so I could cheerfully have let him continue for the rest of the evening.

But then one hand slithered off my breast and down my

stomach to run through my pubic hair and between my legs, and then he was fumbling there, pressing, stroking and digging deep inside me, before the hand withdrew and reappeared at my head, where he offered me his shining fingers, steeped in my juice: a taste I love. When I had licked his fingers clean, instead of returning to caress my breast, he unzipped himself, unbuckled his belt and pushed his trousers and underpants down his legs. His shirt was tented out in front of him, but when he pulled that away, his erection was there, level with my eyes and waving just in front of my face. Without a word, he drew me across the table (was this why they kept it so smoothly polished? So they could slide people like me across it?) until I was right on the edge and he could feed the tip into my mouth.

Someone else's hands took the place of Derek's, working between my legs. Fingers, I don't know whose – nor how many – had pushed up inside me and were sliding in and out with a slow regular insistence that would have done nothing except that all the while other fingers were working on my clit, and from time to time a tongue would circle that, lips pinching me and nibbling before releasing me again. I could feel myself getting steadily wetter and would probably be dripping by now, certainly I could smell myself, the scent wafted across on the evening air.

But I had no chance to consider them as Derek pushed himself even deeper into my mouth, so deep that I was almost choking. His erection was not specially long, but was gloriously thick so that when I reached up to steady it with my hand, my fingers barely circled round him. Even so, he grew bigger in my mouth, and the foreskin, loose and sloppy when he had started, was stretched tighter. I could see the other two now, crowding round to watch, stupid grins on their faces, and Jack casually reached out to fondle my breast as he stood there. I slid my hand down from Derek's cock to his heavy swinging sac beneath, held that, cradled it in my palm and felt him tightening as his arousal grew. For a while I took him right out of my mouth and ran a few long laps the whole length of his erection, but from the quivering in his thighs, he seemed to be getting dangerously close to orgasm and I pulled him back deep into my mouth again. His eyes were shining, his face flushed and glistening and as it all got tantalisingly close, he started to pull away; except that by now I was not willing to let him go and held on, even reaching round to grab hold of his buttocks and pull him closer.

'Oh no,' he gasped as his sac tightened suddenly, and again he tried to pull back, just as his cock twitched up for the first time and he got clear as the first jet shot up and landed in a line across my cheek, my eyebrow and into my hair. 'Oh fuck,' he groaned in dismay and the other two just laughed; I think Roy even slapped him on the back as he gave up trying to hold back and instead struggled to push his erection back into my mouth, his hips bucking against me as the rest of his spurts shot up into my throat in a short sweet shower that I swallowed down.

When it was finished, he smiled down at me sheepishly. 'Sorry, love. I didn't mean to do that. In fact, I had meant to finish off somewhere entirely different. Still. Next time, maybe.'

He turned away, awkwardly trying to pull up his trousers, stuffing his half erect penis back into his pants while Roy grinned at him and slapped him on the back.

'Done already, Del?'

'Bugger off,' but the other two only laughed.

From what Gill had implied, she had only used her hand on each of them; already this had passed the point that I had expected or intended, and I certainly did not want it to go any further. I started to sit up but didn't have time to move before Jack stepped forward. 'Just a minute, Abbie, love,' and he was unzipping his trousers as he stepped up to me, pulling out his erect penis and, just as Derek had done, aiming for my mouth, resting the tip on my lips and then, quite gently, pushing forward.

And like Derek, his hand reached down to fondle my breasts and then further down to explore between my legs, his open palm running up and down my pussy, making small circles and from time to time, pausing to let a couple of fingertips focus on my clit, running tiny rings round that, steadily, insistently and also effectively. But he wasn't going to make the same mistake as Derek and pulled away, swivelled me round across the table and pulled my knees up and spread me wide open. Until then, Jack had only unzipped his fly but now, as I lay there entirely exposed and watching him, he unfastened his trousers and pushed them down his legs, but that was as far as he went. His cock pushed out from between his shirt tails, shining from my spit, as he pulled me right up to the edge of the table and pressed the head between my lips and pushed.

He sank in so smoothly and easily. The table was perfect for a man of his height: the angle was right and he was gloriously hard and I was achingly wet. It could not have been more perfect. Presumably, this was not the first time he had taken a woman across that table, nor the first time there had been people watching him to do it; certainly he was not at all inhibited. Conversely, this was the first time that I had ever done this with other people watching me and it was gloriously exciting, adding an indescribable intensity to the simple rhythm of his actions. And it was so simple: his hands rested on my knees, holding me open as he stared down between my legs where he was pushing forward and back at a smooth, steady unchanging pace. He didn't speak, although occasionally his mouth worked and he would glance up at me and raise his eyebrows in a friendly conspiracy, before focussing back on the place where we were joined. He ignored my breasts, available right in front of him and quivering with every stroke, my nipples reaching up erect and greedy. He was not distracted by anything, as if I were as insignificant as the two men watching, as the little white clouds drifting across the sky behind his head, as if this were a job he had been given to do and until it was done he would work at it steadily, professionally, almost unemotionally.

I could not be so detached. I could not ignore, or keep from glancing at, the two men standing either side of me: one flushed from having me, the other waiting to have me next. And they were not just seeing me naked, but witnessing this most private of acts, seeing the effect on me of what was being done to me, smiling whenever I could no longer hold back a sigh of pleasure, and if Jack had no interest in my breasts, the other two both did, and each of them from time to time reached out to run his fingers round my nipple. But mostly I watched Jack. My pussy was stretched tight round him, so that, although there was no direct contact with my clit, every long smooth thrust pulled me and released and pulled me again ,and that was more than enough for my pleasure too. It was only then that it struck me that his small size was not reflected here: maybe that was what gave him so much confidence.

Nothing seemed to change his pace. Ridiculously his tie

was swinging back and forth with every movement of his body, and every time he pulled back, his pale cock came into view, as ringed about by its own little fringe of red hair as was his face. But if his pace didn't alter, his expression did. That was growing increasingly flushed and tortured, and when his breath broke into low grunts, I realised that he was not nearly as fully in control as he appeared. And then he gave one louder grunt and that was it: pressing my knees even flatter, at last his pace doubled, and he was pounding at me with the ferocity of a bull as he shot his semen into me.

And as suddenly as it started, so it finished. He pulled out and released my legs with a cheery slap across the thigh. 'You're a good one, you are!' and with no more ceremony, he started tidying himself, pulling up his trousers and looking round for his beer can.

I hadn't really noticed what the other two men had been doing during this, but as soon as Jack pulled away, I knew that Roy was going to start, and as that thought came to me, I looked round and there he was, lurking, grinning, smirking; his eyes wide and expectant.

He sauntered up to where I was lying, my feet still flat on the table, my knees still up and wide apart, my sex still wide open to his eyes, and to more than his eyes. I wondered what I now looked like down there: open and supremely wet and glistening certainly; but was Jack's sperm now trickling out in an obscene display of my greed? I felt flushed and radiant. Jack had been good, even if he hadn't quite gone long enough for me; Roy, on the other hand, looked like the kind of man who would make very sure his lady was entirely satisfied.

He held out his hand. 'Turn over.'

'What?'

'Turn over onto your stomach.'

When I rolled over and slithered round, there was a neat pool where I had been lying, now smeared across the polished surface.

'Lovely.' One hand rested on the middle of my back, lightly but unarguably holding me in place. There was also a prolonged fumbling of some sort behind me and I guessed he was taking down his trousers. Eventually he leaned down, pressing me even flatter against the table. 'Lovely arse you've got, Abbie. Quite gorgeous!'

'What are you doing?' I no longer had any confidence in what was happening behind me.

A low, gurgling laugh came from behind me before he leaned down close again. 'I'm getting ready to fuck you in the arse.'

Immediately I struggled to get up. 'I don't want to do that. I've never...'

'Oh, but I've heard that you do. I've heard that you rather like this. I've heard....' and then I felt the end of his penis against me, nuzzling between my lips where I would accommodate him if I had to, pushing and sliding in shamefully easily, but with only a little sigh, he carried on. 'I've heard that way might even be your favourite,' and he casually pushed himself deeper into me, pulled back, and pushed in again. 'Is that right?'

'No!' I protested, 'I don't....'

'Well, that's not what is being said round the club.' His movements continued their same insultingly slow pace. 'So once I'm good and slippery, I'm going up there to try. Then we'll know, won't we? First of all though,' he was deliberately timing his words to the rhythm of his slow thrusts, 'first we'll get nice and wet and get you nice and ready. Although, it seems to me that you're about ready now.'

'I'm not!'

'Then what was that little squeal about just now? Why are you so slippery down here? Why can't you keep still? Huh? I think you're ready and I think we'll give it a try about now.' And he slowly pulled out further and further until he was out completely when he pulled me even closer, lifted my bottom higher and nestled the tip of his penis right into my bottom. He started to push against me and I screamed.

'Wait!' I struggled to get up and he stopped. 'It's too soon, too tight.'

'I like it tight!' And he laughed, running his hands across my back and taking a handful of my bottom cheek to squeeze.

'It's too dry. I've got some stuff in my bag.'

'In your bag?'

'Yes.'

'Why?' He sounded amused as much as curious, but I think more than either he wanted to humiliate me by stripping away any secrets.

'In case I need it, in case I.... Look, I just have. Please?' There was no need for them to know all the details of our private life: besides, those three probably wouldn't even know what dogging meant.

So I scrambled down off the table and went to collect the tube, feeling the cold intensity of Jack and Derek watching me as I scurried naked round the room. When I brought the little tube back, I offered it to Roy but he wouldn't take it, just stood there, shamelessly, naked from the waist down and with his erection eagerly pointing towards me. When I did nothing either, he offered a vague nod which took in my nakedness, the tube of *Bodyslip* held out in my hands and his erection bobbing between us. He was not going to take any part. And ultimately, the effect was purely for my benefit; if I wanted his entry into me to be made easier, it was going to be up to me to make it so.

I took hold of his cock, surprisingly cold to the touch and squeezed a small worm of jelly onto its tip and ran my fingers round to cover the whole surface. Nobody in the room moved or spoke or even, as far as I could tell, breathed. I squeezed on some more, and with my full open hand, rubbed that the entire length of him, ensuring there was nowhere left uncovered. Roy smirked down at me, and although I know I was only doing this to put on the lubricating jelly, and it was more for my benefit and comfort than for his, if I had just been masturbating him, would it have looked any different? It was rather a nice cock.

But even if it wasn't specially thick, it was quite long and Roy was too eager. I didn't trust him to treat me as gently as David would have done, so although I hated having to do it, I knew I needed to apply some to me as well as to him. I squeezed another little bit onto my finger tip and, dropping into a half-squat, slowly worked that finger round the entrance of my bottom and finally right into it, as deep as my finger would reach, opening myself in readiness and lubricating the whole area. Then I turned, bent over the table and offered myself to him again.

His hands came down and rested on my bottom, his thumbs digging in and peeling open the cheeks to inspect what he was now being offered. A couple of times I felt the cold wet tip of his penis bouncing against my skin but he made no effort to take things any further. He peered at me closely.

'Actually, I think we'll have you face up. I like to see who

I'm doing, if you'll pardon the pun.' And his two friends did snigger at his frightfully clever joke.

I stood up, sat on the table and, under his half smile, lay back and opened myself to him. For a minute he just stared and then, one hand casually and nonchalantly working up and down his cock, just to maintain the erection, his expression said, because my being stretched naked, greased and waiting, before him, that would not otherwise be sufficient temptation, he stepped forward. He took hold of my ankles and pulled them right up over my head, peered casually at what was now so fully exposed and turned to Derek and Jack.

'Would you mind lending a hand, lads?' and he offered them each an ankle to hold, folding me further back, further exposed, further open so that Roy could again lay his penis against the heart of my bottom. With his hands on my thighs, he pulled me closer and pressed forward with his hips.

And of course it was much easier that it should have been: he slipped inside far too easily to maintain my pretence of this being unusual for me. His hands gripped me firmly as he slowly, slowly, half an inch forward, quarter of an inch back, pushed deeper and deeper into my bottom. And once he was in, whereas Jack had practically ignored me, Roy was quite the opposite. His hands were everywhere: over my breasts, pinching my nipples, running across my stomach, pushing through my pubic hair and sometimes even tugging at tufts of it. From time to time, he would work one finger up inside my pussy, and that would be running in parallel to his penis in my bottom. But he never gave much attention to my clit; I was left peeled open to his view, to the two men stranding at my shoulders, each holding up one leg, and I could feel the cool air brushing across my clit, but I needed more than air and eventually I gave in. I reached down and started masturbating. One hand pressing my lips wide open, the other rubbing hard across my clit, just as I would have done if this had been David, and I closed my eyes and didn't care what they all thought.

But I didn't have long enough. It was soon obvious that Roy was struggling not to come too quickly; he had lasted well, but when I squeezed, he could hold on no longer. He pulled back briefly, and then with a few short stabbing thrusts, collapsed onto my chest, hugging me, cuddling me and groaning out his orgasm without restraint.

The other two released my ankles and I hugged Roy against my breasts, running my free hand across his broad shoulders, the lines of muscles in his back, and reaching down as far as I could towards his buttocks. But my other hand was still busy: I know what I like, and how to do it best, even if he was finished. Before he stood up, he leaned forward and kissed me. 'Thank you. That was really rather good.' And he grinned at me as he stood up, but I was too busy to smile back, and if his arrogant selfishness had been enough for Gill Harmer, I was sorry for her.

So I stayed there with my thighs spread wide, my hands between my legs, one hand clutching myself and the other circling, squeezing and rubbing at my clit with a glorious brutality. And I didn't care that the three of them were all standing round watching me, Roy, I dimly noticed, already struggling back into his trousers. Let them watch, let them see me at this lowest level of obscenity; I wanted them to watch; I was shameless; I was magnificent. I was full of Jack's semen, I could feel it in me and trickling out of me. Roy's too, deeper and even more forbidden. Even Derek's: the smell of him still in my hair. And lying there, spread open for them all to see,

I brought myself to a wonderful shaking climax which rattled through me, startled them and finally, thankfully was enough.

Afterwards, I climbed to my feet and began reaching for my clothes, but Derek stopped me. 'Just a minute, Abbie.' Looking round, he was holding a small camera in his hand. 'We like to have a couple for the archive. Could you just pop back onto the table?' And he arranged me as I had been before, on my back and spread open to the world, and then bent over the table, close up, even though I could feel myself leaking as I stood there. 'Lovely,' he said as the flash scattered round the room. 'Lovely.'

When he was done, they all stood watching me in complete silence as I shuffled back to my side of that horrible table, retrieved my clothes and started to dress again. I heard but didn't catch a quick mutter from Jack as I was stooping to gather up my underwear; it would be sodden by the time I got home. Collecting my trousers and shirt I saw Roy's red finger marks on my breasts; I would have to think of something to explain that to David. Only as I was pulling on my shoes did Jack speak at last.

'Do you think, Abbie, that David will want to play in the team next season?'

'I expect so.' I looked up and frowned round at them all. 'Why?'

'Nothing,' Roy said casually. 'Only we start the main selection process in April, so it's as well to come and see us early to make sure there's a place.' From the top of a cupboard on the side he brought forward the club's fixtures diary and started flicking through the pages. 'How about April 12th? We've got Annie Sanderson coming then, but there's nothing to stop us seeing you both together.' He turned to me. 'Is there?'

The following night, Wednesday, I waited eagerly for David to come home. I could almost picture his arrival as he struggled to squeeze his grin down the hallway, sauntered up to the living room door and stood there, rocking a little unsteadily.

'Guess who is batting at number three on Saturday!' he would chirp. 'I knew those idiots would eventually see sense.'

But instead he was quiet, and said nothing until I prodded him. 'Well?' I asked.

'Well what?'

'Are you in the team on Saturday?'

He frowned, just a momentary tightening, but suddenly I knew it: those bastards had still not included him. But I was wrong; it wasn't that at all. 'Oh no; No, I'm not. I told you, didn't I? I've resigned from the Cricket Club. I told Jack Cattermole after the match last Saturday. In fact, I have applied to join another club based near the office and I am seeing them on Saturday; they did ask particularly whether you could come along too.'

DIANA'S TALE: MRS BEAUCHAMP

Mrs Beauchamp was a very kindly woman; she reminded Diana of the teacher who had taken her very first year at primary school. Soft and round both in figure and manner, she was motherly – in fact she was easily old enough to be Diana's mother – and that was particularly reassuring for an application such as this, going right across to America. But today the atmosphere was decidedly strained. They were sitting where they had always done in the front room of Mrs Beauchamp's own house, the room she used as her office, but the woman was not at all at ease. Her neat cotton dress was no tighter than usual, but she seemed to fit it less well. Her make-up was as carefully applied as ever, but today it seemed less effective in portraying the experienced serenity which had previously give such confidence. She seemed flushed, tired perhaps, or harassed. She had fussed over the cups of tea, the chairs, had made sure the window was open and that the door was shut. Now she was fiddling with the papers, busily reshuffling them as if she were unwilling to meet Diana's eye.

'Now, they are a bit funny about some of the girls they select to have as carers.'

'What kind of funny?'

'Well, not funny, dear, so much as particular. They do insist on well brought-up, clean-living girls, and they have heard some strange stories about English girls; about their being rather wild: punky and that kind of thing. They don't want anything like that.'

Diana was sure she wasn't "anything like that" and said so, quite firmly.

'No, of course you aren't, but you see your clients, your patients will be very respectable people. They are all retired, and many are quite elderly, some even bed-ridden. Yet they are used to having everything they want, just as they like. And of course, they are very conservative.'

'Yes, I understand.'

'Extremely conservative.'

'That's all right, Mrs Beauchamp. I promise I won't shock them and will never sing *The Red Flag* while on duty!' Mrs Beauchamp managed a smile, but a small one, rather less than Diana had hoped, so she went on. 'You did say that I had all the qualifications.'

'Oh you do, my dear, you do. It's just this last bit. It would be dreadful if you got all the way over to Utah and they sent you straight back.'

'Send me back? Why on earth would they do that?'

'They can be very funny. They sent back one girl last year because she had a tattoo.'

'I don't have any tattoos. You asked me about that.'

'And another one was rejected, fortunately before she made the journey, because she had a piercing.'

'I only have my tummy button. Well, and my ears.'

'Ah, yes,' and Mrs Beauchamp twitched a little. 'I don't think they would like that; not the tummy button.'

'I can take it out. Frankly for this opportunity, I will take out my earrings too if they would like me to.'

'I don't think that will be necessary, but the tummy button might be a good idea.'

'Okay. I will remember before I leave.'

'Yes, well I have to certify that to the agency in Salt Lake City.'

'Okay. So certify it.' Yes, Diana decided, there was something very wrong.

'I have to check each applicant personally. And sometimes – frequently – they ask for photographs as well.'

'Yes you said.' Mrs Beauchamp was still doing no more than glancing at Diana, and this prevarication showed no signs of coming to a focus. 'I am a bit confused actually, Mrs Beauchamp. You said I would need photographs for the work permit; that is partly why I am here today. You said that I could have them done here; that there would be someone here to take them. What is the problem if we need a few more prints for the agency too?'

'These ones are... Sometimes the agency needs more personal ones.'

'Personal?'

'Intimate.' Diana frowned, the little face wrinkling up as she listened. 'Complete pictures of all of you. Of you all over, I mean.'

'Do you mean...? What, sort of in my underwear?'

'No, dear. Not even your underwear.'

'What?'

'Yes, dear. In your birthday suit.'

'No!'

'I'm afraid so.'

'Bloody hell! I'm not doing that! What on earth do they want them for?'

'Well, as I say, they have had people with strange tattoos and things; piercings in odd places. They are rather insistent.'

'I see.' Mrs Beauchamp fussed about with more tea

although Diana really wished she would stop and let her consider properly what all this really meant. Mrs Macklin! That had been the teacher's name, and now that she remembered that detail, her face came into even sharper focus and they did seem incredibly alike. Eventually Mrs Beauchamp came and sat down, this time on the settee next to Diana. She even patted her knee.

'I know it's not nice, but... Well it's just that they are so very particular about this.' She patted the knee again, a sort of circular pat this time which was not that far off being a stroke. 'Will you mind, dear?'

'I don't know, to be honest.' And she really didn't know, although if Mrs Beauchamp said it was necessary then it would be rather silly for Diana to make a big fuss about it. However, the thought that had hit her first, and which kept bouncing back to the front of her mind, was that presumably at some stage Mrs Beauchamp would see the photographs. Then what would she think? Diana was not ashamed of her body; she knew she was quite attractive and sometimes she even thought she was better than that. Even so, she could not stay entirely unmoved by the prospect of Mrs Beauchamp seeing pictures of her breasts; and not only her breasts. Well, it made her quite nervous; she felt her pulse running a little faster, her skin prickling with the anticipation, and bizarrely a slight fluttering between her legs. But there were also other considerations. 'Who would take these photographs?'

'Naturally we would not want a man present for that sort of occasion. Certainly not. I have a lady who comes in to do these: Miss Gilbert, Elaine Gilbert. She always does them, for all the girls. She is ever so nice, dear: perfectly safe. And of course I would stay with you all the time. Just to reassure you, be a friendly face.'

So Mrs Beauchamp would see not only the photographs, but would actually see her in the flesh while she was naked and having them taken. So would this other woman. But no men: that was... What? Disappointing? No, not really. If he had been a nice looking young man then Diana might not have minded so much. But if he had turned out to be nasty, then it would be much better if it were only Mrs Beauchamp and the other woman.

As well as those two, there would obviously be the agency people looking at the photographs. The fluttering felt a touch more insistent, and was coupled by a growing dampness. Her nipples felt tighter; her heart beat faster.

'I suppose I could.'

Mrs Beauchamp beamed. 'That's the way, dear. Well done. Shall I give Elaine a tinkle now? She runs Mirabelle's. You know them? Just along behind the stationers? I always have my hair done there. Perhaps she could pop up.'

'Now?'

'Yes! Why not? Let's just get the beastly business over and done with, shall we?'

'But I'm not ready. I was all in rather a rush this morning, you see. I didn't do up my hair or anything. I thought it was just going to be like a passport photograph.'

'Oh don't worry, dear. Elaine will tidy it up for you. There's not much she can't manage in that line. I'll ring her right away.'

Ten minutes later Elaine was striding in: a slim woman of thirty, or perhaps a little more, with long blonde hair pulled into a tight pony tail and very sensible trousers, although she probably called them slacks. All of this was contradicted by a frivolously loose striped shirt and a lightness in her makeup that seemed to welcome people to look rather than intimidate them by arrogant display. She dropped down a large black case and took Diana's hand; a good four or five inches taller, she nevertheless held herself perfectly straight, smiling down with an easy honesty so that Diana could only smile back, feeling herself drawn in as if they had been the closest of friends for years.

'Hello, Diana. Lovely to meet you. Helen has told me all about you.' Even after she had begun addressing Mrs Beauchamp, Elaine kept hold of that hand, her eyes wandering up and down Diana's face and body, weighing and assessing. 'Is it the usual sets for Saint Martha's, Helen? Good.' And her smile was so reassuring, and offered with such calm confidence and warm contentment that Diana found her pulse going even faster. And when the hand, after a momentary squeeze, was finally released, Diana was actually sorry, even though the squeeze had caused another little jolt and more warm dampness that seemed to have no justification.

'We often do them in here, Diana.' Elaine purred on. 'The white wall makes a good background for the head and shoulders shots and it is private, and comfy for the other ones. Is that all right with you?'

So they moved one of the chairs back – 'Will that be enough room?' – and while Elaine sorted out her equipment and set out a big white umbrella, Diana stood up against the wall and Mrs Beauchamp fussed over Diana's hair and even, using her own lipstick, touched in Diana's lips. Finally Mrs Beauchamp was satisfied, and Elaine had added her own touches to Diana's hair and she too was satisfied so Diane faced straight out while Elaine gazed through her viewfinder at the girl and took two, three, four photographs for the application forms and then, after stepping forward to adjust Diana's hair again, her fingers, long slender fingers, brushing it down on one side of her face, Elaine took just a couple more to be on the safe side, and if one or two were not needed for St Martha's and remained in her own collection, what harm could there be in that?

So those were done, which only left The Other Ones. And nobody knew quite how to start. After a glance exchanged between Elaine and Mrs Beauchamp, Elaine excused herself a moment, a moment long enough to allow Diane to be helped over the hurdle.

'Right, then,' Mrs Beauchamp steered her back to the settee, putting on her smiles and motherliness again. 'Shall we just slip these things off? I'll give you a hand,' and she dropped down beside her, immediately reaching out for Diana's buttons: Mrs Macklin all over again.

'It's all right, Mrs Beauchamp. I can do it myself,' and she tried to regain control but it was completely ineffective.

'Of course you can, dear, of course you can. But you must let me help you where I can.' The buttons were popping open steadily and Diana could now see the front strap of her bra appearing as the shirt was teased open. 'There we are! Easy as that!' and Mrs Beauchamp was pulling it out of the waistband of Diana's jeans, pushing it back over her shoulders, clearing it away.

'There. And what a pretty little bra. I do like the little rosebuds; how charming! Such a pity you have to take it off.' However, she managed to overcome her regrets and reached round for the fastening, was smoothly unhooking it, pulling it away, even though Diana automatically brought her arms up to protect herself, covering her front and trying to hold onto the bra.

'Are you sure we need to do this, Mrs Beauchamp? I mean I have already told you that I don't have any tattoos or anything, so really I don't see why you need to do this.' But even if Diana did not understand the reasons, she did understand the results, and would have been mortified if everything had stopped at that point. How long had it been since she had been able to be naked like this, to be looked at and examined, pored over, and of course pampered?

'I think we should be on the safe side, dear.' Mrs Beauchamp was tugging at the bra straps as Diana's arms held the cups firmly clamped over her breasts. 'You never know,' and then she carefully lifted Diana's arms away and the bra fell free at the same time. 'There you are! How very pretty, Diana dear! What lovely little breasts you have! I bet all the boys are in love with you, aren't they? Lie back, dear.' And Mrs Beauchamp's hand reached out, and at the same time as it guided Diana back against the settee until she was not far off horizontal, it also enfolded the nearer breast, enclosing, supporting and stroking in a way that could have been maternal and no more than affectionate, even the gentle caress as her thumb passed over the nipple, even when she moved from this breast to the other, again stroked the little nipple to eager excitement, all of that could have been dismissed as mere womanly admiration except that at the last minute Mrs Beauchamp's head bobbed down and she planted a light kiss right onto Diana's nipple.

'You are so lucky, my dear. You have the most wonderful little breasts. So neat and firm and absolutely adorable.'

And perhaps Elaine was listening outside because the door flew open without warning and Elaine was in there with them, her face flushed, eyes flaring bright and anxious and she took a place on Diana's other side. 'Now,' she said, words ready to cover any awkwardness as she made up any lost ground. 'Are we nearly ready?' She picked up the bra which had been discarded on Diana's lap, and smoothed it out, feeling through her fingertips the residue of body warmth from its cups. For a moment, she even concentrated on that. 'This is very pretty, isn't it? How sweet!' But once it was carefully folded and placed neatly on the side table, her focus turned back to Diana herself. She took hold of the girl's upper arms in her hand and twisted her round until they were facing each other.

'Very pretty!' and her fingers, beautifully manicured fingers, Diana noticed, although the nails were all kept curiously short: presumably necessary for her work, these fingers brushed Diana's hair away again, smoothing it back, and then the fingers moved on to her cheeks, and round under her chin, and even right over her lips, so that for an instant as they grazed past, but hesitated, oh, only for a second but hesitated, Diana was deeply tempted to pucker her lips, to allow the tiniest of timid kisses to be swept away on the fingertips.

But she didn't. She waited, feeling curiously at ease in the warmth of Elaine's comforting smile; although she was conscious of having no top on, of her breasts being bare, and knew that her nipples had responded as eagerly as her nipples always did, she was not ashamed or embarrassed. Behind her Mrs Beauchamp fidgeted, cleared her throat and Diana caught a glance thrown from Elaine, even the fraction of a frown creasing the perfect smoothness of Elaine's pale forehead. It was gone as quickly, and the gentle smile, showing only a sliver of her neat white teeth, returned to wrap itself round Diana once more.

Meanwhile Elaine's hands continued. Running down Diana's arms, they continued across her shoulders and slowly all the way down her arms to the hands, where for a moment they paused, holding both her hands and raising them slightly to improve the view of her front and, of course, of her breasts. 'Very sweet! Now lift your arms up, Diana, up over your head. That way it shows off the shape of your breasts so much better,' and she lifted the hands herself to bring them right back onto the top of the settee behind them both. But then she frowned. 'Oh! Oh dear!' And as her hands slipped down Diana's arms, they came up to her armpits where they stopped. 'It is a bit bristly here, Diana, isn't it?'

Diana would have brought her arms down, indeed quickly tried to do so but was immediately stopped by Elaine returning them to her preferred position and holding both wrists in one of her hands while the other gauged the pale stubble in Diana's armpit and Diana flustered through an explanation.

'Yes, I didn't realise... I mean I didn't know we would be doing this today.'

'Maybe,' and there was only the slightest criticism in Elaine's voice. 'Maybe, but a girl should always be looking her best and ready for any eventuality. Otherwise it is so easy to be caught out.'

'Yes. I'm sorry,' and Diana genuinely was sorry. She felt that she had let down not only Elaine but the nearly-Mrs-Macklin too.

'Never mind. I can take care of that for you before we do those pictures.' And then she released Diana's wrists and instead passed her hands up her body until they could sweep in and enfold her breasts, swirling light circles across her, lightly pinching her nipples, and gently squeezing the whole breast. 'You do have very lovely breasts.'

'Thank you. But...' While not embarrassed at her situation,

neither was Diana certain of where all this was leading, and the uncertainty prevented her finding quite what she should be asking.

'Hmm?' Elaine really did have a lovely complexion, but it would be much easier to concentrate on what Diana should be asking if only the woman would stop stroking her. 'Hmm? But what?'

'Why are you doing this?'

'For the photographs.'

'Yes, but why are you touching me?'

'Don't you like it?'

'Well, I mean I don't know. It's just that...'

'Your little nipples have pushed up, haven't they? I think they like it.' And again the finger tips gently pressed on the pointed pink nipples, raising them out. 'Don't they?'

'Well, yes, I mean it feels very nice, it's just that...'

'Then, that's all that matters. If it feels nice to you, then I am glad to be able to do it for you. Now, my dear: let's have a little look at this piercing in your navel, shall we? How does that fit in?' And although Diana suspected that the subject would come back to her breasts in due course, it was a relief just for now to be on safer ground. The two women peered closely at her stomach, fiddling with the little silver ring before Mrs Beauchamp sat up.

'It's very pretty, I'm sure,' although from the tone Diana guessed that she was very far from sure, 'but I don't think the Agency would like it. Could you take it out for us?'

So Diana slipped it out, and the women checked the place again, their fingertips running over her skin so lightly that she giggled.

'Actually, I do think that looks better, you know. It looks

more natural without that thing,' and Mrs Beauchamp made another wide sweep of her hand across the soft smooth stomach where the ring had been, a sweep which inevitably and to nobody's surprise, extended right up Diana's front until it met her breast again, where it rested for a second, feeling the hard little bud of the girl's nipple poking against her palm.

'Right, now I can confirm that the top half of you is clear of any tattoos or anything. Shall we check the rest of you?'

Almost immediately two pairs of hands were fighting for control of her jeans zip. Evidently Mrs Beauchamp won for Elaine squatted down in front of her and started ripping open the velcro of her trainers, peeling her socks off, and when at last Mrs Beauchamp had managed to unpop the stud and opened the zip, Elaine took hold of the bottoms of the legs of her jeans and pulled. Mrs Beauchamp helped work them down off her hips, but it was all so smoothly done that Diana began to feel control slipping away from her and made a grab for her knickers before those too could be pulled away.

'And these?' Mrs Beauchamp took hold of the thin elastic waistband and pulled gently while Elaine stood watching, silently smoothing down the jeans, folding them, before laying them on a chair where, Diana now saw, her shirt was already draped over the back.

'Do you need to?'

Elaine sat down in her place again, her hand resting on Diana's thigh, near the top, very near, so that with her forefinger she could reach out and stroke the little sprays of rose buds that covered the gentle swelling in the front of Diana's knickers. 'We should really,' she said.

'It is for the Agency, dear,' Mrs Beauchamp added.

Diana didn't dare look at either of them, stared straight

down her body at her hands gripping the front of her knickers, at the single slender finger tracing little circles on the front. Nobody else moved or spoke, and for a few seconds there was perfect silence.

'Are you going to touch me there, too?' Diana asked softly.

'Yes. You see, dear, we do need to check.' Still nobody moved.

'Will you need to touch me there a lot?' The room had gone completely still; even that one finger had stopped its circles and was now just resting on her leg.

'Well...' Mrs Beauchamp started but her voice faded away.

Elaine took over, her fingertip now just lightly scratching up and back along the thin cotton. 'Would you like us to?'

Diana bit her lip, still clutching at the only item of clothing left to her and feeling her heart racing. 'Yes,' she whispered.

Then she simply let go of her knickers: released the elastic and raised her hands to let them do as they would. Straightaway, Mrs Beauchamp reached across to start pulling them down, and Diana even lifted up her bottom to help, but while Mrs Beauchamp busied herself with disentangling the knickers, Elaine had already moved into position.

'Well, this is all rather wild, isn't it?' Her voice was kind enough as she ruffled her fingers through the heavy curls which were now the centre of all attention, but again there was no hiding the slight trace of criticism. 'When did you last trim here?'

'Not for a little while: it never seems to work very well.'

'Why not?'

'It goes all stubbly and itchy.'

'Even so, lots of girls do find it much nicer to trim themselves just a little. Much more hygienic, too.' Her fingers were still twirling through the hair, just touching the skin beneath. 'And of course, often their boyfriends prefer that too.'

'Do you have a boyfriend, Diana?' Mrs Beauchamp ran the back of her hand gently down Diana's stomach into the soft, slightly damp, valley at the top of her thigh and on down her leg.

'Not really. Not just at the moment.'

'Or girlfriend?' Mrs Beauchamp continued hopefully.

'No.'

'Pity.'

Elaine now moved her hand onto Diana's thigh and curled it round until she had squeezed down between her thighs and could draw the quivering legs apart. 'May I just look at the lower bit?' and she drew it further towards her while Mrs Beauchamp did the same on her side, and Diana felt her legs being spread wider and wider apart. She could not remember ever having sat in so indelicate a position, certainly not when she was naked and with two other people in the room. Elaine's fingers were running across her skin. 'Yes it is a bit stubbly, isn't it?' The frown was sympathetic, but the tone disappointed as she rasped across the delicate damp skin.

'It's difficult to reach properly,' Diana tried to explain.

'I know. When I was working, the girls used to do each others'.'

'You were working?'

'Of course. Before I switched to this side of the camera, I was working on yours.' Elaine's fingers continued running softly up and down through the growing dampness, but there had been something in her remark which had caught at Diana's attention.

'Mine?'

'It could be yours if you wanted it. Wouldn't you like that? To have people admiring you all the time? Being photographed wearing wonderful flowing dresses?'

'I suppose so.'

'Or elegant, delicate lingerie?'

'Yes.'

'And sometimes being photographed wearing nothing at all?'

'Yes,' and neither of them missed the shiver that ran right down her body.

'Good,' and Elaine leaned down and dropped the lightest possible kiss onto Diana's half open mouth. 'Would you like me to trim it for you now? And do your armpits?' But when she had bent down, the shirt had ballooned open and for one tantalising second, Diana had caught a glimpse of Elaine's breast, not her bra, but her breast: smooth, golden and, tantalisingly free of any sort of paler tan line. The implications of that rushed in, knocking everything else out of her mind until she realised the room had fallen silent and the two women seemed to be waiting for her to answer something.

'Sorry?'

Elaine smiled, an oddly knowing smile as if she knew more than she was letting on. 'I asked if you would like me to trim it for you and do your armpits.'

'Would you mind?'

Elaine smiled. 'No. I'd love to.'

Mrs Beauchamp went to fetch towels and when she came back, Diana felt as if she were in hospital. There were scissors, a razor and an aerosol shaving cream, as well as a flannel and, last of all, she brought in a large bowl of hot water. Diana was made to sit forward while they arranged a towel under her shoulders and then lift her hips while they spread one under her bottom.

They worked very well together, and once satisfied with the arrangements, the two women returned to their places, one on either side, and started on her armpits. Mrs Beauchamp carefully washed and then applied the shaving cream, and Elaine lightly set to with a neat purple razor. When each armpit was done, and rinsed, and patted dry and checked for smoothness with their lips – Mrs Beauchamp under her left arm and Elaine under her right – and even a little talcum powder had been sprinkled on as if she were a baby, Mrs Beauchamp went out to change the water and Diana was allowed to feel the result for herself.

'Better?' asked Elaine.

'Oh yes. It feels lovely.'

'Good. Now, let's see what we can do down here. Feet up on the seat I think.'

Diana obeyed, planting her feet on the seat and opening herself as wide as she could to this woman, feeling no awkwardness at all at being so exposed; indeed she felt almost as if they were friends. As Elaine started snipping with the scissors – without even waiting for Mrs Beauchamp to come back – Diana felt entirely at ease.

'Did you trim yours, Miss Gilbert?'

'Please call me Elaine. Yes, of course I did. In fact for several years I shaved it all off completely.'

'All of it? Why?'

'At that time, ten years ago or so, it was just becoming the daring thing to do and so I was rather in demand. And for some photographs, some poses, a girl does look so much nicer like that.'

'Do you still shave it all now?'

'Not quite all, although I do trim it quite severely, but now it's for my benefit and because some of my lovers prefer that.'

'Oh,' but it seemed strange to think of her like that, and while Diana tried to order those thoughts in her head, she found Elaine staring at her; staring and then leaning low to whisper warmly right into her ear.

'Would you like to see?'

'Could I?'

And Elaine nodded, with a mischievous smile. 'Just quickly.' And immediately she stood up, unzipped her trousers at the side and pushed them straight down her hips to reveal first a smooth pale tummy and then a narrow strip of neatly cropped pale brown hair, little more than an inch wide. Diana stared, and Elaine pushed the trousers a little lower so that the point where the vulva opened out came into view, and there the hair stopped entirely. Elaine's lips were now plainly visible, and as Elaine seemed to be pushing her thighs as far apart as the constricting trousers would allow, and also pushing her hips forward firmly, Diane could even see in to where the puffy inner lips were hanging down. She was just going to ask about that too when the outer door slammed and Elaine hurriedly pulled her trousers back up, rezipping them as Mrs Beauchamp's feet marched down the corridor, so that she was quite composed and squatting properly in her place with the scissors in hand when Mrs Beauchamp arrived with the bowl.

'Here we are now. Oh! Oh Elaine! You've started already!'

'Only just, Helen. Just getting the longest bits off while we waited for you to bring the water. Do you think you should just give it all a bit of a wash?' In no time at all, Mrs Beauchamp was wringing out the flannel and wiping it carefully and extremely thoroughly all across Diana's tummy, over her pubic hair, down her thighs and even as far as her bottom. In fact Diana was rather glad she was doing this because if there was now any trace of moisture in that area, she would be able to explain it away as having come from the washing. Mrs Beauchamp smiled, beamed even, as she worked. 'We want you nice and clean now, don't we?' She held out her hand for the can of shaving cream but Elaine was already clutching it firmly.

'I'll do this, Helen dear.'

'That's all right, Elaine; I don't mind.' And after a moment Elaine silently surrendered it into the waiting hand. A short squirt produced a neat spiral of white foam, which Mrs Beauchamp was about to transfer to Diana's stubble when she suddenly sat back on her heels, the foam quivering in her upturned palm. 'Do you know what, Elaine? I think it might be best if we gave Diana a bath! She could have a proper make-over, do her hair, everything. What do you think?'

'Oh yes! What fun! That would be wonderful. What do you say, Diana?'

'I don't know. It doesn't really seem necessary just for these few photographs.'

'Oh, but you want to look your best, dear, don't you? And it's always nice to have a few extra pictures to keep. Or for other occasions.'

'Other occasions?' What other occasions could there be when she might want to have photographs of herself with nothing on?

'Yes,' continued Elaine, 'you never know.' But her smile suggested that she did know and Diana would soon find out, so Diana really didn't want to admit her ignorance. 'Besides, you aren't expected to be anywhere else this afternoon, are you?'

'No, but...'

'Well, that's fine then.' Mrs Beauchamp promptly closed

the argument; the two worked so smoothly together. 'Let's go up to the bathroom, shall we? Come along.' And she quickly wiped the foam off on a towel and reached out her hand to help Diana stand up, although Diana was not sure there was not an element of staking a claim as well.

She was beginning to get more used to this, but there was still something bizarre about being led naked through a strange house by a woman who she did not really know all that well, and while there was another woman whom she scarcely knew at all following on behind. Even so, she padded on down the corridor and up the stairs. They turned left into the bathroom, and at last Diana was released so that Mrs Beauchamp could turn on the taps. It was a big room, probably originally a bedroom when the house was built but now with a fashionable cast iron bath in the Victorian style with basin, bidet and toilet to match. They all three crowded into the bathroom and stood watching as the water gushed into the tub, but this only made Diana conscious of all the teas which had been pressed on her earlier in the afternoon. The other two women were huddled together in discussion over which of the array of oils should be added to the bathwater, while Diana fidgeted, squirmed, and finally spoke.

'Would you excuse me?'

'Yes, dear?' Nobody could accuse Mrs Beauchamp of being inattentive. 'What is it?'

'If you would excuse me, I need the loo.'

'Oh, yes. Of course,' and Mrs Beauchamp promptly moved out of the way, even helpfully raised the seat cover, but she didn't leave the room and nor did Elaine. They waited and Diana waited, and eventually Diana had no choice but to ask them to leave.

'Please, I would rather have a little privacy for this.'

'Oh nonsense, dear,' scoffed Mrs Beauchamp. 'It's a perfectly normal function that any young woman must perform. Quickly now because your bath will soon be ready.'

And in the face of that Diana felt as if she was being unreasonable in continuing to object, so she sat down and eventually was able to blot out the two cheerfully watching faces enough to relieve herself.

Mrs Beauchamp's comment was entirely in keeping. 'All done? Good girl.'

But when Diane reached for the toilet roll, Elaine stepped forward. 'Shall I help you with that?' and without giving her a chance to reply, Elaine tore off some toilet paper, pushed Diana's legs open and started wiping her. She was very careful to do it thoroughly, to the extent that Diana did rather wish she would stop, only Mrs Beauchamp was standing stroking her hair and Elaine was smiling happily as she worked, and it seemed quite rude to suggest that really she had been wiped enough. Eventually it was Mrs Beauchamp who called a halt by pointing out that the bath was now full. And it certainly was: the biggest bath Diana could ever remember being in and so full that once she had been helped to step in, helped to sit down and helped to lie back, she was completely covered by wonderfully scented water into which, at the last minute, Mrs Beauchamp had sprinkled some rose petals.

Diana was allowed to lie and soak for a few minutes while the other two sat, Elaine on the bidet, Mrs Beauchamp on the closed toilet, and chatted inconsequentially of all the other girls who had gone to work at this same place in Utah and what fun they had all had there. But she was not allowed to lie for long; Mrs Beauchamp busied about again and gathered up a flannel.

'Right now. Let's get you clean.'

'Shall I do this, Helen?' and Elaine picked up the soap.

'No, dear. I can manage.'

'I just thought...'

'If you are going to shave her, perhaps I should do this bit. That's only fair.' She plucked the soap out of Elaine's fingers and started at once to work up a lather. She was thoroughly efficient when she started her work, briskly washing Diana's legs, back, arms and body. For hygiene reasons, as she explained, she made particularly sure that Diana's breasts were clean and properly rinsed, and that she could not feel any soap left behind which, if you weren't properly careful, could cause a rash. Of course it was even more important to make sure she was clean between her legs, both at the front and, almost more so, at the back. Naturally it was essential to rinse very thoroughly there as well.

Elaine watched the whole operation in thin-lipped silence, although she did help just once: when Mrs Beauchamp went out of the room to fetch some towels, Elaine also checked that no traces of soap had been left in any delicate places, although it did seem to Diana that when Mrs Beauchamp returned with the towels (and, curiously, some white cotton gloves), she was not at all pleased to find that Elaine was questioning the thoroughness of her work.

But she said nothing, and while Elaine returned silently to her post, Mrs Beauchamp equally silently helped Diana out of the bath and then dried her; everywhere; thoroughly. At last she draped the towel over the rail, but Mrs Beauchamp was not yet finished: she turned to the gloves, or – as it turned out to be – the one glove, and picked it up carefully. 'Now dear. The white glove test.'

'What?'

'The white glove test. To make sure you are perfectly clean, inside and out.'

Diana stared as Mrs Beauchamp worked the thin white cotton onto her hand. 'I don't understand.'

'Your bottom, dear. Just to make sure you are clean in your bottom.' She had now taken up a tube of some sort and was squeezing a thin worm of jelly onto her finger. 'Surely you have done this before?'

'No. Never.'

'Well I must say I am most surprised. All the girls would be checked like this when I was young. Never mind. The best way is if you just come and lie over my lap,' and she patted her thighs in case Diana was unsure what a lap was.

'I am sure I am clean.'

'Well we will soon know, won't we?'

'But I don't see why you need to check. You were actually extremely thorough in washing me just there.'

'That! That was not a particularly thorough wash at all, my dear. Indeed if that is what you would define as "thorough" then I fear we may find that you are not as clean as we would like.'

'But honestly...'

'Look, dear, I have already explained that the Agency is very concerned to ensure that the girls we send to them are clean in thought, word and deed. If you still want this appointment, well...' she let the words trail away and smoothed down her skirt.

Diana took a step forward and then gingerly lowered herself down onto the ample lap spread out for her and allowed Mrs Beauchamp, with her one free hand, to wriggle her about until she appeared satisfied that she was properly in place. 'Right now do relax.'

Diana felt the cheeks of her bottom being pulled open, at which she automatically tensed up. 'No, dear. You must relax.' And when she had managed that, but immediately felt the finger tip pressing right against the very centre of her bottom, she tensed up again, at which Mrs Beauchamp tutted and Elaine came and held Diana's hands, also encouraging her to relax, explaining that Helen had only a very slender finger which any girl's bottom would easily be able to accommodate, even one – and here she craned forward to check – even one as sweet and delicate as Diana's. Eventually, with that encouragement and even though, as Diana told them, she had never in all her life had anything pushed up into her bottom before, she was able to relax enough for the finger to push through and slowly, coldly and slimily, slide further and further in until Diana was sure that Mrs Beauchamp must have either switched to using something different or else that she had the longest fingers in the entire world.

But at last Diana felt the other knuckles touching her bottom cheeks and she knew that at last the finger was as deep as it would be going and, sure enough, it now started to slide back out, so slowly and reluctantly, until at last it came free and she could feel her bottom was her own again.

'Oh dear.' Mrs Beauchamp was obviously not happy.

'What's the matter?'

'Well I am afraid, Diana, that you are not as clean as you had been claiming. Just look!'

Still face down over Mrs Beauchamp's lap the manoeuvre was not easy, but Diana twisted round and saw the hand in its neat white glove and the single finger pointing straight up in the air with a long dirty stain extending all down one side.

'Oh dear,' she whispered and felt the shame rushing to her face. 'I'm sorry; I did think I was clean.'

'Not clean enough, that's for sure.'

'Shall I get back into the bath?'

'That will not do. Not for this. You had better stand up, dear.' And once Diana had got back to her feet, Mrs Beauchamp, looking as worried as she ever had, opened a cupboard beneath the basin and withdrew an apparatus of rubber tubes and china bottles that looked to be as Victorian as the house itself. 'We will have to clean you properly. Elaine, would you mind taking her into the bedroom for me while I prepare the solution? Put a towel under her.'

Diana allowed herself to be led out, and was gratified that when she apologised to Elaine as well, Elaine told her not to be too disappointed because it was not unusual for a girl to fail the white glove test. That was some reassurance as she found herself being brought into a large, over-decorated and gaudy bedroom, in which a large, over-decorated and gaudy bed took pride of place. In the centre of the pillow reclined a large rag doll, who Elaine reverently lifted out and placed comfortably in a chair so that the pink bedspread could be covered with towels and Diana could be arranged, face down and stretched flat, in the centre. On consideration, Elaine felt that her bottom needed to be raised up a little, so a pillow was folded over, Diana lifted up her hips to allow it to be slid under her, and then she settled back down again, feeling even more ashamed of the indignity of her position.

'Lovely,' said Elaine, tickling her fingers across Diana's bottom and even up and down the groove between her cheeks. 'What a perfect little bottom you have!' and before Diana knew what was happening, Elaine had actually planted a kiss right in the centre of each cheek.

A few minutes later Mrs Beauchamp appeared with the china bottle, proudly emblazoned *Dr Elphick's Wonderful Scientific Cleanser, Patented*, set that on the chest of drawers beside the bed and unwound a long red rubber tube on the end of which dangled a creamy white nozzle. A squeeze of jelly from the same tube was applied to this and Diana braced herself for the insertion of that into her bottom. Her cheeks were spread open again, a finger tip traced a short path around the area and after only a few tries, she was able to relax enough to allow the nozzle entry into a place which she had never previously regarded as an "entry" for anything. Even so, she was startled by the sensation when Mrs Beauchamp turned a small tap at the base of Dr Elphick's bottle and immediately felt a surge of warm liquid flowing into her bottom.

'There!' pronounced Mrs Beauchamp. 'That should do the trick!'

It took several minutes for the liquid to trickle in, and as it slowed Mrs Beauchamp lifted the bottle higher to increase the flow until at last it stopped, and when the bottle was shaken, a marble inside rattled noisily to show it was now empty. The nozzle was then removed gently, Diana was allowed to stand up and Mrs Beauchamp led her back to the bathroom and carefully sat her back down on the toilet.

'Good! Now, wait a couple of min...'

But Diana could not wait a couple of anything and almost immediately the full flow emptied out of her in less than a tenth of the time it had taken going in. Mrs Beauchamp sighed deeply.

'Sorry, Mrs Beauchamp. I couldn't help it.'

'No, dear. Well, back into the bath and rinse yourself off. Then we'll see how you are.'

She got back in again and sat down but Elaine came up to help, kneeling down beside the bath to rinse her, fluttering her fingers in the little groove between the cheeks of Diana's bottom and even, with a 'Relax!' whispered softly into Diana's ear, gently pressing her forefinger right inside before letting her out.

'Quickly now,' barked Mrs Beauchamp and under her stern scrutiny, Diana dried herself off but was dismayed, when she turned from re-hanging the towel, to see Mrs Beauchamp working another white glove onto her hand. Without a word she sat down and patted her lap. Diana lay down where instructed and the miserable operation was repeated. Diana waited nervously as the finger was being slowly withdrawn.

'Better,' concluded Mrs Beauchamp. 'Much better.' She sighed, although that seemed more wistful than contented. 'I suppose I should now let Elaine have you to complete the coiffure.'

She directed Diana back to the bedroom where Elaine was waiting, having fetched the comb, scissors, shaving cream and razors in the meantime. She smiled cheerfully and patted the bed. 'Up here, please!' and patted again.

Together they arranged Diana: knees up and feet spread wide – although she was allowed to prop herself up on her elbows so she could watch what was being done – and all being entirely satisfactory, the process started. First, in long slow sweeps, Elaine combed out the main bush of her pubic hair carefully and then trimmed it back to little more than half an inch long. Elaine then stepped aside and Mrs Beauchamp came forward, wrung out the flannel, washed the whole area again and applied the shaving cream, thick lanes down each side of her bushy triangle, down the insides of her thighs and – as far as she could tell – all over the part underneath that was hidden from Diana's sight. This was carefully rubbed in with Mrs Beauchamp's slow gentle fingers but always under Elaine's constant scrutiny, and all the time the two of them were discussing between them whether there was enough cream, whether it was in the right place and whether it had been sufficiently worked into the pale curls. When even Mrs Beauchamp had to admit that nothing more was needed, she stepped back, now took up the rag doll and sat down in that chair herself, cuddling the doll on her lap so that both she and the doll would be comfortable as they watched Elaine take up the razor and set to work.

It all took a long time, but then Elaine was being very careful, rinsing the razor frequently and pausing to apply more shaving cream from time to time. The two strips down each side of the front were done first, not taking off as much as Elaine had done for herself, but producing a much neater and more focussed expanse of hair than Diane had before which, at the top and each side, ended in a definite line beyond which she was smooth and hairless. When this was finished and Elaine moved to the area right between her legs, Diana could no longer see what was happening and lay back, closed her eyes and enjoyed the feeling of the fingers dancing over her skin. This seemed to take even longer as fingers spread the shaving cream carefully right across the hair; fingers stretched the skin tight while the razor lightly scraped down; fingers checked the result for any remaining bristles, running softly up and down her thighs, the delicate hollows between the tops of her thighs and her lips; and at times fingers skittered right along the lips themselves. Here in particular, the care was exquisite and faultless to the extent that Elaine pressed her own fingers into the slit between Diana's lips to ensure that the razor could not touch any of those soft tender places between them. She even kept her guard there when she was not actually shaving at all, but maintained a steady light pressure coupled with the suggestion of a slow circular movement which was not merely serenely relaxing, it was also thoroughly seductive.

Eventually there was no patch of skin left which had not been tended and Elaine put away the razor, took up the flannel and completed a final wash to rinse away any last traces of hair or shaving cream. 'There! Done!'

Immediately Mrs Beauchamp jumped up and came over to see. She plumped herself down on the bed and bent down to inspect closely, checking not only that it was all now pretty to behold but equally importantly, as she emphasised, that it was all smooth and soft to the touch. Her fingers stayed there, running up and down the length of Diana's vulva, stroking lightly and continuously the full extent of her lips so that Diana could actually feel herself blossoming under the touch: the swelling, the opening, the moistening: all so gracefully induced and so persuasive that Diana hoped it would never end. But it did, because Elaine interrupted them.

'Shall we do the rest of the photographs now? I think we might as well do them in here as Diana is looking so comfortable on the bed. Shall I fetch the camera?'

She came back with that while Mrs Beauchamp was still clearing away the shaving equipment and towels, and Diana had taken that opportunity to stand in front of the long oval mirror on the wardrobe door to see properly the result of Elaine's work. She now had a neat fluffy tuft, small enough to be easily covered by a single hand and appealing enough for any hand to be anxious to reach out and cover it. She was standing like that, her hand drawn to cover herself and her fingers curled through to where, she discovered, they naturally came right in contact with bare skin, and warm, damp, enticing skin too, when Elaine returned.

She grinned at Diana's reflection. 'Like it?'

'Yes. It's really pretty, almost as pretty as yours.'

'Why thank you!'

But standing there, a nagging puzzle came back into Diana's head from what Elaine had shown her. 'Elaine? Don't you wear knickers?'

'No. Never. Hate the things.'

'Why?'

But Mrs Beauchamp came bustling back in and instead of answering, Elaine asked Diana to hop up on the bed again while she herself collected the camera and put in a fresh film.

'We'll start with you sitting up,' Elaine hurried on, 'and turned to face me. Sit up straight. Shoulders back.' Diana sat and turned as directed.

'I wonder,' mused Mrs Beauchamp after a few had been taken that way, 'whether it might be better if Diana's nipples didn't look quite so sleepy.'

'Sleepy?' Diana glanced down to check but they appeared all right to her.

'Well,' continued Mrs Beauchamp, 'you know. Flat. Soft.'

Elaine peered over the top of the camera, squinted and tilted her head. 'Perhaps you're right, Helen. If they were a bit more pointed it would look more... professional.'

'Shall we do that for you dear?' but without waiting for a response, Mrs Beauchamp had reached over to run a hand across Diana's breasts, gently stroking them, even lightly pinching her nipples until the desired effect was received and the softness and the flatness had been replaced by darker, firmer little cones, greedy for more attention and so provocatively brazen that Mrs Beauchamp could not resist bending down to kiss the nearer one, and having kissed, to draw it into her mouth and run a dozen tiny laps of her tongue right round it.

'There!' as she straightened up again.

'Now the other one?' asked Elaine, and almost at once Mrs Beauchamp bent down again to take the other nipple between her lips and lick across its nut-hard tip, releasing it eventually as wet and shiny as the first. Several more photographs were taken, some of Diana's head and shoulders (although all these invariably included her breasts) and some much closer up of little more than her breasts; some, very close, showed only the nipple itself.

'Now would you settle back, please.' Elaine asked as she changed the film, 'lying flat out but still facing me.'

It proved to be as involved a process getting Diana satisfactorily arranged for these photographs as it had for the shaving. Initially she was lying on one side, legs crooked, then the other side, then on her tummy. And then kneeling, but facing away and then, 'still on your knees, dear, but lean right forward onto your elbows. Knees apart and keep your bottom up. Don't worry about our being able to see everything, even right up to the little bottom hole. We know it's beautifully clean now, so there's absolutely nothing to be ashamed of.'

A few clicks later, 'actually, I think you could push your bottom back even further towards me. It really is a quite lovely little thing with those sweet little puckers! Don't be shy!' A couple of clicks and, 'Just push a little more?'

After these were done, the two women decided they probably ought, for completeness, to have a few with Diana on her back; this last had her legs demurely together but then Mrs Beauchamp suggested it might be as well, just to be on the safe side, to be able to show there was nothing being hidden on the insides of her thighs. So Diana opened her legs a little, which apparently was not enough, and in the end she had to open them very wide indeed before Mrs Beauchamp was certain that nobody could possibly imagine she was hiding anything, and Elaine had been able to take some photographs quite close up, to make sure.

Having gone that far, Elaine wondered next whether a few photographs of Diana's lips might not be a good idea.

'My lips?' Even making allowances for everything else, photographs of her lips seemed a little bizarre.

'Yes,' but then she saw Diana's bewilderment. 'Not your mouth, you silly girl; these lips,' and Elaine pinched them lightly between her fingers. 'They might want to see that there are no piercings or anything.' She continued idly stroking them as she spoke, and as they were anyway quite full, she flopped them from side to side with her fingertips.

Mrs Beauchamp agreed. 'And this bit too,' and her hand joined in, stroking the warm soft sides of the hood over Diana's clitoris, even pushing it back so that they could see it poking out, pink and swollen and ready. 'She's so pretty!' And Mrs Beauchamp leaned down and kissed her, right on the tip of her little bud.

'And quite gooey!' added Elaine as she leaned down to kiss the puffy lips she had been stroking.

But they took some more photographs anyway, while Diana held her lips open to show off the shiny wet insides and pulled up her clitoris to show that. For a few silent minutes, she lay there stroking it happily, sighing in the contentment of it all while Elaine crept in closer to capture the moment.

This was almost the end, except that Mrs Beauchamp, wearing a smile that on a woman thirty-five years younger might have been called mischievous, came and sat beside her on the bed, leaned down close to her ear and whispered. 'Would you like a little rub now?'

'A rub?'

'Yes. Just a little rub.' And this time Mrs Beauchamp laid her hand on top of Diana's newly trimmed pubic tuft and curled her fingers down until they were just lightly stroking across the fullness of her lips. When Diana did not respond immediately, but just continued staring down her body to where the rub was being offered, Mrs Beauchamp smiled at her ever so sweetly while simultaneously her finger tip wormed right between Diana's lips and the long slender finger began to push inside. 'Wouldn't that be nice, dear?'

'Well I don't know if we should.' She stared round at the two beaming women. 'Is it all right to do that?'

Elaine came and sat down by her side. 'Of course it's all right, Diana. Many of the girls who come here have a little rub before they go. I think you deserve it after all you have had to put up with, don't you?' Her hand reached out and passed softly across Diana's breast. 'You should let us make it up to you.' Then she leaned down, kissed one breast, kissed the other breast and then turned and kissed Diana right on the mouth, a proper kiss, in which Elaine's tongue slipped through and touched hers, slid round inside her mouth, tugged at her lips and then darted away.

'And besides,' continued Mrs Beauchamp as she moved

up in turn to claim her kiss, not a tongue this time but her lips did reach out to nip at Diana's, holding them briefly in a little squeeze, 'besides, it seems to me that you feel very wet down here. And I think that means you would rather like it.' Another tiny kiss, tiny nip. 'Wouldn't you?' All this time her finger had been embedded deep up inside Diana, but as she has been talking she was easing it back out. She held it up: it glistened. 'See?'

Lying there, one woman on each side, a breast being casually stroked by one of them while the other flaunted undeniable proof of her arousal, Diana knew there was no point in argument. She said nothing, simply lay flat on the bed and closed her eyes, bringing her arms up to cover the shame on her face.

And with her body surrendered to them, she simply let her mind drift. The fingers returned between her legs, running up and down her lips, homing in on her clitoris, circling steadily and unstoppably. For a long time someone, presumably Elaine, was still stroking her breasts, but then she felt the movement of the mattress as she got up, followed by another series of clicks from the camera shutter. The feeling down there grew steadily to something so much stronger than she had managed during those furtive lonely nights at home, and a million times better than the brief brutal encounters with either of the boys whom she had so far allowed into her bed. Instead, every inch of her was tingling. Her breasts still carried the memory of Elaine's touch and her skin could still feel the passage of Mrs Beauchamp's hands as she was carefully washed and dried. All of her had been tended, patted and admired, shown off to the camera to be recorded and revered, and Diana had never been so fully loved. To top it all, there was now a hand working slow circles of magic round her clitoris, seeming to find every nerve that yearned to be touched and touching it until Diana felt ready to burst, and the more she moaned out her frustration, the deeper the pleasure sank into her and the more focussed became Mrs Beauchamp's attention, and when Elaine abandoned the camera and returned, lying down beside Diana, kissing her face and mouth, kissing her breasts and suckling them into her mouth, returning to her face again to kiss her some more, Diana could not resist any longer and let herself be swamped by the most powerful wave of pleasure that she could believe possible. On and on, in a series of shuddering spasms that left her finally wrung out, limp and almost lifeless.

'You're very sweet, Diana,' and Elaine kissed her yet again. 'I'll go and fetch your clothes.'

When she was gone, Mrs Beauchamp leaned down and kissed her. 'There, you see? I knew you would like it. Now, why don't you pop back again one afternoon, hmm? Elaine is a lovely girl but perhaps we could have just as nice a time with just the two of us. You think about it, and I'll see you downstairs.'

When Elaine returned, she gave Diana her clothes, all neatly folded. 'Would you like a hand with any of those?'

'No, I'll be fine.'

'Sure?'

'Yes. Really. Thanks all the same.'

'Right,' but still Elaine hesitated. 'You know where my shop is, don't you? Do come in one day and I'll do your hair for you; no charge and I'll do it myself. And if you need any of the other bits just tidied up, I'd be happy to do those too.' And she smiled, a touch nervously, Diana thought. 'Only it might be better not to mention to Mrs Beauchamp that you are coming.' And at last she went downstairs too and left Diana to dress in peace and privacy.

Back in the front office Diane found Mrs Beauchamp sorting out the papers and stuffing the forms into an envelope while Elaine packed up her camera.

'If you let me have your address, Diana, I can drop these round to you as soon as they are done.'

Mrs Beauchamp looked up sharply. 'No need for that, Elaine dear. Pop them in to me here and I will take them round to Diana.'

'It's no trouble.'

'No, but I will almost certainly have other things to take her anyway; stuff for signing or whatever.' She stared a moment then continued more firmly. 'Just bring them here.'

Diana was quite happy to leave them to sort out who would carry the photographs and let Mrs Beauchamp see her to the front door, pecking a light kiss onto her cheek as Diana stepped out, but suddenly Elaine appeared in the doorway, beaming cheerfully and tossing her camera bag up onto her shoulder.

'Just a minute, Diana. I might as well walk with you as far as the corner. Bye, Helen,' and she kissed the air several inches away from Mrs Beauchamp's tightly drawn smile before turning to link her arm through Diana's. 'Shall we go?'

Diana felt herself being hauled down the pavement at such a speed that Mrs Beauchamp soon had to shout to ensure she would be heard. 'I'll ring you tomorrow, Diana. We need to arrange a date when you can come back here for your medical.'

And although Elaine stopped abruptly, almost knocking Diana off her feet as she whirled round, Mrs Beauchamp's neat green front door was already tightly shut.

JANE'S FIRST TALE: TUESDAY

I t certainly wasn't late but it was Friday, and it had been a long, hot and frantic week. "Sultry" was the way that the man with the nice eyes had described it when he gave the weekend forecast at six thirty. Danny would be late, we'd eat late, so as soon as I came home I stripped off, took a long bath with some pretty smellies, changed into my Chinese pyjamas and flopped out in front of the television to wait for him. Hot weather always makes me feel like this.

So as I say, it wasn't late, only about seven o'clock, but when the door bell rang, I knew it would be Danny, that he'd got away earlier than expected and had forgotten his key – again. I skipped through the little hallway and yanked the door wide open. It wasn't Danny.

The evening was still warm and full daylight. Next door's children were cycling up and down the pavement, and straight opposite Emma and Mark (who bought the last house to be completed) were out in their front garden, laying out some elaborate stone vase feature. But there was a smart white car parked right in front of our house and a stranger standing in our front garden looking down the road towards the old houses. He turned when he heard me, smiled broadly and looked at me: up and down. Then up and down again, so that I wished that I'd put on a dressing gown.

'Mrs Rhodes?'

'Yes.'

'Jane Rhodes?'

'Yes.'

'My name is Douglas. It's about the money overdue on your account with Martine's Boutique.' He had an attractive, very mellow Scottish accent, like that politician who keeps appearing on televison and who, despite being a politician, seems almost trustworthy.

'Oh.' I think I just stared. He was probably about forty, in a neat dark suit, a very dark purple shirt and a tie of almost the same colour. His hair was short, thinning and a bit grey at the temples, but neatly brushed down. He held a black leather document case clamped under one arm, his hands in his pockets, cooler than he had any right to be and I didn't know what to say. I glanced round again and saw Emma watching us. She must have realised who he was, because I saw her nudge her husband and they were both now smirking across the narrow roadway.

'You understand?' the man brought me back to concentrate.

'But Danny, my husband, he's not home yet.'

'Does that matter?' And then before I had time to answer, 'I have spoken to him you know.'

'Oh.'

'Shall I come in?'

I said nothing but took a half step back, letting him push past me into the tiny hallway and on towards the living room. I glanced back once towards Emma: this was her fault. She had been the one who told me about all this, had even tried it herself.

I caught him up. 'I thought this wouldn't be until next week.'

'No. Your husband agreed with me that the sooner this was dealt with the better.'

'Oh.' I must have been sounding utterly brainless, standing

there just mouthing 'oh' at him every couple of minutes, but I had been anticipating a quiet evening of frozen pizza and television, then an early night. 'But I'm not ready for you.'

'We often find, Mrs Rhodes,' and he unzipped the document case, 'that our visits are often more successful if you are not.' He looked up at me. 'There is a temptation otherwise for you to be, what shall we call it, uncooperative? Obstructive?' He paused. 'Even absent is not unheard of.'

'I see. It's just that...'

'When will he be home?' The casualness with which he interrupted me was crushing.

'Anytime. I mean, I expect him any moment. I thought you would be him.'

'I'm not.'

'No.'

'Well, I don't think we'll wait for him. I'm sure you can pass on anything he needs to know.'

'Well, yes but I thought...'

He had pulled a couple of sheets of paper out of his briefcase, stapled together in the top left hand corner they displayed their authority in their neatness. He flicked the top page up and out of the way and peered down at the neat table of figures. 'Three months.' He flicked the page back and absently scanned down the front. 'Nearly four.'

'Sorry?' I tried to see what was written on the paper but he pulled it back.

'Three months since the last payment on your account.'

'Yes. Well, you see, it's been difficult because...'

'It has been difficult, Mrs Rhodes, because we have received no income from you. That is what has been difficult.'

'But you see...'

'There's nothing else I need to see. I see it all here. Balance now due, including interest charges, £1,455. Payments received, nil. And none last month or the month before that.'

He peered over the top of the leather case at me a moment and then sat down. For a few seconds he peered round the room. 'Well, Mrs Rhodes?' He casually crossed his legs. 'Please sit down.' He had no right to be offering me a seat in my own house but I obeyed, sat down opposite him. 'Well, Mrs Rhodes? Are you going to give me the money now? One thousand four hundred and fifty five pounds?'

I said nothing.

'And forty eight pence?'

'I don't have it.' My voice came out at little more than a whisper so that I felt betrayed by its weakness.

'So that's a "No" then.' He folded back the paper again, and made a slow careful note. 'Are you going to return the goods as new, in their original wrapping?'

'I can't! I mean I have worn them. You know, they were...'

'So that's another "No", is it?' he interrupted. 'Things aren't looking very good for you, are they?'

'No. I suppose not.'

'You have a big credit card bill as well, I suppose,' he prompted.

'Yes, yes I do.'

'I thought so.' He shook his head sadly; the ballpoint pen clicked and he made another note. The pen clicked again.

'What can I do?'

'Are you likely to have the money next week?'

'Well I might. I...'

'Realistically, Mrs Rhodes. Is that likely?'

'Well, I mean, I can... That is I could...'

'I think "No" is the word you are looking for.' He slipped the papers back into his case. 'What did you expect would happen? That we would simply say never mind? That I would walk away, forget the whole thing?'

'What can I do?' I repeated.

'Well...' he sucked his teeth. 'I like to be understanding, of course, because these things can happen to anyone, but it so easily gets out of hand.' He paused, I think just to frighten me. 'If you cannot repay the money, and if the failure just slides by, overlooked and unmarked, well...' He shrugged. 'It just tends to tempt further failings.'

'I see that, but I mean....'

'So we prefer any transgression to be marked. Yes, marked in some way.' He slid the papers carefully back into the briefcase and slowly pulled the zip all the way round.

'Marked?'

'There has to be some form of punishment, of restitution. And, in a sense, of compensation.' And he paused again, his eyes fixed on me, staring. 'I suppose if I were to be entertained, amused in some suitable manner, I might be able to leave this until, say, next week.'

'I don't know what you mean.'

'Oh come on!' He laughed. 'Of course you do. You're not that naive a woman.' He tossed the leather document case down on the table and leaned back. 'Stand up.'

I stood and waited.

'Sweet little slippers.' The comment might have been sarcastic, but I let that pass.

'My husband gave them to me. I've always liked frogs.'

'So I see. And the pyjamas?

'No, I bought them.' They were pretty ordinary, chequered

in various shades of blue, but nice and warm.

'At Martine's?'

'Yes.'

'You understand that I will have to take back everything you have ordered from us?'

'Yes.'

'Including those pyjamas.

'These? But I'm wearing these.'

'Yes, I can see that. You'd have to take them off.' I simply stared at him, but it was while we were both considering the implications of his remark that I finally heard a key in the front door.

'That'll be my husband.'

The man simply raised his eyebrows. 'In the nick of time.'

I hurried to meet him in the hall so that I could explain what was happening. 'The man is here...'

'About the Martines account,' the voice called from the living room. 'Which is overdue.' Danny pushed through, I followed and the man had not stirred from his position, although his face wrinkled into a self-satisfied smile as we came back in. 'We have however, made a little progress on the background. First, we have established that your wife does not have the money to pay what is due.'

'No, well...' started Danny, but the man just carried on.

'Second, that there is no realistic prospect of her having it within the foreseeable future.'

'You see...' Danny tried again, with the same result.

'And third, that she will have to return our property if she is unable to pay for it.' Silence. 'And you are not able to pay on her behalf.'

This time Danny did not even try.

'So, we were just seeing whether there was any alternative recompense that she could offer.'

'I see,' but Danny didn't see and he looked from the man to me and back again. 'What kind of recompense?'

'Well,' the man let out a long bored sigh, 'as a starter, she was just going to take off her pyjamas.'

'I wasn't!' I protested. 'I hadn't agreed to do that!' I turned to Danny. 'I hadn't said that. I hadn't said anything.'

Danny looked bewildered. He dropped his shoulder bag onto the floor and ran his fingers through his wild hair. 'Jane?'

But he was ignored, just like before, just like I had been. 'So, Mrs Rhodes. Shall we continue? Please would you come back here?'

I shuffled back to the place in the middle of the floor but that didn't mean I was going to undress for him.

'Good. Thank you. Now please take off your pyjamas.'

'Why?'

He laughed, almost scoffed. 'Why, Mrs Rhodes? Why? First, because since you have not paid for them they are not your property: they are in fact the property of Martine's Fashions Limited and must be returned to their rightful owner. Second, because...'

'Yes, but...'

'Second, Mrs Rhodes, because I want to see you without them on. That is why. I should have thought that was fairly obvious.'

'But then what?'

He laughed again, a sound which was I was starting to find intimidating. 'Then what? Then what, you ask me? Please, Mrs Rhodes! One step at a time. Let's not be greedy.'

'But I don't know what's going to happen!'

'You do know what's going to happen first. You are going to take off your pyjamas so that I can see what you have to offer.' And then for the first time his voice dropped down to something more like friendship. 'Will you do that?'

'I could, I suppose. I mean, if that was all.'

The man smiled, a slight tilt of the head in acknowledgement of my agreement and dismissal of my question, and then he turned to Danny. 'Are you going to stay here to watch this, Mr Rhodes, or would you prefer to withdraw?'

Danny stared from me to him and back, one to the other but no help was coming from either of us. I didn't know, and I don't think the man cared. 'I don't know.'

The man opened wide his palms. 'It's all the same to me only – as they like to say on the television – if you don't want to know the outcome, you had better look away now.'

I suppressed my giggle, just, but Danny had noticed it. 'Jane?'

I turned away.

'Jane? What shall I do?' I tried to be helpful, but not knowing what was going to happen, how could I tell? I tried to smile but couldn't immediately think of any words to say anything. Danny slumped down onto the end of the sofa, his head down in his hands, but he was staying in the room.

'Right then, Mrs Rhodes. Please continue. Let's have the top off, shall we?'

I don't know why but I'd expected something more subtle than that, that he would not be so direct, but he simply waited. For a second I looked over to Danny for some support or guidance or even an instruction, but he was no more help to me than I had been to him. He didn't even look up.

'Now?' I asked, but the man didn't even bother to answer so I lifted the top up a little way, pulled my arms down inside the sleeves and then took a deep breath and pulled the whole thing over my head, tossing it down onto my chair. My breasts quivered.

'Not bad,' said the man. 'Not bad at all. Quite a big girl, aren't you? Come closer where I can check you over.'

He was being deliberately insulting, because they aren't 'not bad', my breasts; they are very good. I have received loads of complements about them, and not just from men but from friends and people at work. I took a single step forward, but he just pointed down to a piece of carpet almost between his feet until I was standing only a foot in front of him. My breasts were now level with his eyes and as he scrutinised me, as close as any man would ever want to be, I felt – saw – my nipples hardening and knew he could see it too. And he knew why. After an age his hand reached out to touch me, quite slowly and I heard a little gasp from Danny as he saw what was coming next. Then the hand touched: long fingers wrapping round my ribs and running up to my breast, winding their way round them, running up over the top and curling down underneath, skimming over my nipples and pausing to enfold them and pull them, gently at first but steadily harder until I cried out to him to stop.

The man laughed and released me, but not without a pat, a hard stinging pat, on the side of my breast. Then his fingertip traced down my stomach, tickled into my tummy button for a second and hooked into the waistband of the trousers but there it stopped. 'Now these.'

I glanced over at Danny. 'Please...?'

'And if you have anything on under them,' he continued,

ignoring me completely, 'we'll have that off as well.'

I didn't move. I couldn't.

'Do you have anything on under them?'

'No.'

'Really? Nothing at all?' There was an accusation that wasn't justified, but he pulled the waist out a little way, out and down, just enough so that he could peep in. Then he pulled a little further and glanced down. 'No. You don't, do you? But you're a nice wooly little thing, aren't you? I like that.'

Over to the side, Danny's head shot up. For a moment he stared, was about to speak, sat with his mouth working silently and then it was all just too much. He scrambled up out of his seat and strode out.

The kitchen door swung shut and the man released my pyjama elastic at the same moment. 'Right,' said the man, 'now that we are alone, I think we should have these off, shouldn't we?' and he plucked at the elastic again.

'Look,' I started, suddenly anxious how Danny was going to be reacting to all this, 'I'm not sure about this.'

The man leaned back, considered a moment and frowned at me. 'Isn't it a bit late to be worrying about that, Mrs Rhodes? I mean you have a certain problem here. And you do not seem to have much of a solution.'

'Yes, I know, but what about Danny? He's...' I couldn't think of how to describe what must surely be so utterly obvious. 'He's upset.'

'Upset?'

'Yes!'

A frown flashed across the man's face and as quickly cleared. 'Well yes. I imagine he is. I mean he has suddenly found you are quite seriously in debt. Most men would be very upset in that situation. But surely that's something you should have considered earlier, don't you think?' He plucked at the elastic again. 'Hm?'

In the silence while I searched for a defence he plucked at my pyjamas again. 'Come along. Let's have these off.'

He could have pulled them off himself, he was close enough to have done so, but maybe he liked watching me do it, or wanted to humiliate me more by making me do so.

'Look,' I was clinging to the waistband now, my fists clenched tight and clutching the flimsy security. 'Look...'

He reached up to my breast again, running his palm across me in rough sweeping strokes that squashed my nipples flat and then let them fly up again. 'Don't play games, Mrs Rhodes. I am going to have the rest of your clothes off and it is not going to be any better for you if you waste time.' He sat back again for a second, quietly considering me. Then simply: 'Off!'

So I obeyed him, afraid of what would happen if I didn't, kicking off my slippers, pushing the pyjamas down and away and then dropping them on my chair with the top.

'Come closer again. Don't keep scurrying away.'

I stepped back to the appointed place and stood with my hands clasped in front of me, the very smallest protection, but even this annoyed him.

He slapped at my wrists, pushing my hands out of the way. 'Don't be silly, Mrs Rhodes. Before we are through, there is not going to be an inch of you that I won't know intimately, so there is absolutely no point in this pathetic attempt at modesty.'

So I let him have his way, and waited while he ran his hands up my sides, over my breasts again, lifting them, cradling and weighing them. Yes, I am a "big girl" as he has said and he was clearly someone who appreciated that in a woman. But he did now have all of me on display so he then moved on down and through my bush, his open palm running back and forth, the fingers curling in underneath.

'Nice and wooly,' he mused. 'Can't stand a woman who chops and butchers the whole thing as if she were ashamed of it.' He made me turn round and his hands roamed across my bottom, up and down the groove and pushed through between my legs, pressing against my lips, then turned me back again, but made me part my legs this time so that he could explore better between them, pressing open the lips to peer at my inside ones, running the backs of his fingers back and forth along the valley.

Satisfied with this at last, he had me turn around again, my back to him, and stand with my hands on my head and my feet apart, as if I was just a naughty schoolgirl. I couldn't hear him moving, or even breathing for some seconds but when his voice came out again he was perfectly calm and steady, and then a light pressure, it must have been a fingertip, started wandering slowly across my bottom.

'Have you been beaten, recently, Mrs Rhodes?'

'Beaten?'

'Whipped? Caned?' The finger was tickling along the crease at the top of my thighs.

'No!'

'I rather thought not. It does seem to me that it takes a more direct discipline to teach young people how to handle money these days.' The finger stopped and pressed harder before being lifted away. 'Well, it's time. I'll beat you now, I think.' The fingertip was back swinging back and forth tracing sweeping paths across both cheeks of my bottom. 'Would your husband like to witness that, do you think?'

'I don't know.'

'Then you had better ask him.'

Danny was sitting at the kitchen counter, his hands clasped in front of him, but he turned when I came in, flinching when he saw I was now completely naked.

'Did you hear that?' I asked.

'Partly. What's going on?'

'He's...' I couldn't look as the full picture was laid out in front of him. 'He is going to beat me now and he wants to know whether you want to watch.'

'Christ!' He stared up at me, his eyes running all over my nakedness but flickering as if he was fighting tears, and then he buried his face in his hands and turned his head back down to the floor. 'Christ,' he muttered again.

I began to feel sorry for him, because he was not to blame for any of this; the responsibility for everything was entirely mine. I wanted to reach out to him, hold and be held by him, but the fate waiting for me in a room just a few feet away stood between us: unforgettable and unpassable.

'Well?' I asked.

'What?'

'Do you want to?' He peered up at me, forehead wrinkled, eyes anxious and worried. 'Do you want to watch?'

He immediately shut his eyes, screwed them tight, and made a sound that could have been disgust or even an attempt at a laugh. Some seconds passed while he considered the question. 'Do you want me to?'

'I don't know.'

We both waited in silence for the other's answer and Danny

broke it first. 'Yes. I suppose I do.'

I led the way back to where the man was still sitting exactly as I had left him. He smiled to see Danny trailing behind, glancing meekly round and then taking back his position on the end of the sofa.

'Excellent. Now, Danny, I wonder if you'd be so kind,' here he paused, dug into his trouser pocket and produced a little bunch of keys which he held in the air, 'to fetch the tawse from my car. It's on the back seat.'

'Tawse?'

'Yes.' I had heard about these, common in Scottish schools, but I had hoped for more explanation.

Left alone with the man, our earlier conversation seemed so mundane, and yet it had provided some kind of link, almost a bridge, between me standing naked and shivering and him, sprawled relaxed and comfortable in my living room. Yet he barely noticed my nakedness, simply waited calmly for this strap to be fetched for him.

'Nice little estate this. Lived here long?'

He had his back to the window, but from where I stood I could see it all happening out in front of our house: Danny unlocked the car, reached through into the back and emerged with a long tube – it looked like cardboard – and he peered down inside before he re-locked the car, glancing up and down the empty street before turning back towards where the man and I were waiting. It was all being performed in silence, out there beyond the new double glazing, in the place where I met our neighbours and we talked about our families, our jobs and shopping. And I waited inside, in the private area, but never as private as this. I avoided looking at him, this man who had suddenly turned up out of the blue, marched into my home and stripped me naked, whose eyes I could feel rasping all across me, peering and probing in anticipation of the closer inspection he had already threatened.

Danny shut the door carefully and offered up the long tube. 'Is this it?'

The man pushed forward. 'I would think so, wouldn't you?' And he slowly drew the thing out. I'd never seen a tawse before, not a real one, and although it looked quite harmless, the need to enclose it, hide and encage it, showed it was not so innocent as it seemed.

It was longer than I had thought, almost two feet long: thick leather in a serious deep tan colour and split into two long tongues. He curled back the tips, pointed and pierced, like..., like nothing I had ever known. Maybe he saw my eyes studying it.

'It's called a "Devil's Tail" tawse, for obvious reasons,' and he released the tips so they sprang back up and quivered in the air like the forked tongue of a huge snake.

'Now,' and he slapped the end against his open palm. It was only a light slap but the noise was horrible. 'Now, six is the traditional number for an offence.' He swept it back and forth a couple more times. 'There are four months unpaid so that makes twenty four strokes.'

Slowly he got to his feet and glanced round. 'I think the sofa. That would be best for this. Bending over to start with, I think. Place your palms flat on the seat please, arms and back nice and straight, hands and feet well apart.'

I followed the instructions and Danny shuffled up a little further to give me room: it's only a two-seater settee. As I bent over and spread my fingers out on the settee I was almost touching his leg but I did not dare meet his eye.

'Excellent.' The man's unbreakable easy cheerfulness made things no easier at all, but I don't suppose he thought it would. He came across and rested his hand on my back. 'Excellent. This way, you see, the subject is nice and steady. We can get access where we need to,' and he reached through underneath me to take hold of my hanging breast, the one nearest to Danny, and squeezed it hard, 'and anywhere else where we'd like to,' and now his other hand slid down my back, across my bottom and right in between my legs to pinch my lips. 'And of course, a clear shot at the target,' and with that he brought his hand down really hard on my bottom. I leapt up, or tried to, but he must have been expecting it, because he immediately pushed me back down again.

Danny started up too: the crack of the spank right next to him must have startled him as much as it did me, but he quickly turned back again: staring at the floor and unable to watch but unable to leave. Then the man picked up the tawse, stood back, and tapped the tips on my bottom a few times.

'Twenty four.' Tap, tap, tap and then the first stroke landed. It was bearable. I didn't scream; I didn't even cry out; it was all right. All my worries about whether I could take this were swept away and I almost smiled. But then came the second one, and almost immediately the third, and that was when I realized that it is the repetition that makes the pain grow. Twenty four strokes is not like suffering that first stroke twenty four times: it is having that first stroke doubled twenty four times. I think we were up to four, but the whole thing felt like one, but one that was four times worse than that first easy deceit. Five times worse. Six times worse. He paused.

'That's the first month taken care of.'

'Please? Please can I...?'

But he had already started again and I gave in and cried. Danny reached over and covered my hand with his as seven, eight and nine came down. I couldn't concentrate, could only feel the increasing throbbing building up in my bottom, one great band of agony across both cheeks. The tears were rolling down my face and dripping off my nose, and I could feel my whole body trembling, shaking with every stroke but trembling between them. I realized he had stopped.

'That's twelve. Short break before the rest?' His hand was running over me still, underneath to scoop up my breasts again, deliberately squeezing hard enough to hurt, to make me cry out again, and flicking at the nipples with his fingernail. 'Why are these so hard?'

I was still sobbing and did not answer. 'Hmm?' and he flicked at me again.

'It's the pain,' I explained, pulling away.

'Oh yes? A likely story.' But at least he released me.

For a few moments I could not stand up, but when I turned to get a tissue to blow my nose, I heard Danny's gasp. I suppose from where he had been sitting he would not have been able to see the tawse landing on my bottom. Now he could see the results and his shock did nothing to make me feel any better.

When I came back from the kitchen, the man was back in his chair, the tawse lying casually on the carpet beside him. 'What about a cup of tea, Mrs Rhodes?' The nerve of the man was staggering. 'You might like one yourself.'

I didn't feel strong enough to argue, and was glad of anything which would put off the second twelve: if there was no tea on offer, he might just bend me over again. Back in the kitchen I shuffled round filling the kettle and tried to peer over my shoulder to see what Danny had seen, but I could not see clearly. Touching it carefully with my fingertips did not produce any blood – surprisingly – but I could feel deep ridges all across the surface, horribly tender and hot to the touch. Low voices came through from the living room and though I could guess well enough what they were talking about, I could not hear any of the words. The conversation stopped the moment I went through with the tray and Danny avoided my eyes when I handed him his mug.

'Oh, Mrs Rhodes, before you sit down, if of course you want to sit down, would you come over here. Turn round and let me have a look at how we are doing so far.'

I turned to present my bottom to him and felt his fingers crawling across me, tracing much the same path as my own had done earlier, along the rows of agonised weals which stretched right across the whole of my bottom.

'Lovely!' and he actually slapped me. 'You're doing very well. The tawse is a very effective instrument; better in many ways than the cane since there is much less risk of breaking the skin. Now drink up and then we can get on.'

I stood to drink my tea, facing them both because there seemed no point in pretending shyness after all they had seen, and I was more embarrassed about the state of my bottom than about letting them see my front.

We drank in silence but I could not make the tea last forever and as I put down my mug the man smiled with oozing cheerfulness. 'Ready to carry on?'

I was about to go back into the same position when he stopped me. 'We'll have you differently this time. If you would stand up, Mr Rhodes, I would like your wife lying on her back on the sofa, head up this end.'

He arranged me how he wanted, even having me lift up my bottom so that he could slide a cushion in underneath me. I was stretched out on my back and I could not see what he had in mind. He was surely not intending to beat me on my stomach, or my thighs, or even, for heaven's sake, on my breasts. I could not have stood for any of that. He perched on the arm next to my head and without a shred of embarrassment his hand came out to grope my breasts.

'Very lovely breasts you have, Mrs Rhodes. What a very lucky girl. Nice and big without being too baggy yet nice and responsive.' He continued kneading them as he spoke. 'Now I hope you are learning your lesson from this.' They were quite rough, his palms, as they scoured across me, from one breast to the other and back again. 'This punishment, once it is finished, has enabled me to put off the repossession of the items for a week. I will be back next Friday and will not be willing to be so lenient then. Is that understood?'

I nodded and muttered the appropriate response.

'Good. Now then. Let's get you into position. Bring your legs up and over and perhaps Mr Rhodes you would be good enough to help by holding her feet there. Oh no! Nice and wide apart.'

And there I lay, on my back, with my knees pulled up nearly to my ears so that I could hardly have been more exposed if I had tried. Danny was holding my feet and, as he had been instructed, was holding them well apart so that I could feel the cold air blowing across my skin, over the hot bruises of the tawse and even the delicate skin right between my legs.

'That's much better. Now. Let's have a proper look at you.' "Look" of course meant feel. His fingers ran down my thighs and pushed between my lips, pulling them apart, pulling even at the inside ones, and when Danny pushed my feet even further apart, peeling the lips open and the man peered down at me. Then his fat stubby finger ran along the valley and pushed in, further in, and finally right inside. It stayed there, twisting slowly, turning and flexing, rhythmically pushing gently deeper and then back again.

'You are very wet, Mrs Rhodes.' His thumb was pressing at my clitoris as he continued to pull me open and expose the full seeping shame of my reaction. Danny towered straight above me and was also watching closely as the man fingered me, almost masturbating me. I shut my eyes. A few moments later the fingers withdrew but then moved further back and pulled at my cheeks, tugging and stretching as if he was trying to prize open even my bottom. Again his finger, cold and wet with my own juice pressed at the highly delicate place but could not get through and finally gave up. He stood up and went to fetch the tawse.

'Right. Last twelve. These ones will be rather harder, I'm afraid.' He pressed my legs further down onto my chest, then again: tap, tap, tan and then fire. I screamed, I heard myself do it but I could not believe the pain of that single first stroke. It felt as if there had been no interval, that this was building up right on top of all the earlier strokes so that my whole bottom had been burnt open in a single stripe. There must be blood now. The next stroke was worse: on new skin, almost the backs of my thighs, but they were stretched so tight that there was nothing to absorb the shock of the tawse. The next one similar, then back on my bottom again. At every stroke I cried, twisting to get away from him yet held tight by Danny's hands on my ankles. He did not pause, or slow down and I had completely lost count when he suddenly said 'Last one. Let's make it count, shall we?' and the final shock ripped across my bottom.

When Danny released my legs, I curled round into a ball and tried to shut everything out but that was not to be allowed. I was finished, but the man, Douglas, was sliding his tawse back into its tube and sitting down again. 'Is there any more tea?' and he calmly held out his cup. I didn't move but thankfully Danny leapt up and took the cup out to the kitchen. We were alone together again, me and the man, and staring at each other across the little room, silent. He slowly got to his feet and stepped across to me, ran his hand down my side and rolled me over onto my back. Then he stopped, but I knew what he wanted and I let my legs fall open.

He reached out, touched me, brushed his hands across my tight nipples and then moved down, but the journey was teasingly slow. Even when he reached my pubic hair he dawdled; running his fingers through the curls: twisting them; tugging them; teasing, teasing, teasing. The longer he lingered, the wider I opened my legs, not as an invitation, I didn't want him, but I did it anyway. When finally he moved on, and smeared the lips apart, he casually pushed his fingers up inside me, slowly stirring them about. Danny came back in, stopped dead when he saw what the man was doing and then tried to ignore it.

'Here is your tea.'

The man appeared not to have heard. 'She is very wet,' he said and continued slowly pushing his fingers up and back.

'I'll leave it here by your chair.'

Still neither of us spoke, but finally he released me and held up his hand 'Do you see that, Mr Rhodes? Dripping wet.'

'Yes,' Danny muttered, standing side by side, the two of

them staring down at me as I lay sprawled on the sofa, legs apart, sex pulled open, my whole body as completely on display as it could be.

'Aroused,' he offered, rolling his tongue around the word which with his slight accent gave the word extra decadence. 'Excited or, as the current slang would have it, "hot for it".'

'Yes,' murmured Danny, 'yes I know.'

'So what will you do?' pressed the man. 'A devoted husband would not dream of leaving his wife like that.'

'No,' Danny said hastily. 'No, I'll, ... I'll look after her.'

'Good,' the man said, returning to his seat, picking up the teacup and stretching out his long legs. 'And you?'

'Me?'

'Yes, you. Are you aroused?' And when Danny didn't, or couldn't, answer he went on. 'Come over here.' I twisted round to see better as Danny slowly shuffled across to stand right in front of where the man was sitting. He set down his cup and saucer and simply reached out to lay his hand directly on Danny's crotch. 'Aha! You are erect.' But Danny had flinched back. 'Take out your penis, man. Let us see if your level of arousal is equal to your wife's.'

After a pause, Danny did as he had been told, unzipping his trousers and pulling out his glorious cock to reveal that it was indeed erect.

'Fine,' said the man condescendingly. 'A little thin, but a goodly length. You had better carry on.'

'Carry on?'

'Yes, Danny; carry on.' But neither of us moved. 'To continue in the slang we were using earlier, to "give her one".'

'Yes, we probably will after you have gone.'

'I'll not be leaving just yet. I think I should make sure that side of things is properly taken care of.'

'I see.' Danny was groping for some sort of base, something solid, but the fact was that I did want him. I wanted him desperately to finish off what that man's beating and groping and dominance had started.

'Come on, Danny. Let's go upstairs.'

'Oh no,' the man said. 'Here is fine. I can see perfectly well from here.'

'Here?' Danny and I both spoke together.

'Come on!' the man practically laughed at us. 'Are you telling me that sofa has never seen a bit of hanky panky?'

'Well...'

'So go on with you.' He stretched his legs out again. 'Just get undressed, lad, and see if you can't make her feel a little better.'

'Here?'

'That's what I said and it won't change if you make me say it another twenty times.'

Nervously, Danny began to undress, folding his clothes with a care I had never seen him show before and laying them neatly on the carpet. All the while, his cock was sticking out of the front of his underpants, quite ridiculously waving about as he moved. Finally he took off his underpants and came over to where I was still lying waiting.

He sat down on the end of the sofa at my feet and started to position himself between my legs, but he had no sooner started than the man stopped him,

'For goodness sake, you're not going to start straight in, are you?' His accent seemed to strengthen with his vehemence.

'Well,' said Danny, 'yes. That was what you said.'

'I told you to see if you couldn't make her feel a little better. A quick "wham, bang, thank you, Ma'am" will not do that.'

'Well, what...?'

'A little foreplay, man! Kiss her, stroke her, fondle her. Lick her cunt for her. Just because you're ready for the home straight doesn't mean she is.'

And that was how it continued. Soon the man brought his chair over and although he did not touch me much, he directed Danny in every move he made and showed him how to do things differently. The way he stroked me, the way he suckled me, best of all, the way he played with my clitoris. For some minutes, they alternated stroking me there until I was so wet and so ready that I had to stop and ask if Danny couldn't please now sink his cock into me.

'There! You see? Now she is ready for you!' and he leaned back, with a warm hearted slap on Danny's shoulder. 'Now go for it, lad, and don't spare the horses!'

And Danny obeyed. With a glorious ferocity which, even though it was brief, was all I needed after so much preparation and so long a build up. Within moments I heard myself moaning for him, begging and when I finally climaxed, only seconds before Danny did too, I startled myself (and probably the Robinsons next door) with my wails.

<hr>

Later I was vaguely aware of movement, of low murmured conversation, doors opening and shutting and then Danny was back, alone.

'He's gone.'

I had nothing to say but slowly unwound myself and got

to my feet. Danny at last put his arms round me and his hands dropped down to my waist, drawing me in against his chest and his groin. Already he was half erect again and in fact we both still had ground to cover. I was just starting to lead him upstairs when suddenly the back door burst open and Emma appeared, her round face bursting with excitement.

'Well?' She completely ignored the fact that both Danny and I were cuddled up together entirely naked: the words were bubbling up too fast to be contained. 'What did you have? What did you think?'

I grinned over Danny's shoulder at her. 'You were right. Utterly amazing. I might have him again!'

Jane's Second Tale: Thursday

I struggled for four days and five nights not to ring him. I didn't even know what his name was, not properly. He had called himself "Douglas" when he first arrived, but whether that was his first name or last – or even if he was one of those people who have the same name for both – I didn't know. That was just one of many things I didn't know about him. The weekend came, dragged, and passed with me still stretched like piano wire. Time after time, I picked up the receiver but always managed to put it down with the number not rung, or only partly rung. I left the receiver on the hook while I dialled the whole number and rehearsed the conversation that I would have with him if ever I dared. A fifth day passed, and a sixth night and I collapsed. When I woke up that Monday morning I knew that I could not survive the day; I knew I would have to phone him so I set myself a time and then I did it. He answered almost straight away, as if he had known.

'Douglas.' That slight lilt pierced me.

'Hello. It's me.' But he hadn't known; the silence said that my voice meant nothing to him, where his meant so much to me. 'Jane.' Still silence. 'Jane Rhodes.' Nothing. 'You came to see me. And my husband. Last week. At our house. We, we...' I trailed away. If he didn't know now, how could I tell him? How could I put into words what we had done?

'Oh yes.' His tone left no space for denial; he knew me now. 'What can I do for you?'

'Well I... I wondered... I mean, is that it?'

'Yes. Of course.'

'But I want more.'

He chuckled. 'So you liked it.' It was a statement, but I answered it as a question.

'Yes. Yes it was...' It was what? How could I possibly describe an experience which had so completely reshaped my opinion of myself? 'Very good,' I offered eventually; how pathetic. Thirty seconds had passed and already he had me feeling inadequate.

'People normally do enjoy themselves.'

'Yes, I imagine so.' We could have been discussing a concert, except that I hope I would have sounded less like a brain-dead moron if that had been the case.

'What did you like? Exactly?'

'Everything.'

'Exactly, I said.' That edge was back, that glorious edge which I could not resist.

'Well. The way you were. The way you made us be. All of it, really.'

'Good. So you are ringing to thank me?'

'No. Well, yes, but also I want to do some more.'

He sounded a bit more interested now. 'Like what?'

'Anything!'

'Anything?' He repeated my reply with a chuckle. 'You couldn't handle,' he paused, 'anything.'

'I could.'

'I doubt it.' He wasn't arguing, just stating facts as he saw them. 'Besides, that was just playing a game: playing parts. You can't play games like that twice; it simply doesn't work.'

'I know.'

'Do you?'

'Yes.'

'Perhaps. Anything more has to be genuine, the real thing.'

'Yes, that's what I want.'

'I'm not convinced you could handle it. You'd question me about everything. You'd argue and protest.'

'I wouldn't!' My protest sounded childish, boastful and he simply snorted and put down the phone, but the next afternoon the phone rang and somehow, as I walked up to it, I knew it was going to be him calling, so that instead of saying my number I just said 'Hello?'

And he must have known too, because he didn't ask who I was, just breathed once, heavily, thoughtful. 'I can use you on Thursday, if you are sure you are ready for this.'

'Yes! Yes, I am!'

'For anything?'

'Oh yes.'

'No games?'

'No.'

'All right. Thursday, 12.00. 42, Warwick Street. Flat 5. Got that?'

'I don't know if Danny will be able to make that.'

'Did I say anything about Danny?'

All the scenarios and consequences tumbled over in my head like a boxful of photographs upended onto the floor. This was going to be something outside my marriage, something furtive and deceitful; shameful and exciting. Had he said anything about Danny? 'No.'

'I'm not asking Danny. I'm only asking you.'

On Thursday I saw Danny off to work and said nothing. The minute he was gone, I began getting myself ready and at 12.00 I was outside the building in Warwick Street.

When he opened the door, I wanted to kiss him; better still, I hoped he would kiss me. It wasn't as if I loved him or anything, but even so: I wanted something. Perhaps an acknowledgement that I was now an element in his life as much as he had bored his way into mine. He didn't kiss me, didn't shake my hand or touch me, simply showed me through to the living room and there was someone else already there. A girl, younger than me, not even twenty, was sitting comfortably in the centre of a long leather sofa. She might have been Asian, with a pretty heart-shaped face framed by a sheet of pure black hair reaching half way down her back.

'This is Milly,' he said and her mouth smiled but her eyes did not; she said nothing.

I said "hello", wondering what she was there for and deciding it had to be the same as me but, in that case, which of us he would take first and whether I would have to do it with her watching me. Most likely, I realized, was that he would want to watch the two of us in bed together, and a part of me was disappointed at the banality of it: although that would be new for me, excitingly new, it was so predictable too, disappointingly unimaginative when I had harboured a higher opinion of Douglas. But that was only part of me: another part felt entirely differently: less than five minutes in his flat and already I was out of my depth. What a childish boast: "I can handle anything." Yes, I had kissed girls before (two), but little more than a kiss and an adolescent fumbling. I was already ashamed.

On a neat round tray on the coffee table stood one glass and two bottles: an almost full white wine with silver condensation on its sleek neck, and a big still mineral water. The girl, Milly, was holding a similar glass, turning its slender stem in her long fingers.

'Sit down,' said Douglas; he disappeared briefly and returned with another bottle of mineral water which he set down on the table in front of me. 'Help yourself,' he said. 'Don't call me until you've finished them; you've got half an hour.' Then he walked out again.

I picked up the wine and was about to pour myself some, but turned to Milly. 'Would you like...?'

'No talking!' he called out over his shoulder, not a shout, just a firm direction to us both. I caught Milly's eye; she raised her eyebrows briefly and then held out her glass so I started pouring but when I had filled it to half way, a reasonable amount, she took the water bottle, topped up her glass to the top and then did the same to mine. I hadn't asked for water, but she hadn't asked me to decide. She seemed to know better what was happening, so I went along with her.

There was traffic noise coming in through the open windows, and I could see the low aeroplanes far out over the roofs making their approach to Heathrow. As each disappeared out of the right hand window, within thirty seconds another appeared in the left hand window, and they flew by and they were all I had to measure the time.

Milly finished her wine quickly and refilled for us both, one quarter wine mixed with three quarters water again. Douglas reappeared once, walked through into the kitchen area and I heard the fridge opening and then the drawers and the sound of a cork being pulled. He came through, a glass in one hand and peeling the foil away from the neck of a bottle as he passed us, barely glancing, barely interested and walked out, returned to wherever it was he went while we sat in silence, and drank our wine and water and waited.

On closer inspection, Milly was older than I had thought. It had been her clothes – a plain round necked sweater, a short plain black skirt with plain black shoes and white socks – that had made her look so young. She was drinking much faster than me: as soon as her glass was nearly empty, she refilled us both and immediately drained half of hers. I wanted to slow down, I had not been able to face breakfast and was already starting to feel light headed, but when I had barely touched my glass, and she had finished hers, she held the bottle as if about to pour and gestured to the glass. I shrugged and drank some, but it was not enough and she repeated the gesture until I finished it all.

There was just one interruption: the door phone rang and Douglas sauntered back in to answer it. 'That's the taxi,' he said. 'Get a move on.' He turned and headed back out again.

'Why a taxi?' I called, but he did not stop.

'Get a move on,' he repeated.

Milly divided the last of the wine into our two glasses, filled them to the brim with water, and picked up hers, holding it up to me in a toast. We clinked the glasses and she held my eye as she drained it all down and then stood up, her hand held out for my glass as I struggled to finish. She placed the two glasses and bottles neatly on the tray before, with one final glance at me, she walked up to the top of the corridor; yes: she knew where to go; she had been here before.

'We're ready,' she called, softly, careful not to interrupt, but just to let him know. She stayed there, at the end of the hall, waiting and I sat on the settee, waiting. Another plane passed the window.

There was a shuffling of chairs and then his voice, distant, turned away and almost tired as if uninterested. 'Okay.' Seconds later he was back in the living room, a quick glance to check the bottles, then, 'Come along.'

'Could I...?' I asked, my voice sounding too loud in the stillness of the flat, 'could I go to the loo first?'

Milly suppressed a giggle, but Douglas was not at all amused. 'Don't be stupid. That would completely ruin the point.'

~

A few minutes later we were in the taxi, he sprawled across the back seat, Milly and I perched on the jump seats, as the taxi wove up through Hammersmith, Kensington, Park Lane and St John's Wood, and I tried to work out what this was all leading to and my bladder wished the ride was less bouncy. At last, in one of the quiet, extravagant tree-lined streets, we stopped outside the sort of house which anywhere else in London would have been converted into eight flats. Douglas paid off the taxi, led us up a brick path and rang the bell. A young man appeared, slim and slightly official looking in neat dark trousers, turtle-neck sweater and short hair. He clearly knew Douglas, and with an uninterested glance at Milly and me, opened the door to admit us all. His task completed, he walked briskly down the hall and scuttled up the stairs.

Douglas carefully closed the door behind us, took off his jacket and draped it over a coat rack. 'Wait here,' he said, starting down the hallway, then paused. 'Get undressed except for your knickers,' and then he too had vanished somewhere into the house.

With him gone, there was almost complete silence: a steady ticking from a grandfather clock, but no voices, no music, no traffic, no machinery: none of the normal sounds of London life. Silence underlined by the steady tick of the clock.

'Where are...?' I began to whisper to Milly, but immediately an accusatory heavy thud burst from the clock behind me as it wheezed its way up to strike a single deep chime. The suddenness had made me jump and I waited, wide eyed, for the chime to die away before I dared risk it again.

'Where are we? What is this?' but she simply shrugged with an ease that suggested she did not particularly care. Somewhere at the top of the house a door opened and a man laughed, startling both of us. Without a word, we each began to obey Douglas's instruction, and started frantically undressing, tossing our clothes onto a chair, a huge wooden thing, with ornately carved back and arms, almost a throne. Milly seemed to be finished in no time at all, while I was still disentangling my bra and then balancing on one leg, trying to take off my tights without them bringing my knickers down too. Even so, even after I was done, we were still alone.

I tried not to look at her and saw her trying not to look at me, but we both failed. Now almost naked, she was much prettier than I had realized; they often say that some girls look better with clothes on and some look better naked. I have always thought I was one of the first sort; Milly was unquestionably one of the second: she was slimmer than she had seemed, with neat pale breasts whose nipples, stark surprised-looking nipples, were puckered up: just as mine were. Her tummy was equally pale: narrow hips with a smooth lean bottom without any sign of a tan. Round her back and chest there was no elastic mark from a bra; presumably she hadn't been wearing one although I hadn't noticed. Her mouth, which before had looked big and greedy was now broad and welcoming; her hair, hanging so perfectly straight, came just exactly to her nipples, so that I had a momentary image of her standing completely naked in a hairdresser's salon while they trimmed her hair to precisely the right length. Her knickers were quite plain, white with blue edges at the waist and round the legs but she caught me looking and smiled again, without shame or embarrassment, simple amusement at my scrutiny.

But I felt heavy and ugly. I had worn a bra and tights, and was conscious of the lines they made on my skin. My breasts are heavier than I would like and honestly look better in a bra. Even though my knickers were daintier than hers, a French culotte style in cream satin, they need the matching bra to set them off. Here, without it they looked silly, sluttish, out of place. I turned away.

The jumble of our clothes on the chair was a mess, alien in the neat perfection of the hallway so that I wondered whether I should tidy them up. But if I did, should I separate them and how would that appear? If I wanted my clothes to have no contact with hers, was it because I wanted no contact with her? Again I was flooded by the realization that Douglas had brought us both here for a reason, and it was almost certainly going to involve Milly and me making love together. I cautiously turned to consider her again, seeing her now not just as another girl, a rival, but possibly as a lover. For all her innocent appearance, she stood there with a calm assured dignity that suggested she could handle anything.

At last footsteps returned and Douglas appeared at the end of the corridor. 'This way.'

The corridor led back into what must have been the servants' quarters when the house was built a hundred years ago. The floors were less even, the ceilings lower, the doors less finely panelled and no longer with brass fittings. At the very end, a pair of half glazed doors opened into a bright conservatory looking out across the garden, across Hampstead and down over the whole of London; all the classic landmarks of the whole city were visible from this one spot. I was still taking it all in when Douglas, sounding for the first time less than totally assured, cleared his throat.

'Here they are: this one is Milly; this is Jane. I'll collect them at, what? Four o'clock?'

'Four should do.' I turned and saw him: no, them. A small old man was sitting hunched in an old-fashioned wheelchair. Small blood-shot eyes stared out at us from a gnome-like face quite lost in wrinkles; the nose was too big, as were the ears, and his spotted pale scalp showed through the last few wisps of white hair. He must have been eighty, but it could have been ninety, and he wore a suit, brown and baggy, made for a much younger version of himself. The shirt, neat, white and fresh, gaped round his skinny neck, ringed by a deep blue tie which sported some red and gold emblem that no doubt marked him out as somebody special to the sort of people who understood these signals. Only the blanket across his knees and the nasty brown bedroom slippers suggested any concessions to acknowledge his age and present circumstances.

Behind him stood his nurse, his opposite. Gripping the handles of the wheelchair with obstinate possession, she stood rigidly erect with the conceit of a tennis champion, as tall, strong and glowing as he was shrunken and failing, and she too stared: blue eyes flaring, blonde hair cropped short, the epitome of Teutonic determination.

'Four should do,' the man repeated, 'if they are ready.'

'They are ready,' Douglas confirmed and then turned round and disappeared back down the corridor. I saw his silhouette against the square of light as the front door was opened and closed and we were left alone.

'Come here.' The man beckoned in our direction to both of us, but neither in particular and I followed Milly's example in stepping forward. 'Come on! Closer!' His voice rasped in irritation until we were close enough for him to touch us, when he stretched forward and a scrawny hand reached up to Milly, ran across her stomach just above her knickers: feeling, gauging her. Then it was my turn, except that he plucked the waist of my knickers away to run his hand just inside them, and despite my near nakedness, the easy accessibility of my breasts or even my pussy if he had pulled down my knickers, it was only my stomach that interested him. His fingers poked in, pressing painfully on my bloated bladder until I gasped and he glanced sharply up.

'All right, we'll go in. Marianne!'

The nurse straightened up, turned the wheelchair smartly and headed for a different pair of doors where she glanced back and, seeing that neither Milly nor I had moved, tutted her annoyance. 'Come on you two. Through here,' and the accent was perfect: the perfection of learning not birth.

The doors opened into a bedroom, and although it held a large double bed, a wardrobe, all the usual furniture for a bedroom, there were no clothes, no pictures, no hairbrushes; none of the clutter of occupation. This wasn't his bedroom. The nurse, Marianne, wheeled him up next to the bed, positioning the chair with elaborate care before carefully applying the brake. With a single flourish, she swept the duvet and covers off the bed, bundled them up and tossed them down into the corner, leaving the bed starkly naked, as naked as me, with just a single cream sheet, pulled tight across the mattress, primed and available for whatever it was I had agreed to do.

'Who'll be first?' asked the man.

What on earth could he mean or want? He could not have the strength nor the mobility to make love to either of us, and yet his question suggested he was considering both. There was no clue on Marianne's face and I glanced at Milly for help. She must have had some idea of what was expected, because she shrugged again, climbed up onto the bed and turned to face us, kneeling with her legs spaced wide apart in the middle of the mattress.

For a few seconds nothing happened; we all watched her kneeling there, those little white knickers with their blue edging stretched tight and a look of intense concentration on her face. She was resting her hand on herself over her round swollen tummy and then as I watched, a dark circle appeared in the gusset of her knickers and I realized that she was wetting herself. She was simply peeing straight onto the bed as she knelt there.

I was hypnotised, unable to drag my eyes away from the way that her knickers filled and the pee soaked through them, running down her legs and soaking the sheet, forming pools in the hollows round her knees where her weight depressed the mattress. At first it was silent, but soon a full stream was bursting through the swollen front of her knickers and pouring onto the bed. Slowly it weakened to a trickle, to drips, a single drip and stopped. I turned to the old man and found him watching her intently, his blurry eyes wide and damp.

'Take them off,' he croaked. 'Marianne?'

Milly sat back on the bed in the middle of the dark puddle she had created, pulled her knickers off and offered them up to Marianne who, with a sneer of distaste showing through her cold efficiency, held out a plastic bag into which Milly dropped them. The bag was carefully sealed up and Marianne returned to her place of power behind his chair. The man's bloodshot eyes finished scrutinising Marianne's movements and now they swivelled round to me.

'Now you.'

Milly shuffled back up the bed and it would have been stupid to pretend I did not know what was required so I simply copied exactly as she had done. Now I could understand the strange expression on Milly's face. Despite my urgent need, it really is not easy to pee in that situation, when you know it is the wrong place, and you are not sitting or squatting and there are people there, and anyway you still have your knickers on. It goes against everything your upbringing has taught you, and the impatient shuffling of the people waiting for you to perform only makes that worse. But there is also basic biological need, and eventually the pressure in my bladder outweighed my manners and I was able to release a little, and that made the rest so much easier, although the different style of my knickers meant that rather than filling them as Milly had done, a single strong jet shot straight down one leg beating into the mattress, splashing everywhere and hissing like a fire hose.

When I stopped, I took the knickers off, dropped them into the plastic bag Marianne held out – a different one for each of us, I noted – and sat back.

'Now,' said the man, 'who will be top?' He turned to us, something on his shrivelled face which was perhaps meant to be a smile, as he peered from one to the other. Again I had little idea what he was asking but again, thankfully, Milly took the lead, got up off the bed and stepped forward.

Marianne had put away our knickers – it didn't look as if I would ever see them again – and turned her attention to Milly. Half hidden behind the old man's chair, I could not see what they were doing until Milly stepped forward and if she had not looked so magnificent, I would have giggled. She was now wearing a dildo, black straps wrapped firmly round her waist and thighs and meeting where a shiny black shield covered her pubic hair. From this a pale ivory phallus jutted obscenely towards me, bobbing like a greedy bird with every movement as she came over and, still without a word, climbed back up onto the bed beside me.

I had told Douglas I could handle anything, and he had scoffed at my naivety. He had warned me that it would not just be more of the same, but I had not understood how different it was possible to be. I had never imagined it would be to let an old man and his nurse watch me pee into my knickers. When I saw there was another girl, I had thought he would want to watch us make love. That would have been something I could handle; images of making love to another woman had crept into my quiet fantasies many times. This was entirely different: I was to be fucked with a dildo in front of a silent, passionless audience by an equally silent partner. Last week Douglas had talked to me: taunted and teased me, certainly but he had talked, had acknowledged my humanity. The coldness of this wizened man robbed me even of that. I glared at him but he was not looking at me; at the nurse then, but she remained quite unmoved. Then I would ignore them both, obliterate them and I lay back to welcome Milly.

At first this could have been with any lover. Her hand stroked at my breasts as she leaned over and kissed me. First it was just a simple kiss; on the mouth, yes, but a kiss on the mouth is nothing so very special, even when it's from a girl as naked and as appealing as Milly. But then I felt her tongue pushing in and it became so much more affectionate, more passionate: a kiss such as I might have received from Danny, but with a gentleness that I would never have known from him. And I responded, surprised myself by responding without hesitation. She was pretty and she tasted nice and her body was soft and comforting. The hard plastic penis butted against my leg from time to time, continually reminding me it was there, but Danny's cock does that and I have never minded then so why should I mind now?

When Milly's hand left my breasts and started down my body, I could see her breasts better; so small, with tight little nipples in a pink so brilliant she might have used make-up. I wanted to touch them, and found myself grinning at the realisation that now I could. They were warm and soft, yes, but certainly firmer than mine, and the nipples had screwed themselves up into little knots that longed to be kissed. So I kissed them, suckled them into my mouth and gave little nips such as Danny does to me. It was a slight shock to remember that this was not Danny's hand that was tracing up and down my pussy, sliding softly across the lips, slipping down the outside and then slithering back up inside – right inside – pressing onto my clitoris, stroking me, pinching and squeezing me so that I felt myself opening and starting to flow.

Milly felt it too, pressed me harder, smeared my lips open wider and pinched my clitoris tighter, milking it like Danny does and pushing her fingers right into me.

Then she stopped, lifted herself right on top of me, and let the tip of her plastic cock knock at the entry.

'No, no!' screamed the man. 'Make her wet first.' And although Milly and I both knew I was already dripping, she grinned at me and squirmed obediently down the bed until she was lying between my legs, and her kisses hopped up each thigh until they met at the top, a kiss landed on my lips and a tongue pushed out to lap me, sucking me right into her mouth and slurping at the juice I was offering her. Clearly she was not new to this.

Unable to reach any part of her, I had started squeezing my own breasts, pulling at my nipples and pinching them; I do like them being roughly treated at this stage. I was also finding it hard to stay still, and the longer Milly stayed there licking me, the worse that was going to be. Suddenly, I don't know what she did, but it felt as if all the feeling had been doubled, trebled. She was still licking me, her whole mouth clamped over me, her fingers inside me, another finger tickling at my bottom and even, I am almost sure, pushing inside there, and without any warning, I suddenly came. Not a huge racking, shaking one that builds up slowly, rolls by and fades away steadily in a succession of little repeats. This was a single hammer blow, different from anything I had ever known, that crept up out of nowhere, hit me once and knocked me flat. I sat up, almost unsure what had happened, while somewhere down between my legs, Milly was still lapping gently and, yes, there definitely was a finger twisting in my bottom, and she was grinning up at me over the hedge of my pubic hair.

'Come along, now!' commanded the man, possibly disturbed at our breaking from his script. 'Fuck her! Fuck her!'

I was ready for this, more than ready, so that as soon as Milly climbed back up the bed, positioned herself in the classical way with her elbows either side of me and she lay the tip of her prick against me, I seemed to draw it straight in. And it did feel good, but since I know I will never come from that alone, I reached down a hand to stroke my own clitoris while she steadily pushed in and back, hard and fast with an intensity that Danny could not have maintained for more than a minute or two; an artificial cock does have its advantages. I would have liked to stroke her, and although I could, even if awkwardly, reach her breasts, it was much nicer having her lying right down on top of me so that her breasts scraped against mine with each thrust, and rubbed even better when I lifted my chest to receive her. I could reach her bottom, a sweet little bottom, not much bigger than Danny's but so much softer and smoother that it was wonderful to stroke.

But best of all was stroking myself, at a pace that I am familiar with and which works for me, and having her smirking down at me, toying with my breasts, kissing me sometimes, but deep dark eyes laughing to me as she thrust steadily into me and saw from the reaction on my face what she needed to do. And she did; she simply continued with that gorgeous hard cock while I was swept away again, brought on to come again, softly this time: slowly, softly, gently but deeply satisfying.

It was only afterwards that I remembered we had an audience, and I am not sure if they even realized that I had come. Milly stopped thrusting into me – she knew – but she kissed me and I was getting used to her kisses, sweet and sensual but with no lack of passion for all that, and for some while she simply kissed me while one had gently played with my nipple. The man interrupted us again.

'All right,' he said, and sniffed down at where we were lying. 'That will do.'

We both sat up and Milly went to be unbuckled out of the harness. It was not until this was removed and she turned back to me afterwards that I saw her properly for the first time and discovered that she was completely and immaculately shaved: so perfect she might have plucked it all. As she was standing and I was still sitting, her tummy was almost at my eye level, and I had a perfect view of her little pussy opening up from a pure smooth puffy mound and widening out immediately to enclose the neat ridge of her clitoris hood and lips. It was so clean, so innocent and beautiful, I wished that I had been given the chance to touch it as she had to me. She saw me staring and although I looked away quickly, she had seen.

'Next thing...' growled the old man, but Milly interrupted him.

'I need to pee again,' and both he and Marianne stopped short and stared at her. And at me.

'All right, then,' he said. 'Back on the bed. Over her.'

Now she didn't look at me, just pushed me further back on the bed and lay me down flat, slid me over into the middle of the mattress and arranged me neatly with my arms by my sides. Finally, with a glance towards our audience, she pulled my legs apart, for no reason that I could see since it was my top that he was closest to, but maybe it was just for her benefit, because her hand grazed up my legs as she turned and for one short moment brushed across my open pussy. Then she climbed up, and came right up the bed until she was right beside me, then swung one leg over and knelt there, right over my head, her knees by my shoulders. In front of me, directly over me, gaped her open sex.

I'm not specially innocent. I have slept with four men, or five if you count uncompleted attempts, but never a girl. I had never seen another girl so close before; I had never even seen myself quite that clearly. She was just a few inches in front of my eyes, her legs spread over me, her pussy peeling open to show me everything, and even here there was not a trace of hair: instead I was being shown her clitoris, covered by a long plump hood and after that, her tight little inside lips: tiny, skinny little lips that were hardly there at all but which her fingers worked at eagerly enough, burrowing in, sliding them apart, showing off the smooth glistening pinkness inside, spreading wide the tiny inside opening and then she just stopped. Her bottom lowered a few inches nearer to me and stopped again.

And then a small drop appeared right in the middle, a drop which almost immediately became a spurt, and suddenly I was being showered in her pee. I quickly shut my eyes but could not escape. The stream splashed down straight onto my face and since Milly deliberately wiggled her bottom, it landed everywhere, soaking me. Her legs were either side of my head and as soon as the flow had started she had leaned forward, her hands on my shoulders, pinning me flat and helpless. Eventually I felt it all stop and although she had not moved, I dared to open my eyes. Straight in front of me, entirely filling my vision, was her open sex, shining golden drips still shimmering on her lips, splashed on her thighs and even on the pale cheeks of her bottom. My whole face felt sticky and the smell of her pee was so strong I was unsure whether I was smelling it or tasting it. I started to try to get up, but she simply lowered her bottom even further until it was almost resting on me.

The rasping voice of the old man came through. 'Clean her up,' and my arm was prodded by a boney finger. 'Lick her.'

So I put out my tongue and did that, tasting the salty sourness of the drips hanging from her lips, sweeping away the splashes from her thighs and reaching up also to clean her bottom. For a few seconds, I even licked the front part round her clitoris, not because it was wet but just because I had never done that and I would probably never get another chance, and besides: she was so smooth and gorgeous.

Milly lifted herself up and climbed off me so that I was able to sit up at last and wipe my face down, even if only with my hands, but I could do nothing about the pee still running out of my hair. The nurse and the old man appeared not to have moved during the whole thing; he still glared angrily at us; she still grasped the handles of his wheelchair as if they were her only link to life.

'You?' and his stare fixed on me.

'What?' I asked.

'Can you piss, girl?'

'I don't know. Maybe.'

'Well can you or can't you?'

'I think so. Yes.'

'Go on then.'

Milly hadn't waited to be told; she glanced over towards where the old man and his nurse were waiting and then lay down flat, just as I had been made to do, sweeping her hair out in a halo round her head and then carefully placed her hands by her sides and then she too, whether as display or invitation I don't know, opened wide her legs and waited.

I moved across, squelching over the sodden mattress, until I was kneeling over her, then I too lowered myself down until my pussy was right over her; for a few seconds her big, dark eyes stared up at me, and then knowing what was going to happen, she shut them and waited. Having done it once with people watching, it was easier this time and I was just so eager to go.

The old man was craning round and snapped at his nurse to move the chair so he could see better as I felt my muscles open and the stream shoot out, splashing all over her face. In a strange way it was enormously liberating, watching the yellow pool form round her head, soaking her hair.

When I was finished, I didn't wait to be told, just lowered myself down to receive Milly's tongue to clean me up, licking my skin and noisily sucking the last drops off my straggled pubic hair.

The old man finally stopped us. 'All right. That will do.' He jerked his head back, a signal which Marianne understood for she released the brake and ran the chair back a step or two but then stopped. For a moment, neither of them moved, both staring at us, considering. Finally the man raised his white hand and a wiry finger pointed at Milly. 'That one.'

And Marianne, with a transparent nod towards Milly, immediately whisked the chair round and wheeled the man out of the room away from the conservatory. At the door she paused, checked that Milly was climbing off the bed and preparing to follow and then her eyes swivelled round to me. 'Wait here.'

I had no idea where Milly was being taken, but I was certainly glad that she was the one who had been chosen and that my time was over. I also hoped that Douglas would be pleased with me; I had coped with it all, even though it was nothing like I had been expecting and Douglas hadn't even been there. Maybe this would mean I would get other chances.

It was at least five minutes before Marianne returned, summoning me to follow her back down the hall, passing the chair where my clothes lay, still jumbled up with Milly's.

'I might as well bring these,' and I started to gather them up.

She peered round slowly. 'Not yet. I do not know that we are finished with you yet.' And she continued upstairs to what I assume was her room. She closed the door behind us, sniffed cautiously at my lank sticky hair, and headed straight through into a crisp white bathroom and turned on the shower.

'I don't care for all that stuff; you will need to wash yourself. Are you still needing the lavatory?'

'Yes, actually. I do rather.'

'Go on then,' and she nodded towards the toilet. Well maybe she did not "care for all that stuff" but she didn't leave me to take a pee in private; in fact she positioned herself right in front of me and watched very carefully. As soon as she heard me finish and I reached for the paper she stopped me. 'Stand up,' and she reached down between my legs, running her fingers along the pussy and then holding up her hand to examine the shining streaks it now carried. 'Hmm,' her nose wrinkled in disgust as she rinsed her hand. 'Now into the shower. Get on.'

She pushed soap and shampoo into my hands, reminded me again to be quick and went back to the bedroom. It was a pleasure at last to be left alone and even more of a pleasure to wash. Afterwards I dried myself, wrapped the towel round me and walked back into her room. She was sitting by the bed, thumbing through a magazine.

'At last! I told you to be quick. There is a hair dryer there,' and she nodded at her dressing table as if it was of little significance but I felt her eyes on me all the time I crossed the floor, picked up the hair dryer and a rather pretty wooden hairbrush. 'Take off the towel,' she said.

'The towel? Why?'

I think I knew at once I should not have asked that. She put down the magazine, got to her feet and came to stand beside me, looking down her long nose at me. Calmly she reached up to where the towel was tucked in above my breasts, and although I grabbed at it, she was incredibly strong; she shoved my hands aside as if I had been a child, unravelled the towel and pulled it away. Then she slapped me, just once, straight across my bottom. I yelped but she only laughed.

'Do not be insubordinate,' and then slapped me again. 'I prefer you to be naked.'

I watched in the dressing table mirror as she returned to her chair. This time she did not even pick up the magazine, simply settled into the chair, her hands resting casually in her lap, relaxed and calm, and crossed her long legs. One foot was gently swinging to and fro and for some minutes while I dried my hair I felt her scrutiny on every move I made.

But the foot stopped swinging.

'Turn round. No, the other way. Face the wall.' I turned, presenting my back to her, although I don't suppose it was my back she was looking at, and for a long time she said nothing. 'What is your name?'

'Jane.'

'You have been beaten recently, Jane.'

'Yes.'

'When?'

'About a week ago.'

'With what?'

'A tawse.'

'A tawse? Very good! By Douglas?'

'Yes.'

'Yes, he likes the tawse. And he knows how to use it properly.' I could not comment on this and said nothing so for some minutes more she watched me, mostly in silence; mostly, but not always.

'Did you orgasm just now with Milly?'

'Yes.'

'Did you? Good! When?'

'Well twice actually.'

'Even better. When?'

'When she was licking me and then again with the strap-on thing.' She absorbed that in silence, still watching intently until finally my hair was as dry as it was going to get. I switched off the hair dryer and put it down.

'Good,' she said. 'Now come over here and bring me the hairbrush. Here. Right here. Right by me. Good. Now lay yourself down across my lap.'

'What are you going to do?'

'I am going to spank you.'

'To spank me? Why?'

'I have already told you not to question me, not to be insubordinate. Just do as you are told and lie down.' She took the hairbrush out of my hand, smoothed out her neat blue skirt, took hold of my wrist and jerked me down.

It is so shameful, upended like that: my hands scratching at the pale pink carpet in front of me; my feet scrabbling for a grip on the carpet behind; and in the middle, raised up over her lap, offered up for whatever she chose, my bottom. She ran her open palm across me then a single finger, tracing perhaps the marks Douglas had left.

Then she began spanking me. It was not unbearably hard; I felt I could cope, but it just didn't stop. Carefully alternating between one cheek and then the other, she kept up the same steady pace, on and on, the same hardness, the same unchanging unavoidable sting which built up and built up until I couldn't take it any more. It really did seem worse than the tawse because at least that had varied in weight and speed, and I had known there was a limit: it would end. This spanking was just eternity and I started to cry.

At first I don't think she even noticed, so focussed was she on the single task she had set herself. When she did notice, mercifully she stopped, although her hand continued sweeping round the surface of my blazing skin. 'Are you crying, Jane?'

'Yes,' I said. 'It hurts! It really hurts!'

'Sit up,' and she helped me up onto her lap, sitting me comfortably there and hugging me against her breasts. She stroked my hair, my cheek, wiped away the tears with her fingers and even kissed me, lightly, once on each eye. 'Of course it hurts. It is meant to hurt. But I will stop if you want me to...'

'Oh yes please!'

'... but when I stop with my hand, I will start with the hairbrush. You will receive twenty-four with that. Now: think carefully, my little Jane. Do you want me to stop, or to carry on?'

'Neither,' and so she slapped me: hard straight across my breast and then equally hard across the other one, right on my nipple.

'Ow,' I wailed, clutching myself but she pulled my hands away and held them, both gripped fast in one of hers, in my lap.

'That was not one of the choices.'

'I don't know.'

'Choose.'

'I don't know. I don't know what the hairbrush will be like,' and I realized immediately that had been stupid because she reached across to the little table and picked it up.

'Turn over,' and back I went, face down over her nasty knees, a couple of cold taps first and then the full force of the strokes coming down, one on each cheek: vicious stinging blows, much more painful than her hardest hand spanks, as bad as the tawse, and I could not ask her for twenty-four of them. 'Well?' she asked, and did two more, one on each cheek, just as hard, before once more stroking circles round my bottom.

'With your hand,' I gasped.

'Sure?' but she was only teasing as her hands floated over my skin again, then both palms together which drew my cheeks apart and for a second she stopped as she peered inside. 'All right.' And she took up the steady rhythm, again.

I tried not to cry but it was so unrelenting and almost immediately I was in tears again. She stopped spanking although her palm could still not quite leave my bottom alone and this time her other hand came round to my breasts, just the way that Douglas had done, and I wondered if he had taught her. Maybe he had spanked her, although it was hard to imagine the majestic Marianne over anybody's lap. The way she stroked by bottom could have been a part of – or even a relief from – the spanking, and she had never tried to touch me anywhere else down there, but the way she touched my breasts was different; she was simply fondling me. Then her hand ran up and down my spine and that too was more affectionate than anything else.

'Shall we do the hairbrush ones now?'

'No.'

'After that it will be over.'

'I want it over now.'

'We just have to do the hairbrush.'

'Why? Who says we have to?' I knew I was sounding like a child but she was treating me like one.

'Choose.'

And I thought back to the hairbrush. Yes they had been horrid, as bad as the tawse. As bad, but not worse, and I had managed to take twenty-four with that. 'All right. But not too hard.'

She did do them hard, and I suppose I had known she would whatever I said, but at least she was quick and before I had properly got my breath back from the first one, she had already done six. She didn't even stop after twelve, just carried on, one after another, holding me firmly on her lap with one muscular arm wrapped round my waist. I was crying, kicking and struggling but she held me tight and ignored me.

'There,' she had stopped. 'That's all of them.' Her hand circled down under me to reach my breasts again, stroked them briefly and then released me. 'Now, go and fetch yourself a tissue and blow your nose.'

I climbed up off her lap and stumbled over to the dressing table for a tissue. I blew my nose, wiped my eyes – my make up was virtually gone – and turned back again but as I did so I caught a glimpse in the mirror. The dressing table was one of those fancy ones with three angled mirrors along the back, so I turned round and could see my bottom fully.

'God! Look! I'm so red!'

She didn't seem surprised. 'Of course, but you have done

very well.' I touched it and felt the heat all across my skin and in the background saw Marianne sitting quietly watching me, the hairbrush lying carelessly beside her. 'I hope you are pleased.'

'Pleased?'

'Yes, pleased. It was hard and many girls would not have taken it so well. You did well. Now you may masturbate.'

I turned and stared. 'I'm sorry?'

'Now you may masturbate. After that you will feel much better.'

The woman really was incredible. 'Thank you, but I do not want to masturbate.'

She stared at me for a few moments, sniffed and then crooked that nasty long finger again. 'Come here, Jane.' The tone was resigned, sad more than angry, but her stillness as I crossed the room was the more frightening for that.

When I was standing straight in front of her, she reached up and her fingertip flicked idly at my nipples, first one, then the other. 'Look. Your nipples are erect.' And she stared into my eyes until I admitted they were. 'Now lie down on the bed.' And inevitably however I lay was not right. She sat down next to me, pulled my hands down by my sides and dragged my feet apart, and the long fingers moved up to dig between my thighs.

'You really should trim some of this, you know. It is most unattractive to be so hairy.'

'My husband likes it.' It was a childish pout perhaps but it would do no harm to remind her that I at least had a husband.

'He probably merely lacks the experience to know better. There!' and her fingers rasped up and down between my lips until, with no concern for me at all, she succeeded in pushing one spiny finger right inside me. 'There, you see? You are sopping wet. Of course you want to masturbate. Please don't be disobedient.'

'I don't want to. I don't...do...that.'

'Don't be ridiculous. All girls masturbate. You do it; your little friend Milly does it...'

'Do you do it?' I asked, and straight away regretted being clever as her face clouded and she slapped me again: once on each thigh, followed by once on each breast.

'Do not be impertinent, girl! Do as you are told.'

So I reached down and started, and really it was not so difficult. I closed my eyes and closed my mind to her, but there were still plenty of images whirling round for me to latch on to: of Milly fucking me and kissing me; her kneeling over me, seeing her tiny lips bubble open and that first shimmering droplet appear; the surge when she had let it all go; that old man, coldly directing us from his wheelchair; even of the dreadful Marianne watching us: those cold blue eyes consuming every single thing we were made to do; of being upended over her lap while she alternately beat and stroked my bottom, fondled my breasts and cuddled me to her when I cried; the soaring rush as each blow had landed on me; all of it combined to build up to a glorious collage and like a child on Christmas Day, I did not know which new toy to bring forward and play with first. All were so magical and enchanting; each was more exciting than any other and the appeal of each kept barging in, surpassing the appeal of the last one. I knew I was squirming disgustingly on her bed, could hear the squelching slurping noises that my fingers were stirring up and the gasps from deep in my throat, and suddenly it happened: it was all too much, too good, too extraordinary and I seized up, clutching myself and sobbing out the joy of the relief as it all burst in one glorious whirl.

I stayed lying there, comfortable and relaxed. I did not look at her, managed to avoid meeting her eye when she stood up, and I deliberately turned my head away when she stopped to turn and stare at me with an expression that warned she was about to offer some further criticism or insult. She had been moving round the room, I had vaguely heard the sounds of that, but then I heard a zip running and could not keep from looking round. She was standing beside the bed, stepping out of the neat uniform dress. As she turned away to lay that neatly over a chair, I was treated to her full broad bottom in opaque dark tights and the sturdy black strap of a sturdy black bra. Her shoes were gone already and as I watched, her hands came back to unhook the bra. Then that was gone. Her thumbs hooked into the waist of her tights and they, together with a substantial pair of black knickers, were briskly swept down her legs.

She turned round and for a moment stood towering over where I lay, heavy round breasts, with long pointed nipples, a full mature stomach and nearer to me than that, a neatly trimmed bush through which her thick heavy lips, the direct opposite of Milly's, were clearly visible. But she didn't join me on the bed. Instead she returned to settle back in her chair, her long finger crooked out and beckoned towards me. 'Come here.'

I obeyed her: she was no less powerful naked than she was clothed and either way was not someone to be disobeyed, although I had no idea what she had in mind for me: it could be to go back over her lap for another spanking: it could be anything. As I got close, it became clear. She nodded downwards and her legs drew wide open.

'You know what to do, Jane.'

'Not really; I've never done that!' I protested but I was already kneeling down.

She smiled. 'Really? How sweet!' and she patted my cheek. 'Just use your imagination.' And her thighs slid a little further apart.

Before today I had never realized how different girls can be, just always assumed that everyone was pretty much like me. Milly had been quite different, now this woman was entirely different again. For one thing, she had huge lips. Mine only just appear when I have my legs together; hers had been visible when she was standing up and when seated as now with her thighs apart, they pushed forward: ripe and succulent.

And everything was proudly on display, for underneath there she had no hair at all, so I could see every detail of her, every little fold and pussy, all glistening in anticipation. When I put my tongue out, she was right there and it was just her, her skin: pink and shining with her wetness; a warm, strong stickiness that coated the insides of her puffy wrinkled lips, that trickled down to me; slightly sour, but this was special and intimate and all the more exciting for that. And her lips had already puffed open so that a droplet had formed right in the little vee where they met at the bottom. Even so, she used the fingers of one hand to peel herself open even further, while the other hand wrapped round my head and pulled me more firmly in.

She was gazing down at me, her lips half open as I lay my hands on her open thighs and moved in as close as I could. The feeling on my tongue, the taste, the softness, the wetness all invited more and I tried to remember what it was that Milly had done. I put out my tongue further, lapped gently against her, but when she slid further down in the chair, my tongue had nowhere to go but deeper inside, so deep that her thick floppy lips pushed against my mouth as if she were kissing me. I suckled these too, as Milly had done with mine, sucking and almost chewing on them, milking her sweetness into my mouth and pinching them together with my lips, rolling them apart with my tongue. She groaned and hugged my head in even tighter while her own head rolled back.

When she pulled me up a little higher, it was her clitoris that was drawn into my mouth, its succulent silky covering as loose as her lips so that I could push my tongue right underneath, lap all round there and even at the smooth hard knob of the clitoris itself, huge and swollen. She groaned again and her thighs stretched wider.

And Milly had used her hands, so I did that too, running them up Marianne's thighs right to the top and pushing in not just between her lips but right deep inside, one and then two fingers right into her warm tunnel. Although one hand was still round my head, tangling into my hair, pulling and controlling, the other had gone back up to her breast where it scraped over the whole area and kneaded against her nipples, squashing them hard into her body. Even so, I'm sure it was my tongue that had the real effect, for she kept directing my head from her clitoris to her lips and back again, pulling me still closer against her, pressing herself harder against me as she squirmed in her chair, sliding down lower to open herself wider and drag more stimulation from every scrap of contact with my mouth.

And when she came, in a rolling, groaning, shudder that clamped me so tight I could scarcely breathe, I was scared at the effect I had produced, at the total loss of the dignity which had possessed this proud woman earlier, and which now deserted her entirely as she sprawled back naked and abandoned and choked out her pleasure in rasping, agonised gasps.

Afterwards she sat gazing down at me with a serene smile on her face while her hand stroked my hair, ran down my cheek and cupped under my chin. 'You are really quite a sweet little thing, aren't you?'

'Thank you,' I whispered.

'I really wish I could have you for longer. Still,' and she got to her feet, taking my hand and drawing me up with her, 'back into the shower, with you I think.'

'I really don't need a shower, although I would rather like to wash my face.' I smirked. 'I'm all sticky, and I must smell ever so strongly of you.'

'Oh, I'll wash your face, my dear, in the shower. I need a pee.'

MILLY'S TALE: THE NEW GIRL

I was early arriving at Douglas' flat. Being early normally makes him as cross as being late, but this time he seemed reasonably placid so I risked asking what was happening.

'It's something I'm arranging for a friend of mine: Arthur Garrett; do you know him?' Douglas knows everyone, of course, certainly everyone who matters. He knows who is organising the parties, the exhibitions, the outings and the clubs. And he has a wicked imagination so any invitation from him is a thing to treasure.

'No. I don't think so. And who is this other girl, Jane you said? Who is she?'

'You don't know her,' and then he turned to go out but paused. 'She is new to this, so go easy.' When he came back he carried a bottle of Chardonnay in one hand and Evian in the other so I could see where this was heading. I started to drink.

The girl, Jane, arrived about ten minutes later and looked terrified. She either hadn't asked the right questions or she was being deliberately kept in the dark but either way, I didn't say anything. Even when she tried to make conversation, Douglas promptly put a stop to it. I don't where he finds them, perhaps he advertises, but then I can never exactly work out how he came into my life either. Anyway, Jane looked quite sweet if you like that kind of look: round, blonde and angelic, innocent anyway, a bit out of her depth but perhaps she would learn. She was wearing a wedding ring, so maybe she was only taking a break from domestic bliss; she was certainly a fair bit older than most of Douglas's friends: at least twenty-five.

It was not until we were at the house, standing in the hallway, that he made us undress, partly anyway. The hallway was quiet, as it always in these houses, so Jane was completely spooked when a clock struck just behind her. I saw her: watching me while I undressed, but it didn't take me long: I was wearing what Nikki calls my "semi schoolgirl" with short black skirt and ankle socks. I never wear a bra so the whole lot came off pretty smartly while this Jane was still struggling with her tights. She was much bigger than me: more curvy with big pillowy breasts and a big bottom.

When we finally went through to Arthur Garret, I realized I had met him before, but then at his age, he is ninety-two, and in a wheelchair, he does rather stand out from the other people I meet and play with. We had been introduced about a year ago, at a party down on the south coast, somewhere near Brighton. It was a private affair that I had gone to with Emma, but I vaguely remembered what he liked, so all that wine and water slotted into place. This time he had a nurse with him, called Marianne apparently, a tall and severe woman of at least thirty but she knew how to look after herself. I suppose caring for an invalid does keep you fit; it certainly tones up the physical strength and with her short blonde hair and hard blue stares, she was someone I could rather fancy. I caught her eye a couple of times and I think she felt the same.

We did the usual thing, much as Emma and I had before, and I expect Jane will have told you about that. If this was, as Douglas had implied, her first time, she did well although the knickers she had chosen were completely unsuitable. Once those came off, she looked much better, quite hairy because she did not shave or, as far as I could see, even trim her pubic hair to any noticeable degree: another of Douglas's kinks. First we both peed then the old man brought out the strap-on; he let us decide who would take which part, but of course I was already halfway into it by the time little Jane had even worked out what she was being asked. Marianne helped me with the straps and, yes, she did take the opportunity to grope me, to "check it wasn't twisted" and slip her fingers into my cunt; I gave them a little squeeze as a promise of what she could have later if she wanted. Women like that always have that effect on me.

Jane was interesting but, I think, completely inexperienced. I went down on her first and she certainly enjoyed that: I had her squirming in no time. Her lips were not all that big, bigger than me of course, but everyone keeps saying how tiny I am, but she did have a lovely prominent clit which fitted my mouth just perfectly. When I started in with the dildo, she played with herself happily enough, enough to make herself come again. I very nearly did too, just from the whole situation: the old man watching; Marianne watching; Jane's being new to me, possibly even new to girls altogether and lying on top of her in a pee-soaked bed; it isn't something I get to do every day. Afterwards we lay there and I gave her a couple of deep kisses while the old man and Marianne watched us. I had hoped to be able to take the dildo off and have Jane lick me but he wouldn't allow that. However, I had a good guess what he would like: just as someone like Marianne brings out the sub in me, those like Jane have the opposite effect. Her softness, plumpness almost, with dark innocent eyes and neat curly hair just seems made for the role, so when he started to break things up, I offered to pee again.

It was wonderful seeing her pretty little face screwed up underneath me as I knelt over her, although even then I am not sure that she had gathered what was happening, and I am afraid I did rather forget Douglas's request not to be too hard on her. All that neat blonde hair, freshly brushed and curled, how could anyone resist it? Once I had made that a complete mess, I aimed my pee all over her face until her make-up was running and she was totally covered. Both the man and his nurse were impressed: I caught them whispering together. I dropped straight down on her so she could lick me, after all she had already come twice while I was still owed my first, but the man didn't let me stay for long. Then the dirty old bugger wanted her to go too, so I had to take hers but I made the most of it; managed to maintain eye contact with the nurse while we were getting into position, so she knew who I was doing this for. I also opened my legs really wide so she could have a better look at what I could offer her if she wanted it. Once Jane started, and given her inexperience I had been afraid we might have been waiting for hours, it was not too bad; there is something magical about lying underneath a girl, seeing her cunt right in front of you and waiting for it to start opening up and showering you.

Afterwards I was licking her while the old man sat watching us, drooling and trying to decide. I was confident that he would choose Jane: golden, busty, nice big bum and I remember how much he likes bums; in Brighton he had spent nearly half the evening with his finger up Emma's bum. I was confident, but I was wrong. Could he tell I would have preferred to go with the nurse? Maybe he could and maybe that was part of the game, certainly if this had been Douglas that would have been the way; he couldn't be Douglas's father could he?

However, after considering both of us, he summoned me to go with him while Jane was told to wait. Marianne led us through to a different bedroom, which I think was his; certainly it was in regular use and had a bathroom leading off.

Once Marianne had gone, he beckoned me over and played with me for a few minutes, his scrawny hand scratching at my breasts, mauling me, pinching me and worming in between my legs but more at the back than the front. Since we were clearly waiting for something or someone, I asked if I could use the bathroom to take a shower; if nothing else, it would keep his hands off me.

'In a minute.'

'But I smell, and I feel all sticky. That girl's pee...'

'In a minute,' he repeated and continued prying between my lips, making me bend over the end of the bed so that he could pull open my bottom, examining and sniffing at me, scratching right there at the opening and trying to make his finger wet enough in my cunt that he could push it up my bum.

I was bent over like this when the door burst open and the young man who had first admitted us to the house came in. At least, I think it was him, but I could be wrong because he was immediately followed by another man, and they were not just brothers but twins. They were so fresh: lean, fit and scrubbed. Like angels from an old painting, immaculate and unblemished, they appeared somehow other-worldly. Their hair was tastefully trimmed and perfectly brushed, their bodies slim and athletic, chests smooth and tight without any of that dreadful pecto-fanatic rubbish. Best of all, they were both entirely and unashamedly naked so I could see everything: their flat stomachs, narrow hips and identical little cocks waiting for me: sweetly sprouting out of neatly trimmed little bushes and resting comfortably on their balls. The two of them had come charging in as if they had been engaged in some game together, but that gaiety evaporated at once and they stopped in front of the old man's chair when he glowered at them.

'Where have you been? I've been waiting.' This was harsh, because he had been putting the time to good use.

'Sorry!' answered one of them. 'We didn't know you were ready.'

He grunted and finally pulled his finger out of my cunt so that I could stand up. 'Well go through to the shower,' and he waved at the boys. 'One of you push me.'

He led the way through into the bathroom and that confirmed that this was his own bedroom. It was all converted for his use, not only with gleaming grab handles everywhere, but also a big open-sided shower that you could take the whole wheelchair into.

He had himself parked directly in front of that and directed us forward. 'There now: in you go. You!' and he pointed at me, 'kneel down in the middle.'

So it would be this, and I calmly knelt down while the two men stood on either side. Automatically, I reached up for their cocks, one in each hand, warm and at this stage, baby-soft.

'No, no!' the old man butted in angrily. 'Leave them alone. Let them do it.'

And do it they did; first one started, then the other, a few drops then a steady warm stream all over me again, across my shoulders, over my breasts, forming a puddle in the valley between my thighs. 'And her head!' the old man directed. 'Open your mouth, girl! Drink! Drink!'

I don't know why, but I don't like doing this with men. With girls I don't mind so much, although even there I would rather be giving than receiving. Here I had no choice, so I turned to one of them and opened my mouth to let him direct the stream right in, letting it fill my mouth, overflow and run down my chin, my breasts and my body. I swallowed down a mouthful, and opened my mouth to show the old man I had done so, before turning to the other side for the same thing while the first twin soaked my hair and my back in his warm pee.

When they were finished, he did allow us to turn on the shower and the two boys had fun washing me, washing me with great care. And, yes I washed them too, bringing both their cocks up to good erections, sliding back their foreskins to rinse the pink underneath, soaping their tight firm buttocks; I didn't waste the opportunity. We dried each other with the big fluffy towels piled up beside the shower cubicle.

'Right, now to bed,' and the man spun the wheelchair round himself before calling to one of the boys to "Push, Robert, damn it! Push!" as we returned to his bedroom.

'Now,' he said, wheeling himself up to a position close beside the bed, 'get her up on here and give her a good fucking, front and back.'

Maybe I should have expected this, but I hadn't and although I am happy with most things, happiest of all when there is another girl involved, there are some things I don't like and I don't like anal. Which meant there might be a bit of a row in a while, but that needn't be yet and it needn't necessarily be at all. Twins aren't only a male fantasy, and these two had already looked very appealing, certainly up to the task and ready for anything I offered them, so I was quite confident I could keep their minds off my bum long enough to keep me happy and – between my hands, my mouth and my cunt – ensure they were satisfied too and left in no condition to upset me by going places I did not want them to stray.

On the bed, I settled down between them and took one cock in each hand. They were happy enough with a breast each and their hands soon found their way down between my legs. Clearly they not only knew what they were doing individually, this was not the first time that they had played together as a team. They did not take long to come up firmly erect again, not fantastically big perhaps, but having the two of them, young, slim and flawless, made up for that. Even so, while one cock in each hand is nice, two in my mouth would be better. I scuttled down the bed to be level with their hips, and managed to draw them close enough together that they understood what I proposed and came right up so I could have both.

Of course it is actually pretty difficult and hard on the jaw muscles, but I managed it for long enough until the old man wanted to see more.

The boys knew how they wanted me arranged; they spread me flat on my back and then hauled my feet right up over my head and wide apart so that the old man, sitting directly in line must have had a completely unrestricted view of me. He even reached out to prod his bony fingers into me again; first into my cunt and then, when it was all wet, he tried once more, and again with no success, to get it into my bottom. Eventually, with a burst of frustrated muttering, he nodded to the boys to carry on.

Simon – I was starting to be able to tell which was which now – settled down at the top of the bed and took over holding my legs. However, he did also kiss me, rather nice kisses actually, with enough of his tongue to be meaningful and not too much feverish dribble. He also leaned down to kiss my breasts and for all they are not the largest in the universe, they are sensitive and if someone suckles my nipples with any expertise, I quickly find myself falling into his (or her) hands. Enough so that I reached out for his cock and quickly had that back up and gorgeously erect. I was strongly tempted to take him all the way: I do like girls, but an erect cock is a compliment that cannot be misunderstood.

Meanwhile, Robert had moved down to the other end of the bed where my cunt was stretched open for the world, and seconds later, long sweeps of his tongue were running from halfway down my bottom right round the opening, across my anus, over my cunt and right up to my clit; a second time; a third. And with each new sweep, the tongue pressed slightly deeper in, now separating my lips and skimming up between them, even a little press as it passed across my anus. Then he focussed. First on my bottom, licking carefully all round the opening and his tongue pushing right at the centre with a persistence that I could not keep resisting. Eventually I felt the tip slide through and inside me, opening me and wetting me. From there he moved up to my cunt; licking over, round and along the sides until I felt myself swelling and opening.

And at that point, as he stood up, I saw that he had been working his own cock in his hand. He presented it to my cunt, pushed in and I simply devoured him. He smiled at me, leaned right down and took his brother's place in kissing me, and when my feet were released, he wrapped his arms round me and rolled me over on top of him. I must be naive because it took me a couple of moments to grasp the significance of this, and it was the feeling of Simon's hands spreading open my bottom and his tongue pushing into my anus where Robert's had recently been that alerted me. I clamped up, squeezing my bottom and started to struggle up but Robert held me tight.

'Don't struggle,' he whispered into my ear. 'Just relax. He will be very gentle.'

'But I hate that!'

'Just relax,' he repeated, and his cock began a more purposeful movement in and out of my cunt, catching somewhere wonderful inside me and, because my legs were spread so wide apart, tugging at my clit with every move.

Already the tongue in my bottom had been replaced by a finger and that, God knows how, had slipped in past my opening without any struggle, and after a few gentle rotations had slipped back out again. The old man wheeled himself closer and I felt his hand clawing across my bottom, and his finger nail now scratched at my anus before finally he got what he had been hankering for all day and he too had pushed inside, a harder and more angular intrusion than Simon's. For all that, I was quite happy to let his finger stay there as long as he liked, because when I did feel him starting to pull out, I knew the next push was going to be from Simon's cock.

It was quick, and again it was wet and slippery, so that when he laid it on me and pushed gently, I was able to cope. He slipped the tip in, withdrew, and then with a slow determination, pushed back again until almost all the head was in, and withdrew. The next time the whole head slid in and I felt my bottom close up and hug the thinner part of the shaft behind. Then he paused, giving me time to get used to that and while he paused, Robert slowly pushed in and out just below, with a soothing, calming regularity that helped to relax all of us. After this Simon pushed again, and slowly, smoothly without a break, I felt the end of his cock sliding deeper and deeper into my bottom until his pubic hair tickled my thighs and his balls nestled against me. He leaned right down, kissed the back of my neck and nuzzled into my ear.

'Well done, Milly. Now just relax.'

Between them, they rolled all three of us over so we were all on our sides and that was rather lovely: so much skin contact with Robert all down my front, Simon all down my back and me sandwiched in between. It is a gorgeously sensual and tactile position, where I could exchange deep wonderful kisses with Robert while he hugged me against him, and at the same time Simon was reaching round to stroke my nipples and then one nipple and my clit. And of course I was utterly filled: completely. The two of them started slowly, frustratingly slowly, but steadily the pace increased and we all became lost in the closeness and intimacy of it all. The old man was wheeling his way round the bed but, I soon realised, another advantage of this arrangement was that he could not get at me; I was protected front and back by one of the twins. He could probably hardly see anything except their backs, and their bottoms pushing at me in a perfectly synchronised rhythm. Maybe their bottoms were enough for him; at one stage he did pause behind Robert for some time and the sudden wince on Robert's face indicated something was going on there.

I had never done this before, although I have managed to repeat it since: I like it! And I think they liked it, and they liked me and the whole afternoon had been a succession of experiences, which had all built on top of each other so that I was more than ready for an energetic finale with one, or better still two, men who knew how to treat me. So despite occasional twinges of envy wondering what Jane might be doing with

Marianne, I was soon swept away with it all, with being the centre of their attention, with the old man still watching me being fucked, and with the simple stimulation of the two cocks penetrating me with a growing ferocity that satisfied first Simon in my bottom, Robert soon afterwards in my cunt, and finally me from both of them and Simon's fingers still on my clit.

The two of them slowly withdrew, Robert from my cunt although his cock was still quite firm, impressively so considering the pounding he had just given me, followed by Simon from my bottom. I kissed them both, kissed their cocks, even Simon's despite where it had just been, fondling them as they lay either side of me and their damp cocks subsided to the harmlessness which they had displayed before. It had been a good day, and I was feeling entirely relaxed and satisfied, ready for a bath, a drink and possibly something to eat. I sat up, heading for the shower, and caught the eye of the old man.

He was sitting there with his hands clamped round the handles of the wheelchair glaring as if everything we had done, even though it had – at least initially – been for his amusement, was offensive and demeaning. He scowled at us as we lay there and maybe we were too happy for his approval, but even so we did not deserve this. Finally he grunted at one of the boys.

'Simon! In the desk,' and he nodded towards the opposite wall. 'I should like to see her caned.'

I shot up, and even the boys exchanged anxious glances. 'Caned?' I echoed. 'Why?'

He just smiled. 'Come here my dear and let me explain.' But when I did, and my original "here" was not close enough, his hand, after one brief sweep through between my legs, came round to grasp the cheek of my bottom. 'I should like to see you caned, my dear, because you have a very skinny little bottom which will bruise quite beautifully when these boys take a couple of canes to you. Furthermore, since I get the impression this is not something to which you are accustomed, I anticipate that you will scream quite delightfully while they do it. My only regret is that I no longer have the strength to perform the task myself, but must needs rely on these two somewhat inexperienced youths to take up the role.' He saw my wild stare and for all his age and handicaps, his scrawny hand had incredible strength when he applied it, as now he did to squeezing a handful of my bottom in his long fingers. 'Oh yes, my dear, yes I am indeed what is commonly called a sadist. But then if you did not have similar leanings, you would not have come here today, would you? And it will do you good to be on the other end for once. Let us at least understand one another.' And he released me.

The boys had stayed on the bed listening to this. Now they dutifully and, I would like to think, a little reluctantly, climbed off to fetch what he required from the desk, but he must have planned this from the start for they were lying there ready: two traditional rattan canes with curved handles and long vicious stems. The boys picked one up each, examining them, weighing and balancing them thoughtfully.

'Right,' said the man. 'Bent over the end of the bed, I think.'

'How many are they going to do?' I asked, unable to take my eyes away from the two canes being turned and flexed in the boys' hands.

He hesitated a moment, considering the two of them. One of them swished his cane through the air, a screaming swoosh that anticipated what they would soon be doing to me.

'Six?' I suggested. 'Three each?'

He sniffed and turned his attention from them to me. 'Come here and turn round.' So again I attended by his side while his cruel hands grasped at my bottom and his fingers dug into me. 'Twelve from each of them. Go and bend over.'

I gasped, straightened up and turned to stare at him. 'No! Come on! I can't! I can't take twelve. I have never taken so many.'

For a minute he said nothing, peered at me, watched the boys swinging their canes as they waited to be told. 'Twelve from each of them,' he repeated, 'don't argue, and don't tell lies. Now go and bend over the bed.'

I wanted to remonstrate but in the face of his inflexibility, feared that would only increase the number. I moved across to the bed, thinking that at least the twins would not be hard on me, not after the pleasure I had just given them, but when I tried to convey my fear, neither would meet my eye. I stood up against the foot of the bed and bent over, resting my hands on the mattress.

'Lower than that, girl,' he grumbled, 'and I want your feet apart.' I turned to glare at him, but there was an eager determination in his face and I began to think he saw everything. He had seen that I preferred women, so he had let Jane go with Marianne. He had seen that I am normally dominant so he had the boys piss on me and would now have them cane me. He had seen that I disliked anal, so he had one of the twins bugger me. This would be for his pleasure, to turn me to all that I would not choose for myself. He had been right: the two of us did have similar leanings, did understand each other.

I leaned down lower and parted my feet. 'Better,' he said, and came up to feel me, to rub his hands over me, pinching at my lips, at my clit, at my bottom; pushing his fingers back into my cunt and into my bum, even though I was still wet and slimy from the twins' sperm, and even though it was now seeping out, trickling down my leg. 'Good,' he said, although I have no idea exactly what part of that had been "good". 'We will stop after each six. Off you go, boys.'

I took a deep breath and braced myself as they moved up into position. There was something especially cruel in their being entirely naked; it emphasised the horrible simplicity of the cane which each held in his fist. Worse still, as they stepped up to their places, one each side of me, they were both at least half erect again. I had hoped for a reluctance on their part which would have made them more lenient; instead, both showed clear signs of pleasure and excitement at the prospect before them.

The man had moved back but stayed directly behind me where he would have an unrestricted view of my bottom and of every stroke that landed on it. The twins took their places, the tips of the canes tap, tap, tapped on my bottom and then one of them called 'One' and the first stroke fell. It was agony: a single blazing sheet of agony across my bottom. I gasped ('two') and screamed at them but there was no response. They could see my tears ('three'), but were entirely unmoved. I tried to stand up but was simply pushed straight back down on the bed again ('four') almost falling over and struggling to make my legs work ('five'), kicking out and yelling at them to let me up ('six').

'Rest!' called the man, but I think the rest was for their benefit, not mine. The boys waited in silence but the rasp of the old man's breathing took up the space that the canes had relinquished, and after his breathing, the creak of his wheelchair as he came round to the side of the bed. 'There my dear! How's that, eh? That's something to remember!' I turned to stare at him in disbelief and found, for the first time that day, he was actually smiling: his eyes lit up, his sagging cheeks pink and flushed and he came forward, craning his face as far towards mine as he could while he reached through to grope at my breasts again. 'Very good job they are making of it. Lovely! Shall we continue?' and his chair rumbled back to the end of the bed again. 'Feet further apart, please!' he called, and when I obeyed and looked down between my own legs, I could see him hunched in that horrid chair with his stained hands in his lap, clasping at the blanket in their fervour. Each side of him stood the boys, like bearers on a coat of arms: identical figures, identical canes, identical stance, identical fierce erections.

'Right, carry on.'

I felt so utterly betrayed ('seven'); there was no concern for me in this, just the full intent ('eight') to do as they had been told. Not ten minutes before we had been lovers ('nine') and now they were just as happy to inflict unbearable pain ('ten') as they had been the gentlest kisses ('eleven'). But they were his friends, not mine, would do his bidding, not mine ('and twelve').

'And rest!' the old man called and wheeled himself up to look again at my bottom. I felt his fingers on me, tracing the lines and then of course because I was available to him, digging his fingers up into my cunt again, chuckling at my wetness and the ease with which it could enter. He wheeled himself round to my head, offered me his finger to lick and when I refused just wiped it across my lips and cheeks. 'Juicy little thing, aren't you?' I made no response, so he chuckled again. 'Carry on lads; good and hard.'

This time he did not move away, stayed with one hand clamped round my breast while the boys counted through from twelve to eighteen and I wept all the time and cried afresh at every stroke, no longer able even to pretend any dignity or resolve.

When they stopped at eighteen, he stayed there a while, smiling at me, those horrid fingers still toying with my nipple as he watched me trying to get my breath and compose myself. But he was too eager to see the results to wait there for long and shoved himself back, rolling away down to the end where he sat chuckling like a miser with a windfall. 'I was right, my dear. You mark beautifully. Last six, boys.' And the chair rumbled back against the wall.

I felt the initial taps and determined to close my mind but failed as soon as the first cane landed on me. There was to be no sympathy and they would make the last six even harder than the rest. I gripped the bedding and counted each stroke in my head; as each one hit me it was one less before the end until there were only three, only two, only one, and finally, exquisitely, none. The boys dropped away and I crawled up onto the bed, curled in a ball to let my feelings restabilise, to let the tears finish and to return to the person I had been.

He sat there unmoving, unblinking while I cried and it must have been a good five minutes while the boys huddled in the corner, each of them still clutching his cane in one hand; each of them slowly stroking his brother's cock with the other hand. I heard them whispering occasionally although they seemed now, too late, somewhat awed by what they had done.

Finally the old man sniffed and wheeled away. 'Simon?

Go and ask Marianne to bring that girl down here. There is something I should like to try.'

CARA'S TALE: THE PATRICKS

I sat holding my head in my hands so that nobody else would be able to see that I could not keep my eyes open and convinced myself that, from a distance at least, I looked engrossed in the spreadsheet I had pulled up on my screen. In fact I could not focus on the jittering screen: the tiny numbers were swirling in and out of focus with every wave of nausea that washed across my stomach, and my head pounded slowly and deeply with every weak beat of my pulse. No real work would be possible for several hours, and in the meantime I could let myself be distracted by one of the cleaners, a squat tubby woman who was steadily working her way nearer to me, dragging a squat tubby vacuum cleaner along behind her. She looked to be another "fifty", and I winced at the recollection.

$\sim$

Yesterday had been Greg's birthday, twenty-four no less, and that was what started this running. Greg, Liz and I share a flat and so we all went out to celebrate, even though it was a Wednesday, Liz bringing along her boyfriend, Matt, to make up the four. We started with cocktails, then pizzas, then more drinks, (quite a few more drinks actually), and then headed for the clubs.

But Greg had never been inside a lap-dancing club and Matt would not admit to having been either, so off we went. It was weird, actually: seeing all those girls, most of them no older than me, doing things that I wouldn't have dreamed of doing in all my life. I mean they don't take everything off (at least not up on the stage when they are dancing round those shiny firemen's poles), but they also offered what they called 'private dances' and then, well, you know, everything comes off.

How do I know that? Well, we were sitting at a table and one of the girls (she said her name was Jade but I bet it was really Gladys or something), came round and asked Greg if he wanted a private dance, downstairs. Greg did: that was obvious, but he's a shy lad, Greg: rather sweet really and never having seen one before, he was nervous. But the girl was very attractive, tall with wild golden hair and a friendly little smile that stirred temptation on his face. She was trying to entice him, running her hands through his hair and down his chest and we were all egging him on but the enthusiasm was still not quite able to overcome the fears. He asked Liz to go with him, and when she refused, he asked me. Jade said that was okay, as long as we paid her an extra ten pounds and so I agreed. I admit I was curious, and I just knew that I'd never have that kind of chance anywhere else.

She led us downstairs to a cluster of little curtained booths – some of them obviously occupied – and pulled a curtain over the doorway. Inside was dark and sinful with red lights and red decor, and while I sat to one side she found some music, put Greg into a straight-backed chair and told him he mustn't touch her at all. Then the music started and she began to dance.

Almost straightaway she swirled up close to him, running her hands all over herself and leaning close in as she began steadily unbuttoning her short black blouse. It was quickly peeled away, then the skirt and after a few more turns and spins, the bra. Again she leant in close to him, her breasts almost touching Greg's face as he sat with a fixed grin on his face, hardly daring to move or even to look. She dropped her foot down onto his knee, rubbing her hands down the whole length of her leg, before lifting it right up to rest her foot on his shoulder while she rolled down one stocking, then the other foot on the other shoulder for the other stocking, drawing each one slowly down her long legs and as slowly across his chubby shining face. With only a tiny pair of knickers, she turned her back to him and bending straight from the waist, peeled them down, her bottom stuck out so far that her cheeks were inches from Greg's nose.

Then she stood up, completely naked at last, and turned slowly to show the only part of her that we hadn't seen when she had been dancing on the stage upstairs: the little narrow stripe of curly fluff at the base of her tummy. For a while she kept covering herself with her hands, teasing Greg with brief glimpses but then she finally relented and let him see everything, even lifting her foot up onto his shoulder again as his eyes widened at the totality of her exposure.

She leaned down to murmur in his ear. 'Do you like that, Honey?' and ruffled her hand through his hair and grinned over her shoulder at me. I don't think I was looking too obvious but her glance rested on me a little longer and the smile stayed. 'Do you want to see too?'

But she already knew the answer that I couldn't bring myself to make and she didn't wait. She just walked over in front of me, blatantly naked, swinging her hips and round breasts until, standing directly in front of me, she raised one leg straight up until her ankle was resting on my shoulder just as she had with Greg, then she simply leant back. I could still feel her eyes on me but mine were drawn. I couldn't keep from looking down between her legs at the private bit, the bit we don't even talk about between other girls, or at least not until we know each other very well. And I stared at what she was showing me, and as I stared her hand slithered down and I was mesmerised by those long fingers as they reached down to open herself up. Forefinger and third finger on her lips, while her middle finger skittered across the top of her clit, circling a couple of times round the point and briefly pulling the skin back. I had never seen another girl's sex as clearly as that, displayed just for me, right in front of me for the sole reason that she knew I wanted to see it. I was ashamed of my interest, and yet when that long slender finger pushed on and curled down to dive up inside her, I felt it almost as if it was pushing into me. And I think she knew that. For a moment the finger stayed there, moving fractionally to and fro before she withdrew it again, shining now, and then her hand came up to my cheek, two of her fingers running down to my chin and although that middle finger didn't touch me, it came so close that there was no doubting the scent of her arousal as it passed close in front of me.

Then she moved back to Greg, giving him much of the same treatment, spinning close round him but always just not touching until the music finally ended.

Upstairs the other two asked what had happened, Liz with more genuine interest than Matt so I was further convinced he knew a great deal more than he was admitting. At one point Jade came over to us again and sat with us. I wanted to go with her again, and I think Liz would have done too, but we were both too ashamed to ask. We talked for a little while until she had to leave, but a few minutes later another man was trailing along behind her, smirking as she led him by the hand down to the lower floor.

We stayed there, drank a whole lot more and were still there when the club shut, when the lights came up, the staff asked us to leave and the cleaners appeared, hoovering round our feet and grumbling at our dawdling when Liz and I linked arms and staggered to the toilets on the way out. As we sat in adjacent cubicles, I remember a sequence of ideas coming stumbling through a vodka haze, the sort of haze which has obscured so much that what does emerge seems all the more crystal clear and profound. One discovery – as we giggled our way towards the door – was that all cleaners are identical and fifty. Identical: as if they are popped out of the same pepper-pot mould, fat faces, short round bodies with thick red legs, and dreadful pink and blue print dresses. Fifty: being age, girth and cigarettes per day. Yes, in daylight it does not seem so clever; at the time, Liz and I were all for recording a song on the subject until the lads went all prissy and told us to shut up in case the cleaners overheard us. Honestly! We all piled back to Matt's flat because it was closest, had a take-away pizza and then the three of us went home.

I was horribly hung over the next morning and felt even less ready to face the day when I realised that I'd left my purse at Matt's. I rang straightaway, but he'd already left and when I finally reached him on his mobile he said he'd look for it that evening and bring it over. In the end I had to borrow some money off Liz just to get to work, and when I got there I had to spend quarter of an hour filling out a temporary pass and explaining to the Hitler on the desk that I was the same person he had seen coming into the building every day for the last eighteen months.

There was an urgent report which Mr Pettiman was waiting for, but I was honestly in no condition to do anything. My head was pounding, the world was spinning and I managed simply to fill in the day looking busy and fussing about just enough to keep any of the partners from noticing anything, but it was not until late afternoon, when most people were starting to go home, that I began to feel well enough and sufficiently clear headed to begin putting down any words on paper.

Which was fine until the bloody cleaners turned up again: identical figures clattering about and ignoring my pointed looks, loud sighs and determined concentration as they fussed about and sprayed and wiped and cleaned and vacuumed everywhere.

I had been staring at one of them as her Vacuum Waltz brought her right round to our corner of the office, the Minor Litigation Team, until she was cheerfully dragging her grinning red dalek round my workstation and even banging into my desk.

'Sorry, love.'

My chair,

'Sorry, love.'

And the cabinets,

'Sorry, love.'

But she didn't feel any remorse at all and it came to me finally – as the alcohol subsided at last, almost eighteen hours after my last drink – that this was no accident. She was deliberately staying right round my desk while everybody else packed up, closed down their computers and offered cheery good nights.

And I started to get annoyed. 'Haven't you finished this bit? You'll wear a hole in the carpet.'

'Sorry, love.' A glance. 'Bit hung over are we?'

'No!' I responded with the immediate denial of all those in my condition since time immemorial.

'Heavy night?'

'No!'

'Hung over?' she repeated as if we hadn't just had this conversation.

'No!'

'Nice club that, though. Very friendly.'

'Which one?' My question came automatically but suspicions were stirring.

'The What's It; you know: *Star Burst*. That one.'

'I don't think I know it.'

She finally turned the vacuum off and scanned round the empty office before turning back to me. 'Oh yes. Yes, you do, Love. You know it well enough, 'cos you were there last night. You and your three young friends. I seen you.' She reached into the pocket of her apron and pulled out a packet of cigarettes.

'Um, this is a No Smoking office.'

'Well, this ain't a No Smoking cleaner. Besides, the office is shut.' There was something cold in her voice suddenly, a determination and assurance that hadn't been there previously. 'This club: I clean there an' all, you see.'

'Do you?'

'Oh yes.' A long drag on the cigarette turned into a fit of coughing. 'Yes I do. You probably didn't notice because we all look the same, us cleaners, don't we? Like pepper-pots?' For a moment she stared through narrow eyes, and then the vacuum started up again, banged round the chairs and desks and this time I lifted my feet to let her by. The pale pastel apron was drawn up prim and tight, tied somewhere between her round stomach and wide chest.

'So?' I asked.

'So?' The vacuum went off. 'So nothing, I don't suppose. It's a free country. Only I don't suppose the bosses would be all that keen to hear you was at some lap dancing club. And then so drunk you could hardly keep to your own two feet.' The cloth flicked across a few more flat surfaces. 'Would they? They never like that sort of thing.'

'I'm sorry?'

'Professional decorum, isn't that what they was calling it in the papers last week?'

Yes, she was right about that. The tabloids had been furiously brewing up a scandal about a crowd of Hurray Henries from some finance house who had grossly misbehaved in a club not that dissimilar from the one where we had been, but the idea had obviously lingered in this woman's head and her words had been enunciated with the clarity of rote, of incomprehension: learned for a purpose, not expressed as an opinion.

'I think that was rather different.'

'Perhaps.' She sniffed, pulled a huge aerosol can out of the pouch of her apron and blasted another hole in the ozone layer. 'You can never tell really, can you?'

'In any case,' I said trying to sound decisive, 'I don't suppose they will ever know about it.' I tried to sound off hand. 'I don't suppose they go there.'

'No. That's right. They probably won't. Least, not unless someone tells them.' She blasted some more of the vile-smelling polish across Frankie's desk and stood labouriously rubbing it in. I'd worked in this office for almost two years and in all that time had not exchanged more than three words at a time with any of the cleaners; now this. I studied her as she stood there; over forty, certainly, and under seventy, probably, but it was impossible to narrow the range any more precisely than that; fifty, for all I know. Her own taste in clothing was obscured by the uniform; her hair was mostly shades of grey with the residue of what must once have been a dramatic fiery red, but why was she stopping to chat now?

'Anyway, I've got quite a bit of work to do, so I must get on.' I gathered up the analysis charts and stood up.

'No,' she continued, 'not unless someone tells them.' Her look, stance, slow draw on her cigarette were all designed to challenge me.

'What are you suggesting?'

'Me? Nothing, love. Nothing at all.'

'Are you trying to blackmail me?'

'Blackmail? No, nothing like that.' She paused, but didn't carry on with her ostentatious cleaning. Instead she just watched me for a while so that I knew this wasn't over. 'You're Cara, aren't you? Cara Mackintosh?' She pulled out a tobacco tin, firmly stubbed the cigarette out on the lid and dropped it all back into her apron pocket.

'Yes.' There was nothing exactly sinister about her knowing my name but that didn't much help. There was no need for her to know it unless she had made an effort to find out and that in itself was uncomfortable. I didn't know her name.

'You've lost your pass, haven't you?' And now she did turn away, unconvincingly busy at the dusting.

'Have I?' No response, but I did wonder how the gossip spread like that from the receptionist to the cleaners. 'Well, not exactly no. I left my purse at a friend's flat last night, that's all. Although I'm not sure that is really any concern of yours.'

'No, you didn't. You dropped it in the club' and that was when it all began to spill out. That she'd found my purse at the club, recognised the office pass and rather than hand it in there had decided she would do me a favour and return it directly. Well, no, she hadn't actually brought it with her, but it was quite safe back at her flat and I could nip round and pick it up after work. 'I should be home by 8.30 latest.'

So I got the address – and her name – and finally found Mrs Patrick's flat on the fourth floor of a small block in one of the mass of 1960s council estates that cover much of that part of north London. The lift stank of urine and the stair well was only slightly better, but I trusted to that anyway. On various floors music or televisions were blaring, sometimes drowned out by the shouts, cries and arguments that echoed through the block. The fourth floor was refreshingly quiet.

I was welcomed into a cluttered living room dominated by a vast television screen, thankfully mute, although a silent succession of over-excited game show applicants continued to run wildly around a garish stage.

'Cup of tea, love?' But a mug was being pushed into my hand before I could decline. 'Chuck that on the floor.' She nodded her head towards an unopened carton containing two dozen bottles of supermarket baby-lotion that occupied the sofa. 'Them's our Karen's. She's pregnant.' Her explanation offered me a vision of "Our Karen" craving baby lotion sandwiches, but my confusion must have shown. 'She's dead worried about getting stretch marks so keeps coating herself in that stuff.' She sniffed. 'I don't suppose all that lot'll make no difference, but she reckons it will.' She settled down in the chair opposite me, lit up a cigarette which immediately set her coughing, lit it a second time, and stared over her tea mug for a long minute. 'So, what goes on at these clubs then?'

'Oh, those.' I caught up with her. 'Well, you know, the usual things I suppose.' I couldn't see why she was asking me: I mean she must have some idea, she had been working there for heaven's sake. 'When is Karen's baby due?'

'They dance about and that, the girls, do they?'

'Well, yes.'

'But with no clothes on?'

'That's right.'

'Nothing at all?'

'Well, on the stage they keep their, you know, their knickers on, but downstairs, for what they call "private dances", they don't.'

'You seen one of them, have you?'

'Yes, actually. You see my friend wanted me to stay with him and so I saw...'

'So...' another fit of coughing. 'So, tell me what happens there then.'

It was bizarre sitting in this poky little flat telling some woman whom I had scarcely met about the goings on at a west-end pole-dancing club. And this was more than casual enquiry: it was genuine interest, but why? I could hardly think she was getting off on it. After all, she must have been at least fifty, and without being too catty about it, she didn't look to be someone who took a great deal of interest or care in their appearance. If she was hoping for a job, she had left it a little late. Nevertheless, I answered her questions, outlined what had happened and she listened intently to the end.

'I see.' She finished her tea. 'So, they do take everything off at the end then?'

'Oh yes.'

'And like, you know, show off what they got?'

'Yes.'

'I see.' She put the mug down. 'I reckon my Gavin would be interested in that.'

'Gavin?'

'Gavin: my lad. Well, to be quite truthful, he's really my Tracey's lad, that's my eldest, but since she buggered off, I been looking after both of them: Karen and Gavin. Brought them up from babies, I did.'

'I see.'

'Yeah, and I reckon Gavin'd like to see that.'

'Would he?' I asked, because her comment seemed to be waiting for a reply.

'Yes. He don't get out much, you see. Spends most of his time on that computer of his. Never meets any real friends. Just doing that "surfing" most of the time. Least, that's what he calls it, but I reckon he's looking at saucy pictures a goodish bit of it.'

'I see.' But I didn't really. I had no idea where this was leading, but there was an underlying seriousness in her tone that convinced me it was leading somewhere, and it didn't feel like anywhere that I would want to go. In the silence that followed, while I tried to find a way of changing the subject, of collecting my purse and getting out, she suddenly bellowed over her shoulder.

'Gavin? Come out here a minute!' She sniffed. 'Yes. I reckon he'd like that.'

'Well it's not a private club: anybody can go in.'

'Oh no! Not Gavin. I mean he's still at college and anyway, no, he wouldn't go there. He'd need someone to show him.'

Gavin himself emerged a minute later, a caricature of a computer geek. His eyes, peering out from behind thick black-rimmed glasses, stared at me as if visitors were a rarity, certainly young female ones. His freckled skin was as pale as paint, except for blotches in the centre of each cheek which blushed a fiery red as he licked his lips, pushing back the mass of unruly ginger curls, and sizing me up. He stopped, his shoulders hunched, hands in his pockets, and couldn't say anything.

'Hello, Gavin.' I tried.

'Hello,' he mumbled back, still standing there, still peering but his feet, now shuffling nervously.

'I'm Cara.'

'Yeah. I know.'

I don't believe the debate would have developed much beyond that, but it did not get a chance. At that point we heard a rattling of keys at the door and "Our Karen" came waddling in, as massively pregnant as any woman I have ever seen. With a candy-stripe smock drawn tight across the vast lump in front of her, she was so unambiguously maternal and fruitful that some primitive nurturing instinct was awakened, an empathy of one woman for another at this special time. She flopped down on the sofa next to me; Gavin, I realized, had escaped back to his room under cover of her arrival.

She pushed her hand back through the untidy tangle of reddish brown hair. 'Right that's it. I'm not going out again till this bloody baby's born.'

'When is it due?' I asked by way of making conversation.

'Was due over a week ago; they're gonna do something if it don't come by Monday.'

'You rest dear. You deserve it. Cara, dear, why don't you make her a nice cuppa, eh?'

'Me?'

'Yes, dear. You know how, don't you?'

'Well yes, but...'

'And you're almost like one of the family now, so you won't mind doing your turn in the kitchen, will you?'

It seemed easier to comply than to argue, and I heard them chattering as I waited for the kettle to boil. To be precise, Mrs Patrick was chattering while Karen was perpetually complaining about one thing or another. They were still at it when I took the mugs through.

'Cara, love, you don't mind helping Karen with her skin cream, do you? Only I've been on my feet all day and I'm that tired I don't think I could stand up for another minute. You are a love. Take your tea through.'

I had no time to object before Karen had hauled herself up onto her feet and started moving, so I simply trailed along. It was strange following her: we were not so different in age, almost exactly the same height, only she was at least twice the bulk, round the waist obviously, but also round the breasts and the bum. She waddled down to her bedroom with me following on behind, almost jealous that she, undeniably and magnificently, had achieved her biological purpose as a woman while I was still flirting in night clubs.

We passed a tightly closed door from behind which explosions and machine guns showed the world was being either saved or destroyed. "Gavin" said a small china plaque; "Keep Out" said a hand written addition.

At first glance there appeared to be only two objects in Karen's bedroom: the first was a poster of some red-shirted football team taking up almost the whole of one wall; the second was a double bed taking up almost the whole of the floor. Its pink duvet was buried under a mound of teddy-bears, dolls and a variety of other unrecognisable furry animals.

'Come in,' she said, and pushed the door closed as I squeezed past, squeezed past her and then squeezed past the end of the bed. 'It's so bloody small, this flat. There's no room for nothing.' She put her tea by the bed.

'I've got a towel and that, what I use to stop getting the stuff all on the bed cover,' and she started spreading out a vast orange beach towel with "Malaga" scrawled across it. That completed, she plonked down on the corner of the bed.

'Strewth.' After a few deep sighs, she leaned forward to study first her feet and then me. 'You wouldn't undo my shoes, would you love? Only I don't bend in the middle like I used to.'

I unbuckled them, tatty and insubstantial sandals, and pulled them off as she heaved herself back to her feet. 'The cream's on the side there,' and she nodded at the bottle. 'There's more in the lounge.'

It was a large bottle, at least a quarter full. 'This will surely be enough, won't it?'

She frowned. 'Doubt it. We'll see.'

'How much do you use?' I asked, half laughing.

'Oh quite a bit I suppose. You need to put it everywhere or you end up with them stretch marks all over. Oh, it's all right,' she added. 'Ian nicks them from work so it don't cost nothing.'

And then she started unzipping her dress and pulling it off her arms. I politely turned away and pretended to read the label on the baby lotion as she undressed. For a few seconds she was a billowing mass of pink stripes while she dragged the smock over her head, and then from the corner of my eye, I saw her huge pale body appear, crossed at hips and bust by thick black lines of her knickers and bra.

She dropped the dress on a chair and as I moved to help her stretch out on the bed, she started fiddling with the front of the bra and then that was opened up and fell away. I tried not to stare as her breasts were revealed; I tried but failed; failed completely. They were so full and hard: a lovely pure white skin stretched taut as a drum across round breasts which proudly revelled in their purpose. But what really took my breath was their centres: huge, circular rings, wide and dark, almost dangerous in their intensity and topped with such proud nipples, rigid as fingertips even before she had touched them, rich and dark as plums, pushing exuberantly out from their great vermillion saucers. The bra dropped on top of the dress.

'Huh! That's better,' and for a moment she ran her hand up over her breasts and I wondered whether she was going to want baby lotion on them too. I had never touched another woman's breasts, but this would be different, and I didn't think I would mind if she did ask me to. If the opportunity arose, I could even suggest it myself.

And I must have been staring, because Karen suddenly looked up at me. 'Yeah, quite a sight aren't they? I used to be a C, now I'm a G!' Her hand abstractedly ran across them again, sweeping over the nipples which sprang back up as the palm passed. 'Still, I suppose they'll go back down again. Bloody well hope so. Don't think I could cope with all the stares otherwise.'

And then she calmly hooked her fingers into the tops of her knickers and started pushing them down her legs. I had certainly not been expecting this, and with the two of us squashed into that tiny room, we were almost touching but it seemed to make no difference at all to her. She simply let the knickers drop to the floor, crawled up onto the bed and flopped down on her stomach, squirming down to get comfortable. I picked up the bottle, sat down on the bed beside her and briefly she turned her head back to look at me.

'You may want to take off your sweater. Save getting cream on the sleeves.'

'Oh I expect I'll...' I started.

'Suit yourself,' and she turned her face back down into the pillow.

'Where do you want it?' I asked.

'Like I said: everywhere. All over my back and down the backs of my legs.'

I poured the first pool of lotion into the middle of her back and started rubbing it in gently in spiral swirls from the slight hollow of her back up to her shoulders. For several minutes she said nothing, but a series of regular deep sighs indicated she was contented. 'You're dead good at this, you know. You had training?'

I laughed. 'No, not at all.'

'You're dead good. You wanna go and ask at one of those health places. I bet they'd give you a job,' and after a pause, 'Even one of them legit ones, I reckon.'

I moved down to her legs, first one, starting cautiously at the thigh and working my way down to the ankle, and then the other.

'Right,' I said, 'that's ...'

'Don't forget my bum,' she interrupted.

'Your...?'

'Yeah. That needs some too. I mean, would you want stretch marks across your bum?'

I poured a pool into my palm and then carefully touched her bottom. Her skin felt cool, almost cold, compared to the rest of her, and an even paler patch showed where she had been sunbathing in the past, evidently in a costume which would be absurd on her present size. I lay my palms flat, one in the centre of each buttock, but they were really too large for that, and so I concentrated first on one and then on the other, running small circles across the soft cheeks. It may have been my imagination, but her thighs seemed to have moved apart a little so that as my hands pressed in, her pussy was opened up, offering occasional glimpses of the dark centre deep inside. If you could forget that this was somebody's bottom, it felt quite pleasant: firm and bouncy to the touch and yet smooth. I was rather sorry to finish.

But then she turned over.

I didn't know where to begin on this side. Her stomach would certainly need some, but how low down would I be expected to go? She had shaved her pubic hair but not recently, leaving a uniform unruly stubble that I really did not fancy having to touch. But what about her breasts? Even lying on her back, they pointed up to the ceiling in a way which looked entirely unreal, but the nipples, and their aureolas, were as dark and magnificent as ever.

I started with a leg, carefully at the front of the thigh, but as soon as I touched her, she unashamedly moved her legs apart, exposing the slim groove running down between her legs. I obeyed the invitation to do the insides of her thighs and tried to keep my eyes away from the tightly closed pussy as I worked my way down to her feet. After the second leg, I was faced with her stomach.

It felt strange: not soft and fat but with hard lumps inside, which I could feel moving from time to time. I poured some lotion onto her, around the little dome of her navel, and started working it steadily into her skin over the surprisingly flat top and down the steep sides.

That was when my eye caught a very faint movement. The door was now half open and Gavin was standing there, quietly in the dim corridor peering in through his thick round glasses. He was keeping very still, entirely quiet, but even when he saw that I had spotted him, he didn't look the least embarrassed. At first I couldn't decide whether to point out to Karen that her brother was there or not, but when he continued to stand there, I felt I must.

'Hello, Gavin,' I said.

Karen immediately lifted her head up to peer down over her lump at him, but she made no move to cover herself. 'What do you want, Gavin?'

'Nothing. I'm just watching.'

'Watching what?'

'What you're doing.'

For a second neither of them said anything, just stared at each other with a surprisingly detached patience. 'Well don't touch anything,' Karen said and lay down again. I continued rubbing the lotion into her stomach, but her words swirled in my head. First what she had said: what did 'anything' mean? Her possessions? That was a normal command for any sister to issue to a younger brother, but I was not sure that was the whole meaning here.

And second, what she had not said. What would most girls have done if their brother had come creeping up to their bedroom door while they were lying naked on the bed? Yet she had not been shocked or even surprised at his arrival; she had not even sent him away.

These thoughts were still going round my head when I heard Mrs Patrick come stamping down the passage. 'Here, Gavin, what are you up to?' And there wasn't even any outrage from her. 'You leave Karen alone. She's got enough to worry about without you hanging about.' She had reached the doorway now and shooed Gavin away as she crowded in with us and pushed the door shut behind her. 'Little pervert.'

For a while she stood with her arms folded watching while I continued massaging across Karen's mound of a stomach, reaching right round to the sides, as far up as her ribs and as far down as I decently could, although a couple of times my fingertips did touch the tips of her pubic hair. But the minutes were going by, and I felt I had done this enough, but how could I stop without having to move on to something else? I didn't know what would be expected of me next. Mrs Patrick saved me.

'You done her breasts yet, love?'

'Er, no.' That at least gave me the answer as to whether I was expected to.

'I'll give you a hand, then.' She sat down on the other side and squeezed a great pool of lotion onto the top of the breast nearest to her, then the same onto the one my side. 'There! Such a size these are now, you need a decent amount.' Then she started smearing it round, using both hands to encircle the huge breast, and rubbing in the lotion with a brisk, almost brutal, determination that set the girl's entire body on the wobble. I didn't dare risk such ferocity and was rather more gentle in handling her breasts, lifting them carefully to apply lotion right into the crease underneath. Mrs Patrick had quickly cleared the white streaks, but immediately reached for the bottle again and squeezed a second swirl right onto the dark pointed nipple. This time she was less rough, almost tender, as her fingertips ran little circles round the rich tight peak and slowly the lotion disappeared. Following her example, I also homed in on the nipple. Karen was lying back now, her eyes tight shut, but little puffs of breath from her half-open mouth showed she was thoroughly content. Eventually the breast Mrs Patrick was working at showed no traces of lotion and she stepped back, wiping her hands on the towel.

'That'll do for now. I need to get on: Ian'll be home in a while. Come through when you're done, Cara, love.'

Left alone, I finished that breast, slowly circling the hard dark nipple until there was no trace of the lotion left. One final circle round the full smooth curve. 'There.'

'And my front,' she said.

'What?'

'My front. My fanny.' And she casually opened her legs wide, no longer concealing anything.

'I can't do that!'

'Why not?' and she genuinely seemed not to understand. She even opened her legs a little wider so that I could see her outer lips slowly peeling open, and the thin ridges inside them.

'Why not? I should have thought that was obvious. I mean I just can't.'

'My Nan always does my front.'

'She does?'

'Yes,' and she lay back again, her hands clasped together just above the mound of her stomach, and calmly waited for me to begin.

So I squeezed another small pool of lotion into my hand and began rubbing my open palm across the triangle of coarse stubble at the front, and then finally down between her legs. She felt warm, with a feathery softness like velvet except where the sharp stubble suddenly broke through and even that softened as the lotion soaked in. Down the insides of her thighs, the tendons pulled taut beneath the warm skin. At the back I was reaching as far as her bottom; at the front I was well into her pubic hair.

Without warning Karen lifted her head. 'Nan?' she bellowed down the hall. 'Can you come and show her how to do this? She's not doing it right,' and a few seconds later Mrs Patrick came pushing in again.

'What's the trouble then, love?'

'Can you show her how to do my front? She's doing it all wrong.'

I got a quick disapproving glance while Mrs Patrick shook her head, and then she carefully closed the door before coming back to where I was sitting.

'Here, move over.' She picked up the bottle of lotion, squeezed a good swirl into her palm and rubbed it smoothly between Karen's legs. For a few minutes she simply continued rubbing gently backwards and forwards in slow steady sweeps until the whole area glistened with the lotion. Then she stopped, squeezed a small amount onto the tip of one finger and leaned forward. Delicately she peeled open the puffy outer lips and began applying the lotion directly to the girl's clitoris: deliberately, unmistakeably, directly to the little swelling of her clitoris. To start with the finger tip drew smooth circles round and round, but then began slipping up and over the point and then down along the ridges of her smaller lips. I didn't know what to do: whether I should stay or go, because there was no question what was happening. Mrs Patrick was simply and blatantly masturbating the girl. The fact that I was standing right there watching seemed to make no difference. The fact that this was her own granddaughter did not change things either.

I didn't know where to look. I had never seen anything like this before in my life: I had never seen a girl masturbating, or seen two people involved in anything so unambiguously intimate and sexual.

Karen's hands were now resting over her bloated breasts, her thumbs occasionally flicking at the nipples, but mostly just holding them, cradling and nursing them as if they were injured. She had her eyes shut again, but her head rolled slowly from side to side, and her breaths were steadily getting shorter and shorter while her grandmother continued the same gentle stroking. Between her legs, the lips of Karen's pussy were filling and swelling, and little tremors rippled down her thighs. Mrs Patrick was now using two or sometimes three fingers to run back and forth over the lips, smoothly and sweetly running the full length, but sometimes pausing briefly either at the back, where her middle finger tickled gently at the dark centre of Karen's bottom, or at the very top, where that same finger teased round her clitoris, pressing it down or running fast circles round its peak. And once, just once, stopping to pull at the very tip of skin until the girl's clitoris was exposed, bare and ready, pink and shining, and visible to us both.

She went back to those same slow sweeps the full length

of Karen's pussy, and then for the first time she stopped in the middle and two fingers curled round to bury deep inside her, pushing as hard and deep as she could make them while Karen groaned out her pleasure and pressed her thighs even flatter on the bed, lifting and offering herself up, opening herself as wide as she could, panting and groaning ever deeper.

Suddenly she reached out and her hand grabbed my wrist, almost making me scream in surprise, and I realized it was me she was staring at. Her mouth was open now, her tongue dry but running across her lips as the breaths came in quick short gasps, panting, sighing and heaving, lifting those huge breasts and rolling as she entirely lost control. The hand that was not wrapped round my arm had grabbed her own breast and was pulling at it as if she would tear off her own nipple, stretching and squeezing so that I could hardly bear to watch. But it was not for long.

'Oh God!' and the grip on my arm clamped still tighter. 'Oh God! Oh God!' And her whole body shook from one end to the other, her face deepening to a red almost as dark as her nipples, her heels drumming on her mattress and her eyes now rolling back till they had practically disappeared.

And me? Well bizarrely I was torn. I had never seen any girl having an orgasm before and so seeing this, and the unquestionable power of her response, was staggering. So, at one level I was intrigued, feeling myself almost distant, observing the impact of so patently pleasurable and pervasive an event. Yet there was also another level: this was the most powerful sexual experience I had ever witnessed, and it would be silly to pretend I was not moved by that. And not 'moved' as an abstract emotion, but stirred and inspired and stimulated and, yes, for Christ's sake, excited. Jealous, even. I wanted to be that person who experienced that depth of arousal and satisfaction. Not only because my love life was – just at that time – rather barren, but because this was something for anybody to wish for. And there was a third aspect too. I had been the one who started that massage of her body: of her back, her bottom, even her breasts. It was my hand she had reached for in that final moment of need. I was not entirely an outsider, and I could feel myself a participant both in the provision and, at an inexplicable level, the experience of that total climax.

So I was torn, and probably looked it, felt myself standing there like an idiot when there was certainly a 'right thing' to say at that point, but I did not know what that might be. Karen seemed to be waiting, but when I said nothing – and perhaps my total bewilderment showed on my face – she turned away and released my arm.

Her grandmother smoothed back her hair off her face and Karen smiled back, squirmed contentedly. 'Thanks, Nan. You're the best.' She reached out, took Mrs Patrick's hand and squeezed it. 'I might just have a bit of a rest now.'

'You do that, love. You deserve it after working all day.' Then she leaned down again and kissed her, quite quickly, but the kiss was straight on the girl's mouth, and as she started to straighten up, Karen suddenly looped an arm round her shoulders and pulled her in again for a second kiss.

'Love you, Nan.'

Back in the living room, Mrs Patrick began gathering up the mugs which littered most of the room. 'You'll want to wash your hands; that bloody stuff gets everywhere. The bathroom's through there.'

I did wash my hands and I had a pee, and if I had been at

home, I would not have stopped at that. Washing my hands had not helped ease the stickiness between my legs, and nothing would drive out the image of Karen lying there, offering her self up to her grandmother's caress and squeezing my wrist as she groaned her climax into the pillow. I wanted to get home and hurried back to the living room. 'If I could just collect my purse now, I'll get out of your way.'

'Don't rush off just yet, love. Have another cup of tea. Besides, we was talking about them clubs and what goes on there.'

'Yes, well I think we had rather finished that, hadn't we?'

'No, love. We hadn't. You see I do think Gavin would like to learn about all that stuff: girls and that. But I can't just send him off down somewhere like that. For a start off, he'd get lost.'

At last I felt I was beginning to understand. 'Mrs Patrick, are you asking me to take Gavin down to that club? Because if so...'

'Oh no. No. Not that.' Then she looked me straight in the face. 'I just reckon you could help him a bit. So that he could see what it's all about.'

'Help him?'

'That's right. Show him.'

'Show him?' I was utterly lost.

She nodded. 'That's right! You know, show him what it's all about.'

'I'm sorry, Mrs Patrick, I'm not following you at all.' But that was not totally true; a suspicion was growing that I was not ready to face.

'You see, he's not really very good with girls, Gavin isn't. Well, you seen him; not London's most thrilling man, bless him. Not had no experience, you see, and I think all he needs is to see it for himself and he'd be more sure. I mean he knows the theory and that, seen his sister walking around and knows where all the bits are, but he don't really know the real stuff as it were.' I said nothing. 'Know what I mean?'

'No, actually, I don't.'

'I thought you might show him. Show him where everything is. Like them girls do in that club.'

'You mean...?' I had been right: this was what she had meant. 'You've got to be joking! What do you think I am?'

Her smile crumpled away as if it had been screwed up and discarded. 'Well I think, frankly now love, frankly, I think that you're someone as could show our Gavin a thing or two and perhaps get him out of himself a bit. I mean you've been around yourself, I reckon. Seen plenty, done a fair bit, so it wouldn't be no problem to you. Then I could give you back your pass and we'd be square.'

I stared at her, unable to take in exactly what I was hearing, but realising that what she was implying was that if I refused, I'd be going home without my purse and tomorrow she'd hand it in at work with a highly detailed explanation of where she'd found it. But she was still speaking. 'I don't mean you'd have to do a dance, you know: proper like. I just mean if you could let him have a look. You know, introduce him as you might say.'

'Have a look?'

'That's right.'

'You mean take my clothes off?'

'That's it, yes.' She nodded, watching me closely. 'Just so he could have a look. You know, not do anything. Just look.'

I stared. 'You want me to let him see me naked? You are joking, aren't you?' She didn't sound as if she was, but honestly!

'Oh no. I mean, it wouldn't cost you nothing and it would be so good for him. He wouldn't touch you or nothing, just have a look.' Whereas I could still find no words to say, she didn't seem to know how to stop. 'Then, like I say, you could have your pass back and we'd be square.'

'My pass?'

'Your purse,' she corrected.

'I see.' I considered the ultimatum that I was being offered; she must have thought all this out much more carefully than I had given her credit for, and though it chilled me, I still had images dancing in my head from what I had witnessed in Karen's bedroom not five minutes ago. And there was also the residue from last night of the glorious, glamorous wickedness of a girl's blatantly exposing herself. The two coupled together meant that somehow the idea was not completely unthinkable.

'That's right.' She poured more tea, with such casualness that it was almost artificial and I began to question whether I had gone mad. 'Poor lad: all ready for a girl he is, but just don't know how to get one.' She was fiddling with her cigarettes again. 'Nice big cock he's got and all. You know when he's excited and that. In fact,' and she laughed hoarsely, 'it's like that pretty much all the time. He can't hardly keep it down! Every time I give him his bath, up it comes, like a copper's truncheon. Well, I've told him, and I'll tell you too: he won't never need to apologise to no-one, not with a thing like that. Lovely and thick it is! Long, too. Course, he's not really got the control of it just yet; bit quick off the mark as you might say, but that's just from the habit of it. Bit of practice and he'd be any girl's dream. Just seems such a shame that there's no nice girl getting the benefit.' She took a long drag on her cigarette, squinting through the smoke. 'You got a boyfriend, have you love?'

'Yes,' I said quickly. 'Yes, we're practically engaged.'

'Oh well. Anyway, you wouldn't have to touch it if you didn't want, but I dare say he wouldn't mind if you cared to see it.'

'I don't, thank you.'

She shrugged. 'Suit yourself. But if he could have a look at what's what, well, I'm sure then he'd feel much more confident about getting himself a girl of his own. I had hoped his sister might help him out, but her Ian is a funny one, and then what with her getting pregnant like that. Course he's had the odd glimpse of her, but I can't hardly ask her to show him the whole works, can I? That wouldn't hardly be decent. Not his own sister.' And the comment brought back that image of her lying naked on her bed, her whole body trembling, her hand clamped round my wrist while her grandmother stroked her to orgasm. Another little tremor rippled through my pussy as if in sympathy with the images rippling through my head.

'He would look at me, but he wouldn't touch me?'

'Oh, no. Just look.'

'That's all?'

'Oh yes. That'd be all.' She paused. 'Then, you'd have your purse back and go home.' I frowned, and perhaps there was a touch of refusal in it because she went on. 'Then tomorrow, the bosses would never know about you going to one of them clubs and making a bit of a disgrace of yourself. Nor about you losing your security pass, and telling fibs about it being left at some friend's flat.'

I stared at her. She stared back. 'Where is he?'

'In his room, where he always is. Shall I fetch him out?'

I nodded. 'I'm not saying I'll do it, I'll just see him that's all.'

She sat examining me for a moment, considering my

resistance and perhaps seeing through it all better than I did. 'Right, I'll get him,' but when she returned a couple of minutes later with Gavin shuffling along behind, he was even more embarrassed than before.

I tried him again. 'Hi, Gavin.'

'Hallo,' he mumbled, glancing towards his grandmother for support.

'Right,' said Mrs Patrick. 'I'll leave you two to it and go and see if Karen wants anything.' I imagine it was meant innocently enough, but having witnessed earlier the sort of thing Karen wanted, the remark could only start one train of thought in my mind. As the door shut behind her, Gavin continued standing awkwardly in the middle of the room. He hardly dared look up at me.

'Do you want to sit down?' I patted the settee next to me.

'Okay.' And he dropped down in the chair opposite. He had his head down, but he was still watching me from under his thick brows, his hands clasped in his lap, still and expectant as he waited for me to take the lead. Then he swallowed and glanced just once at the closed door. 'Nan said you were going to take your clothes off.'

'Yes, I know she did. Do you want me to?'

'Yeah!' Like a child offered chocolate.

'Why?'

'I wanna see things.'

'What is it exactly you want to see?'

'Everything.'

'Everything?'

'Yeah.' He glanced at the door again, his sanctuary, and found courage. 'Your tits and that.'

'Have you never had a girlfriend, Gavin?

'No. And your arse. I wanna see that.' He checked my expression, whether his daring words had gone too far, but saw no reproach and wiped his palms down his jeans. 'You know, and your cunt. Everything.'

'Why don't you get yourself a girlfriend?'

'Girls never like me. They just laugh. They say I wouldn't know a cunt if one jumped up and bit me.'

'Wouldn't you like to have a girlfriend of your own?'

'Yeah, maybe. Don't know.' Another glance towards the door for reassurance. 'Go on then. Nan said you would.'

'But you've seen Karen naked.'

'Yeah, loads of times, but not close, not so as I could properly look. Besides, she's different now she's pregnant. Proper girls don't look like that.'

'Proper?'

'Yeah. Normal.'

'So am I normal?'

'Yeah, you're dead fit.' Which was probably as close to either a compliment or a properly phrased request as I was ever going to get from this boy. But if he didn't have the vocabulary to express his enthusiasm, his posture and expression certainly proved it. So I stood up, took hold of both sides of my sweater and pulled it off. He didn't say a word, so then I kicked off my shoes, and although his eyes stared, there was still no sound. Last night, the dim light, gentle music and glamorous fittings had managed to create something mystical and exotic in a girl taking her clothes off. Today, in the cluttered living room of a poky fourth floor flat, there was nothing, and yet my audience now was no less enthralled than Jade's had been then.

I reached round and unhooked my bra, held it for a moment over my breasts and then let it fall slowly, slipping across the skin, catching briefly on my nipples before dropping away. Gavin sucked in his breath. Compared with his sister's, my breasts seemed tiny, even to me, but he was still being shown a woman's breasts and the desire in his eyes was unmistakable.

For a moment I let the bra swing, facing him, watching him, watching him staring at me, trying to consume me with his eyes and the power was intoxicating. My nipples were erect, pointed and as hungry as his eyes. 'Like them?' I grinned at him, even gave my breasts a little shake, and although I did not have Jade's fluency, this was more than he had ever seen.

I dropped the bra and hooked my fingers into the waistband of my skirt, sliding round to the fastening, slowly undoing it and then letting it drop. I stepped out of it and then peeled down my tights, made a deliberate show of bending over to pick them up, my bottom towards him so that the thin nylon of my knickers would be stretched tight across me. Then I turned back, now only the knickers in place. Gavin sat motionless, his eyes focussed on my knickers, his hands laid flat on his thighs and an unmistakable bulge in the front of his trousers.

'There!' I said, waving my hips at him, circling in a free look-at-me movement that he could not help but like. 'There you are. That's what the girls in the club do,' and I swung round again, turning away and bending over. He licked his lips and his voice cracked. 'Take your pants off. Everything. Let me see your cunt.'

He licked his lips again, his hands unable to keep away from the front of his jeans as he focussed on my belly, and his eyes tried to dig through the thin mesh of my knickers. But his eyes were hungrier than looked safe and I was too far from home. 'I think that's enough, Gavin. I think...'

But he just stared for a moment, then without taking his

eyes off me opened wide his mouth. 'Nan!' It was a bellow more than a call. 'She won't do what you said!'

A few seconds later a door down the corridor opened and shut with only a moment of giggling to mark the space in between, and then Mrs Patrick was back. I snatched up my blouse to cover my breasts.

'For goodness' sake, Gavin! What's the matter now?'

'You said she'd show me her cunt and she won't.'

'Gavin! That's not a word I have ever used!'

His expression fell only the slightest degree before he tried again. 'You know, though. She won't show me her front.'

Mrs Patrick glanced about the room, from me to him and back to me again while I adjusted the sides of the blouse to make sure my breasts were covered. She sniffed, stuffed another cigarette in her mouth and lit it, and finally shook her head and plopped down on the settee with a sigh: the needs of the whole family on her shoulders.

'Come along then, love. Let's have your pants off. We ain't shy here, not in this house. We're all of us just as God made us.'

'Mrs Patrick, I said I'd do what the girls in the clubs do and I have. They keep their knickers on except for private dances, and that's what I'm doing. I really think I've kept my side of the bargain.'

'Private, eh? Well you see, I don't know about that. Don't know about that at all.' Her hand reached out to rest on my arm, and the finger nail started playing up and down my skin. 'You see what Gavin needs, is to see what a whole woman is like. Everything.'

'I've shown him practically everything.'

'Not really, love. Least, not if you was to want your little adventure last night to stay private, just between the two of us.' Another flurry of coughing interrupted her. 'And that is what you want, love, isn't it?'

'Yes.'

'Well then. There we are. Private things are best kept private, aren't they?' She reached up and tugged the blouse out of my fingers. Just for a moment the other hand ran across my breasts, a single sweep that covered both nipples and ran on down to lift away near my waist. 'Very nice, love. Lovely little titties. Now: stand up and let's do the rest.'

I stood, but I couldn't move more than that. How could I hope to create, even in my head let alone in Gavin's – or hers – any morsel of the glamour of that club with them just sitting there: one staring unblinking through his glasses, the other grimly coughing her life out every few minutes? Anyway, how much further did they expect me to go? 'What more do you want?'

'Well it's not what I want love. I don't want nothing. It's what young Gavin wants.'

'All right, then,' and I made no attempt to hide my irritation, 'what does Young Gavin want?' We were talking as if he weren't sitting just the other side of the room, listening to every word that passed.

'Well, I think he wants to see all of you. Your bottom and your front and that. The full monty, like.'

'I want to see her cunt.' If we were going to ignore him, he would make himself heard.

'Gavin! I've told you before about using language.' She scowled at him, but switched the smile back on as soon as she turned to me. 'Come along, love. Do you want a hand?'

Gavin was stirred at last. 'I could help her!'

'No! Not you!' I turned and glared at him. 'No, thank you.'

'Here you go then.' And Mrs Patrick reached up, blinking through the smoke which curled up into her eyes from the cigarette clamped in her mouth, and taking hold of my knickers, simply drew them straight down my legs as calmly as if I were a child being readied for bed. In that role I meekly stepped out of them and she tossed them over onto the pile.

'There now! Not so hard was it? Now: let's have a look at you.'

I stood and, under her guiding hands, turned when required to show Gavin my bottom and turned to show him my bush. Finally she was done and patted the settee next to her. 'Sit down, love.'

The covering scratched on my bare skin and I shivered in the cold chill of nakedness in the unfamiliar surroundings of this flat. I pulled up my knees and wrapped my arms round them.

'Lovely. Now just open yourself up a bit, why don't you?'.

I pulled away into the corner. 'What? Why?'

'Let's just show him what a girl looks like down there, hmm?' And her hand came to rest on my thigh and started drawing my left leg towards her and away from the other one, so that I was being steadily opened up. From just six feet away, Gavin's wide eyes, green as his sister's, blinked out through his thick glasses. He rubbed his palms along his thighs again, and I could see now the mound in his jeans which was, as Mrs Patrick had said, impressive. She reached across to push the other leg away so that I was now spread as wide as I have ever been. She turned to Gavin.

'Come and look then, lad. She won't bite.' Immediately he scuttled across the floor and knelt directly in front of me, the staring eyes widening to consume me.

And then Mrs Patrick started talking to Gavin, and it was my turn to be ignored except when I was required to change my position to show him better what was happening. She started with my breasts, showing how the nipples hardened and rose up as she circled them with her fingers, pulled at them until she was satisfied with the effect, and Gavin's unblinking eyes had taken in all he could. Then she turned to my pussy, peeling open my lips to show him all of that as his eyes stared and he watched his grandmother's hands skimming across me, pulling and pressing and opening me out to show where my lips were swelling and darkening with every passing minute, where my pee would come from, where there was now a glistening seepage from the greedy mouth where his cock might enter if only I would let him, but which for now must be replaced by her fingers, pushing deep inside me just as they had pushed inside Karen a short time before, where, finally, despite myself, my clitoris was pushing out and when she peeled back the skin, it too glistened in the dim light. Her fingers slid over there too, small circles running round the tip and longer sweeps of her open hand that ran the whole length of my pussy. I slumped down to open myself wider, and her smile broadened in response as she turned back to me.

'I don't know! You girls! Just as bad as Karen, you are!' and the steady circles intensified, down almost to tickle my bottom, up to push back my clitoris, slithering down my lips, running up between them.

Gavin had moved closer, kneeling between my knees now, his arms brushing against me and his breath whispering along my thighs as he tried to get as close as was physically possible, to see every inch of me which his grandmother offered. He had given up any attempt to hide his erection, or to hide that he was rubbing himself. Mrs Patrick noticed too.

'Gavin!' but there was more amusement than anger in her voice.

'What? You were doing it to her.'

And she laughed again, leaned tight into me while her hand passed slowly and firmly over the whole gasping surface of my pussy. Her voice was almost a whisper: 'Do you want to see his cock now?'

And too much had happened. I was no longer the girl who had walked in here with the aim of collecting a purse and being gone as soon as possible. I had been drawn into this strange family, its bizarre ways and shameless welcome. Her hand would not stop. Or else it might stop if I said the wrong thing. 'All right.'

'Go on then, Gavin. Let the girl see.'

'No!' he protested, jumping to his feet when I had expected him to be as eager to show as he was to see. 'She'll laugh at me.'

'No, she won't!'

'Yes she will. Like Sandra: she laughed.'

'Sandra just wasn't expecting it; not on the beach like that.'

'She'll still laugh.'

'No, she won't,' but Mrs Patrick was tired of arguing, or maybe she hadn't given up hope of making a match, and she reached over herself to the fly of his jeans unzipping them as she continued to reassure him.

'Well she better not,' but by now Mrs Patrick was already working on his tatty Y-fronts. When these had also been bundled down his pallid thighs knees, she pushed away his sweatshirt, and there it was: springing from a thick bush of warm ginger hair was an erection which, as Mrs Patrick had said, would be a credit to any man. It waved wildly from side to side as he stood there, and when she took hold of it and used it to draw him steadily back closer towards me, it seemed only natural to take over, to reach out and wrap my hand round it, my fingers barely reaching the whole way round, to hold it, surprisingly cool and wonderfully firm.

'What do you think of that, then?' Mrs Patrick beamed proudly at this display and delicately I ran my hand up and back the length of his shaft. I also reached out to cup his tightly puckered balls but even so light a touch was too much. He groaned, and simultaneously I felt the first hot spurt splatter onto my cheek and trickle down my chin. A second followed, almost into my eyes, a third onto my breasts and then more onto my stomach and legs. I had let go of him in shock at the first eruption but he now gripped his cock in his own fist and was pounding it with a merciless determination until the last drops oozed into his own fingers.

~

Once he had gone, scuttering back to his room with one hand still holding his wilting cock and the other hauling at his jeans, Mrs Patrick fetched some kitchen towels and helped to clean me up.

'Sorry about that, dear. I should have warned you he does tend to lose control a bit quick. Always has done.' She was wiping carefully and attentively at the dribbles which had trickled down my neck, moving down to my breast, wiping gently round my nipple as she smiled to herself. 'Poor lamb. So enthusiastic he is. Just wish he could get hisself a proper girlfriend.' She moved over to the other breast, although I was not at all sure this one needed it. 'Look at all this! Quite a lad, eh?'

She had reached my pubic hair now, one hand casually resting on my thigh as she dabbed carefully at the flecks which Gavin had sprayed everywhere. Her eyes narrowed. 'You all but engaged, you say.'

'Yes. Yes we're getting married next spring.'

'Pity. You're a very pretty girl; it would have been nice to have a girl like you in the family. Oh well.' She sniffed again. 'There. That's you all done.'

'Thank you.'

She folded up the kitchen towel carefully, but her hand returned to my thigh afterwards, the fingers gently stroking to and fro. 'Anything else, love?'

Yes of course I wanted something else, but this was all too new. Even after I declined, the disappointment in her eyes almost made me change my mind, but she was not one to beg and had already turned away.

She watched while I dressed quickly and finally handed me my purse. I hesitated before stuffing it back in my bag. 'Oh check it if you want. It's all there.'

'No, I'm sure it is,' and I quickly put it away and headed for the door, fumbling with the lock until she came to help me.

'There now. Don't be a stranger.' I didn't even look back as I headed for the stairs and almost ran down them. But in the car park, my determination failed and I did glance up. Two faces were peering out at me from different windows on the fourth floor.

During the following days, I tried never to be alone in the office when the cleaners came round late in the afternoon. I didn't always succeed, and a week or so later I saw the familiar round figure dragging her grinning red vacuum cleaner towards me.

'I expect you've heard.'

'Heard what?'

'They're terminating our contract. Getting someone cheaper to do the cleaning.'

'Oh. No, I hadn't heard. I'm sorry.'

She shrugged. 'Don't make no odds to me. I'll just be cleaning somewhere else.' But she stayed standing by my desk. 'Karen's had her baby: little girl.'

'Oh good.' I had nothing to add.

'You should call by.'

'I'm very busy at the moment.' I indicated the files spread open, the judgements waiting to be reviewed and leaving open whether this was a short term, don't-have-time-to-chat, or long term, don't-have-time-to-visit, excuse. Neither sounded very convincing, but my explanation floated away without apparently making any impact.

'She'd like that. She was asking the other day whether I seen you recently.'

'Yes, well I will go if I get a spare moment, but just now Mrs Patrick, I really must get on.' She stared hard, a stare in which I saw our common history reflected: first the skin lotion, then the demonstration for, allegedly, Gavin's benefit; finally her offer and my rejection. I turned back to the files and felt my face burning until she had steadily vacuumed her way away again.

And then circumstances conspired against me, because less than a week later we had a client on that same estate from whom I had to go and take a witness statement. And, as so often even when we are trying to help, he wasn't at home at the agreed time and there I was: left at a loose end.

The stair well was unchanged: the stink, the litter, even the noise. When I reached the fourth floor and rang the bell, the voice which answered was equally familiar. 'Hang on!' There was a shuffling, clattering then a string of curses and finally the door was opened.

'Oh! It's you,' but Karen just stood there. 'Mum's not here,' she added before another thought came to her. 'Nor Gavin, neither. He's gone to some computer fair or something.' She was wrapped in a garish and unflattering dressing gown, tied loosely round a waist that was substantially slimmer than before but still full. Her pale skin and green eyes looked tired and her foxy hair hung in untidy clumps round her head.

'Actually,' and now that I was there I wasn't really sure what it was I had come for, 'it was really you I came to see.'

'Me?'

'Well, and the baby. I saw your mum and she said it had been born. A little girl.'

'Yeah, Chardonnay her name is. I was just going to feed her.' She stepped back to let me pass.

'Are you sure I'm not interrupting?'

'No: nice to have a bit of company.' The waddle had gone, I noticed as she led me in, but she still shuffled in her bright pink slippers. 'Take off your coat. Bloody boiling in here but Nan says I gotta keep the place like an oven for the baby.'

For me, an only child from a small and insular family, this was all a new world as she got the baby up, changed its nappy and re-wrapped it in warm clothes, then settled herself into an armchair, pulled up the hem of her sweater, opened the front of her bra and offered the tiny baby a tight and bloated breast that was bigger than it was. Its bobbing head wobbled about and then docked onto the nipple and the silence returned. Having a baby of my own was not a prospect I had ever considered with any seriousness, but seeing this here, witnessing the closeness and simplicity of the dependence, I felt the beginnings of a yearning. There was such a naturalness and easy intimacy to the way that the woman satisfied all her baby's needs for shelter and food and warmth. A little traffic noise drifted in: children shouting: low televisions in neighbours' flats: the lift rattled past on its way up or down but for most of the time, the steady sucking and gurgling of the baby drowned all that.

Karen lay back, her eyes closed, the little baby sprawled across her bosom, its mouth fastened tight to her nipple and its whole body rising and falling with each breath she took.

And then it was done: Karen resettled the baby in its cot, but barely paused in the living room, wincing and rubbing at her breasts as she headed back to the kitchen. 'I feel like a bloody cow: reckon I was meant to have twins. Got enough to feed two.'

When she returned, she flopped back down and casually pulled open the front of her dressing gown revealing a sturdy white bra. A little more fiddling at the front and she had unhooked one cup, peeled back the material and her plump, pale breast was pushing out. She squeezed the body of the breast in one hand and pinched the swollen nipple between the finger and thumb of the other hand. Immediately a pure white drop appeared at the deep red tip, sensual and dangerous and despite the reversed colours, so reminiscent of a drop of blood on smooth, white skin. The droplet quivered, filled out and slowly crept down her skin to be wiped away to oblivion on the pad of kitchen towel Karen held in her other hand. It was barely gone before another appeared, and another, steadily increasing to a steady trickle. Finally, as she squeezed still harder, an actual jet carved through the air: thin and sharp arcing down with prolific carelessness.

'It seems a waste,' I heard myself saying, although I'm not sure where the words came from because I could only focus on that gorgeous ripe nipple steadily dribbling its milk as she pinched again. And then I was there, kneeling in front of her and my hand reached up, my fingers took the place of hers and I squeezed gently. Nothing happened.

'You can squeeze harder than that, love,' and this time a droplet did appear, seeping from the long hard nipple, growing and filling until it started to tremble and topple over. This time I caught it myself, on my finger, warm and slightly sticky, and then I couldn't help myself. It was sweet, but not sweet enough. I leaned forward to cradle her breast in my two hands and then put my lips to the nipple and sucked.

Sweet, yes. Sweet and warm, and a thin jet squirting powerfully through to the back of my throat as if this were the most normal thing in the world. And it wouldn't stop: the more I sucked, the more powerful the stream. She had pulled the other side of her gown open and now unfastened the other cup of her bra, gently toying with that nipple as I suckled on the other: quietly, with a calm tranquillity that I could have continued for hours. I felt her hand on the back of my head, holding me, looked up and her eyes were wide with what could have been surprise but I believe was also joy and hope and anticipation. Between my lips the nipple quivered and flowed, and Karen pulled the rest of the gown away, spread wide her legs and drew me in close to her body. Her hand left her breast again and I felt it worming down between us and working its way inside the elastic of her knickers.

And I didn't need to see: I knew what she felt so it was natural for me to do the same, reaching under my skirt to feel the warmth and the wetness; to lie cradled against that breast as it rose and fell with every breath, hearing the drumming of her heart, the first few whispers in her throat and all the while suckling that pure sweet warmth from her nipple.

Except that out in the hallway, the lift doors rattled and footsteps approached the front door.

'Shit!' and for a moment she didn't move as the steps reached the door. 'Gavin!' and then she was pushing me away and reaching at the dressing gown while I scuttled back to my place, smoothing my skirt as I settled back on the settee. Frantically she refastened her bra and grabbed at the belt of her dressing gown as the key turned in the door. We were both composed by the time the boy appeared.

<hr />

Ten minutes later it was all behind me as I made my way back to where I had parked the car. But the memories still swamped my head, memories and one barbed consideration: if Karen had done nothing herself beyond allow me my way, the hasty guilt in her movements could only have come from thoughts and hopes that were less innocent than her actions.

I unlocked the door and slid into the familiar safety of my real world. I would not check just yet to see if our client had returned home, I would call back another day: perhaps even tomorrow.

Some more titles available from the EPS:

The Diary of a Sex Fiend   £9.99

Christopher Peachment

If you're a serious subscriber to political correctness, then this book is probably not for you. But if you are a genial, intelligent and well balanced Renaissance man or woman (as most of us are), then you can do no better than to order this book. In return you will receive a vast repository of acerbic wit, sharp wisdom and an astonishing amount of pithy sexual fact written by the Erotic Review's top columnist, Christopher Peachment.

Rogering Molly & other stories   £7.95

Christopher Hart

From the small market towns of mid-Wales to the narrow streets of ancient Babylon, from a lofty Singapore penthouse (with a rooftop pool the size of Surrey) to a woodland shack deep in the forests of Transylvania, the sexual predators are afoot, and... they're hungry. With an extensive cast of wickedly erotic characters, Hart shows himself to be a subtle master of the genre in these 25 lubricious tales.

The Serving Girl   £7.95

R L Mornington

This is the story of Emily who, while studying, takes up the position of housemaid under the autocratic and mysterious 'Sir". Gradually and intense and highly explicit sexual relationship develops between employer and employee. Everything about this liaison, with its overtones of authority and servility, is extraordinary and unexpected.

The Pharmacist & Her Daughter   £7.95

Esparbec

Meet the luscious, voluptuous Laura, petite bourgeoise and respectable town pharmacist. Meet layabout Bob, her ex-barman toyboy husband. Meet the twins, Laura's incestuously precocious offspring: the beautiful, sexually incontinent Bertande (Bébé) and her anally resourceful brother, Bertrand. And finally, meet Ernest, randy ex-con cousin of Bob, who comes to stay and becomes the catalyst for wild and shocking sexual anarchy combined with superbly erotic, Feydeauesque farce.